JUMPSHIP DISSONANCE

BOOK TWO OF THE JUMPSHIP SERIES

ADRIA LAYCRAFT

JUMPSHIP DISSONANCE

BOOK TWO OF THE JUMPSHIP SERIES

ADRIA LAYCRAFT

TYCHE BOOKS LTD.

Published by Tyche Books Ltd.
Calgary, Alberta, Canada
www.TycheBooks.com

Cover Art by Niken Anindita
Cover Layout by Indigo Chick Designs
Interior Layout by Ryah Deines
Editorial by M.L.D. Curelas

First Tyche Books Ltd Edition 2022
Print ISBN: 978-1-989407-33-2
Ebook ISBN: 978-1-989407-34-9

Author photograph: Erin Laycraft

This book was funded in part by a grant from the Alberta Media Fund.

This book is dedicated to Sherry Peters:
I couldn't have done the middle muddle without you!

CHAPTER ONE

WHEN THREE HUNDRED-odd blips disappeared from her holo tracker display, Diona Jordan figured some orbital shuttle must've blown up. The issue with dropped and corrupted signals was far too sporadic to be the answer.

Diona considered the implications of so many instant deaths as she swiped through holos running computations on her latest nanite experiments. *The only logical explanation is an explosion of some kind.* She mourned the loss of all the nanite gear and materials. These past fifteen years without an Earth society manufacturing anything, she faced the awful truth of being stranded without help. They were attempting to make their own steel and bioplaz here on Mars, to say nothing of creating nubots to repair and upgrade the nano-electrochemical systems they all had injected in them, but it would be so much easier to just buy it and ship it, like in the good ole days of her parents' time. The NECS upgrade she was developing was no guarantee when it came to this new bio-fouling issue.

They left her such a mess.

Instead of a great "new world" colony supplied and supported by Earth's industries, she had no support and the remnants of humanity all begging her to fix everything. Not great when things went wrong, as they had for Luna Base and the Orbitals.

Then those idiots had the nerve to demand food from us, as if Mars was some humanitarian government agency the way

Earth once was.

She paced before the opening in the brick-red regolith that gave her inner sanctuary a spectacular view. Her "away office" she liked to call it. Two enormous windows were divided by a thick wall, and she stood so she could easily see out each one.

The window to her left revealed a forest of pines, spruce, poplar, and aspen that marched on into the distance until out of sight over the horizon. The trees were thick and healthy, the understory dense with wild rose, willow bushes, currants, and more. Above the canopy of trees, rows of massive lights were attached to the underside of the dome, which was covered in the red rock of Mars. These lights simulated the sun travelling across the sky each day, and the protective regolith shell made sure the forest remained shielded from radiation . . . and prying eyes. Not that anyone in the colony would be brave enough to leave their dome. She had made sure of that.

Out the window to her right, through the faint blue tint of the silica aerogel coating that held in the warmth and blocked most of the hazardous radiation, lay the vast, rocky plains of Valles Marineris, with the steep sides rising in the distance, looking much like mountains from this angle. That blue gel made the Martian landscape seem a bit purple, confusing the senses.

The colony lay nestled against the north wall of the cliffs, benefitting from the thermal energy stored there when the distant sun did shine, and protected somewhat from the worst of the storms. This dome was also nestled against the north wall, not far west of the colony, but over an impassable ridge of jagged rock. It was accessible only by tunnel, by air, or by travelling far out into the open plains of the valley, which risked getting caught by a storm.

Her haven. Her shelter. This boundless source of wealth, that was her parents' best legacy. The fact it was to this day still a secret made it even more valuable.

As CEO of SpaceOp and operational director of the Mars Colony, she had the right to keep secrets and test limits. Besides, with the collapse of civilization, she might as well be queen of this forsaken planet. There was no one to stop her.

She watched and waited, still puzzled by the sudden group loss of signals, especially since it happened out near a water mining operation. Could an EMP blast have occurred? Just as deadly as an explosion in space. A mass suicide? Were they so desperate already?

And if that were the case, could she harvest the parts? It sounded macabre, but her nanite experiments could benefit from more tests, and that required more gear.

Diona shook the idea off. She knew better than to allow any chance of that moon spoor reaching Mars. And forget sending them anything—even the tiny probe mechs had been dismantled to be repurposed for repairs to breathing systems and electrical grids. She simply didn't have equipment to send. Once the new upgrades were ready, that should help everyone, even them, but if she wanted to protect *this* colony, she had to put them first, protect *this* attempt at survival right here.

"Mommy?"

She turned from the view. A three-and-a-half-foot tall version of herself stood in the doorway clutching a worn teddy bear awkwardly wrapped in a doll blanket.

"You should be asleep, Thea."

Thea trembled, her eyes liquid pools of hazel and black. Diona hated how the girl cowered under her firm command. How would this child ever be a true Jordan if she couldn't stand up to a harsh voice?

"I try, Mommy, I try, I do. I close my eyes, but the things won't be quiet. Even when I sing."

Diona frowned, moving to herd the child back to bed. She shouldn't have ever told that silly story to Thea, even if it set the stage for later revelation. She sometimes forgot how fragile and stupid children could be.

A flash of memory blinded her; her own stuffed bear dangling, the scream of sirens, the convulsing body . . .

With clenched teeth she fought the vision down. When she could see her surroundings again, her daughter gazed round-eyed from her bed, clutching her toy to her chest like a shield.

Diona crossed the room and sat on the bed. "Come," she allowed, and Thea scampered onto her lap and wrapped tiny arms around her neck. "Stop, child, you're choking me."

"Mommy, what is bio-fouling?"

Diona's heart, having just regained a more normal pace, thumped right back into overdrive. "Where did you hear that?" she demanded, and Thea squeaked in fear.

"Tell me, where?"

But she'd frightened the weak little thing, who now sobbed into her shoulder, soaking her blouse. Diona sighed. Likely Thea heard it through all the medical reports read in front of her. She was older now, paying attention, even at only six. Diona needed to secure information around the child now.

Thea sniffled, wriggled, and settled. Diona went to dislodge the girl to lay her down, but as the banks of artificial lights faded over the Martian forest dome, she sighed and let the increasingly limp child remain in her arms for a few more minutes.

THREE MONTHS LATER, it happened again. Over three hundred markers ceased to show on her tracker app. And one of them was her brother, Stepper, who had been assigned to oversee a water mining facility.

When bio-fouling affected the signal, it tended to stutter. Drifts, as her techs called them, would make signals fade in and out. They were experiencing it now with the earcells dropping calls and losing messages. She was bombarded with demands for that to be fixed, as if she were some witch that could just wave her magic wand and make everyone better. They had no idea how difficult her life was.

If scar tissue formation was the issue, the signal simply faded, becoming less over time but still giving up some data, at the very least telling her where people were. To have all these markers drop their signals in tandem and so abruptly could not be a NECS failure. Those people either died as one in some catastrophe . . .

. . . or somehow had their NECS turned off.

. . . or travelled beyond her reach.

She shook off the last thought as absurd. As much as NECS were designed to eventually take them to other systems and galaxies, nothing like it had ever come to be. The nanotechs at UMars kept assuring her it *was* possible and they would figure it out one day, but she doubted very much it would happen. She doubted even more her brother figured it out. Opening and traversing a wormhole, or "folding" space, whatever, was all a pipe dream.

Except two large groups of people simultaneously dropped off your tracker. What else could it be?

She wanted to dismiss the thought, until she realized her

brother's ex, Janlin, was also in the second group.

Diona retraced the list of the first group to disappear and had her worst fears confirmed. Janlin's father Rudigar Kavanagh was on the list, one of the most talented and frustrating nanite specialists they had. Rudi could make Jumpships real. It was his actual job, in fact, his area of research. And Rudi had head-butted every single idea she tried to get him to work on, always going off to do whatever he pleased and never fulfilling his contractual duties with SpaceOp. It would be like him to team up with Stepper.

Diona cursed herself for missing such an obvious thing. *Time to send a cruiser and rule things out.* She would put the crew under strict decom protocols, and ensure they isolated in orbit for a month when they returned. She had to get eyes on the situation.

The cruiser found little of interest, no bodies or evidence of an EMP troubling the nearby water harvester, no drifting debris, nothing. Diona ordered them to remain on-site and maintain surveillance, ignoring the disbelief from the crew. They thought they were watching a functional, boring, water-harvesting operation.

When 353 signals popped back into existence one day, she was ready.

CHAPTER TWO

JUMP

Janlin held tight to the knowledge that they had survived this before. The universe flattened and spun and sounded out discord as they went both *this* far, and a trillion times more than that, all at the same time. Her head rejected the cognitive dissonance by reaching for the relief of home.

Everyone had made what preparations they could. The *Hope's* systems were once again set to run on autopilot while they regained their equilibrium, and Stepper had them coming in a safe distance from the Jumpship Station and the water harvester. Once this terrible sense of *wrongness* that darkened and blurred her vision released its grip on her mind, she could exult in bringing the first alien to the Sol system . . . and in seeing Gordon with Ursula again.

Memories flashed through her mind, and yet, some of them weren't memories, more memories of a dream? "Little Mousebird," Steve Netchkie's voice said, and she heard the trill of Falco's laughter. Then her father's voice, so gentle, saying, "She's beautiful," and Janlin realized she held an infant in her arms, snuggled close to her chest, but Stepper screamed at her and the baby was gone. "See what you make me do?" he cried over and over, smashing his fist into the table with every repetition.

She groaned, twisting both her body and her mind to find relief. "Sing, little bird," her mom's voice said, and Janlin swore she could smell the chocolate chip cookies she would make. "Sing."

Her mom began to hum a favourite, an old lullaby sung to children for hundreds of years, and Janlin hummed along. The love of those memories flowed through her, calming the storm.

The song faded, and she began to make sense of life. She immediately wondered if it were worth it. Pieces of her felt scattered like a trail of debris behind them, as if little bits of her soul floated through all those light years between Huantag and home.

Janlin groaned. Her head spun and was shot through with sharp pains. Her pounding heart felt too big for her chest. A lightning show flashed inside her skull, and her stomach threatened to let go of breakfast. The screaming whine in her ears subsided, ever so slowly, until finally regular sounds could penetrate.

"Pull it together, girl," she muttered to herself, her voice a bare whisper. She still couldn't see straight, and opening her eyes to check was a bad idea, thanks to the vertigo that made everything jump sideways over and over. A sound did reach her then, a normal sound of someone retching. She swallowed hard.

Something heavy sagged against her shoulder, and she eventually became aware of what—or who—it was. "Anaya?" she croaked. There was no reply.

Thoughts of home, of bringing the Orbitals food stocks, of seeing Ursula again, of showing Anaya, well, everything . . . all suddenly tripped up on new grief for her dad. Rudigar Kavanagh would never again fly, would never get to come home. Sorrow flooded her, anguished anew at his loss.

Breathe, baby, come on, you need to pull it together and be a good host to the Gitane.

Janlin blinked away the blur and sighed with relief when the spinning head seemed to slow.

"Anaya, you're getting heavy," she grumbled. Then fear coursed through her. Adrenaline brought new clear-headedness, and she fumbled with her seat straps. Anaya slumped even more, clearly unconscious.

Stepper's voice called out, "Status?"

Shaky voices replied, here, there, confirming they were home. Janlin could make Stepper out in his captain's chair despite her muddled brain. He blinked at her in return, then his gaze went to Anaya and he frowned.

"She okay?" he said, blinking rapidly. His white-knuckled grip on the arms of the chair showed he was suffering just as badly as anyone.

"My earcell won't work," came Gordon's strained voice.

The buckles finally made sense and she slipped out from beneath Anaya's bulk. The Gitane captain slumped sideways, the makeshift straps unable to hold her up in her comatose state. Janlin touched the alien's face, the leathery scales smooth and too cold.

"She's barely breathing," Janlin called out. "She needs some life support." Gordon helped her shift Anaya to the floor, but he tipped, staggered, then groaned and shut his eyes, holding the floor like a life raft in a wild ocean.

"She's alien," Stepper said. "How do we know what life support looks like?"

Janlin groped for the answers. Anaya's skin seemed drained of colour, and her breath didn't even lift her chest. "Oxygen," Janlin guessed, gripping her own head with both hands. When would the pain stop? "No, better, her own medbay."

A proximity alert sounded. "We are home, right?" Stepper demanded of Danal Goldberg, the helmsman who had replaced Tyrell. He was a big, muscular man that made the helmsman's chair look childish.

"We are home, and that is a SpaceOp cruiser," Danal said. "A welcoming party?"

Stepper swore, leaving Danal looking confused. "We can't outfly them," Stepper said, half to himself.

"It could be here for the water mining," Gordon offered. He knew that SpaceOp was not a part of the Jump program, but most others didn't. He left Anaya with Janlin for a moment and returned to his station.

"Send a hail."

"We're already being hailed," Gordon replied. Stepper pointed at his earcell, and Gordon complied with a frown.

Stepper listened, his mouth becoming tighter and thinner by the second. He met Janlin's gaze and quickly looked away.

"How soon can we Jump again?" he asked Danal. Janlin was sure he must be joking.

Danal looked rather green around the gills. "Everyone is still recovering," he protested.

"How long?"

The shout left everyone silent and grim, and heads turned from the pocket of people peering into the bridge area from the hallway waiting to find out what was going on.

"Anaya could die from another Jump," Janlin said clearly into the tense silence. Steve Netchkie brought her a resuscitation kit and she went to work pumping oxygen into Anaya. The mask didn't fit very well. They needed to get her to her own sick bay.

Stepper continued staring at Danal, waiting for an answer.

Danal swallowed, a muscle jumping in his cheek. "We need time to plot the course and get aligned."

"Do we have the processing power?"

"We can centralize other power sources to augment the main processor."

"Do it, and notify me immediately when you are ready."

Danal looked ready to argue, but the chain of command held. He began tapping at holos with a small shake of his head. "I'll start calculating. What is our destination?"

"Mars."

Janlin and Gordon both sputtered, and many other voices called out in protest. Danal went even whiter, with two high spots of colour standing out on each cheek. Janlin held Gordon back, while wondering why she bothered.

They had all come from Earth's Orbitals or Luna Base, and had people waiting for them—people they had gone on this expedition for. Mars wasn't going to help them, that had already been made clear.

Stepper stared straight at her now. "She'll have them board and take over, make claim to the Jump program and *Hope* herself." He scanned the rest of the listening crew. "I built this. Me. Not SpaceOp, not Diona Jordan, me, my leadership, my ingenuity, my scavenged parts. And I'll be damned if I'm going to hand it over to my sister now. We must Jump. I want her to know she isn't invulnerable out there anymore."

The silence held the shock of revelation to it. However, to Janlin, this was old news. "Another Jump could leave us all dead, and either way, we all want to go home, Stepper. Why not Earth orbit? It's far closer."

Many nods accompanied her statement. Everyone was still feeling the effects. They all knew she was right, even Stepper, if he'd listen.

A commotion started in the hall outside. "Captain Inaba is down," someone called. "He's gone into convulsions."

"Shit, he's having a stroke," Steve said. Another resuscitation kit was run out to them. Janlin continued to pump air into Anaya. She looked over the alien's bulk to Gordon. He gave Janlin a desperate look.

"I can't get my earcell to work. Can you?"

She tapped and waited for the chime. It came, but full of static. She subvocalized Ursula, but instead of a connection, it crackled and faded. She shook her head at Gordon. His face fell.

Steve crouched at Anaya's feet. "What if we bring a supply sled from the loading bay to get Anaya to her ship's sick bay?"

"Good idea."

Stepper was still calling out commands, overriding Gordon's request for a handheld call to Spectra Station. What had his sister said? Janlin shook her head. Any other Captain would've put it up on the speakers for all to hear, but Diona probably dissed him, and the crew didn't know she hadn't backed the Jump program . . . until now.

Things got too quiet out in the hall. "Oh, no," Janlin whispered. Her wrist cramped, and she switched hands on the pump. She was growing tired. Anaya wasn't responding at all. "Please, Anaya. Please be okay."

She kept pumping, willing Steve to hurry with the sled.

"Captain Inaba didn't make it," came the report from the hall after an interminable length of time. An uneasy silence came over everyone. Not a one of them could say they felt great in that moment, after the Jump, and an awareness grew that anyone could suffer the same fate.

Janlin stared at Stepper as she pumped, waited, pumped, waited. His jaw clenched. He would do anything to keep Diona from having *Hope*. His gaze lifted and met hers.

She knew that crazy look.

Steve arrived with the sled, and they struggled to get the Gitane captain onto it. She wanted to stay, to make sure Stepper wouldn't Jump, but she was the only one who had any experience with the Gitane ship. And now Stepper would not meet her eye.

She marched over to him as Anaya was being carried out the door and got right up in his face.

"Don't you dare Jump," she said, "not even a small one. You have one life on your already bloody hands today, don't make it worse."

He scowled, but she took off at a run. Anaya needed her now.

CHAPTER THREE

GORDON AND STEVE staggered back from lifting Anaya onto the medbay platform as Janlin arrived.

She tossed Gordon a Gitane communicator just like the one Anaya had given her to take to Huantag. "Will this work?" Gordon had managed a hacked repair to the first one after Stepper had smashed it, enabling them to reach Anaya in time to save the *Hope* from disaster. "Use it to call Urse."

He brightened, and she turned to the urgent matter at hand. He would get the Orbitals on the horn, while she got this medbay working to save her friend. Nothing looked familiar, or gave her any clue how to begin. She glanced at Steve, who shrugged, looking scared.

She was scared too. What had Anaya done to activate this thing?

"Start praying this thing runs on autopilot," she said, and chose what seemed to be the most obvious "on" button.

Lights came on, and the panel hummed. A blue line appeared and ran over Anaya's length, looking like any other medbay scanner. Janlin sagged in relief. "Come on, Anaya," she said. "Be okay."

"This is Gordon Lewis of the Jumpship *Hope*, calling Spectra Orbital. Do you copy?"

Gordon tipped his head to listen. When nothing came, he adjusted a setting and tried again.

"Is she regaining consciousness?" Janlin asked Steve.

He shook his head. His face was lined, and he looked ready to break down in tears.

"Did you know Captain Inaba well?" Janlin asked softly.

"Yeah, I did, especially after Huantag. But even before . . . we emigrated from Earth together. Did the pre-tests. Drank sake over the news that we'd been accepted by SpaceOp to live and work out here." He shook his head. "That was eighteen years ago. He was the kindest man, gentle but strong-willed, and I never would have survived the Imag without him." He swiped a tear away, heaving in a big breath.

"He told me I did the right thing, believing in Anaya," Janlin said. She watched the machine insert an IV, and fluids began to run down the tube. *Please, let her be okay.*

Gordon rattled out his call once again, and they waited in silence for a reply.

"We copy! Gordon? Is it really you?"

Gordon's eyes glowed bright with unshed tears. "It's me, bloody rights, luv, it's me, I'm home."

Janlin turned to Steve. "Please try and convince Stepper not to Jump?"

Steve headed for the hatchway. "I'll start a mutiny if I have to."

"THINGS HAVE BEEN bad," Ursula said. "Even if we get food now, some may never see a full recovery. And odd things keep occurring with various nanite systems, like the earcells, making us wonder if they will continue to support our health the way we rely on them to."

Gordon looked sick, and Janlin could see his anguish. "We've brought help, Urse," she said, knowing he couldn't speak for the moment. "These aliens, both races, have some magical ways of fixing people up."

"What are you waiting for, then?" she asked, her voice distant and thin over the comm.

"Er, well . . . there's been other complications." Janlin wondered, would starved bodies be able to handle Yipho's anti-viral medication? "And Diona has us under arrest."

"Dumme schlampe."

Gordon's eyes widened, then a scowl grew. "Right, what's she done, then?"

"Fear has grown on Mars, and there's evidence someone is fanning the flames," Ursula said. "Five people from the last group to emigrate there were mobbed and forced out an airlock. They all asphyxiated while the mob cheered." Janlin could hear cold steel in Urse's voice that hadn't been there before. Clearly, they had experienced their own horrors while the *Hope* was gone.

"The group chanted, 'no outsiders, no spores' as those people died." Ursula's voice rose. "They'd been on Mars for months! There was no way they could be carrying the spore. The whole thing was driven by unreasonable fear."

"Bloody hell." Gordon leaned on the console, grey and shaking, with a grim set to his mouth.

"Diona can't afford an uprising of compassion from the Mars population, so she encourages the idea that outsiders are dangerous, and immigrants as untrustworthy and diseased. Then they don't have to help us."

"Too bad I'm not even surprised," Janlin said, shaking her head.

"We'll be there soon, luv," Gordon promised, giving Janlin a look that meant, don't even think of challenging me right now. "We have food, and medicine, and new friends to tell you about."

"Ah! Here I tell all these sad stories and you . . . wait, what? Janlin wasn't joking, you've really met other life? What took so long? One hundred and thirteen days, Gordon. That's what it's been. No message, no Jump home to tell us what's going on, nothing, for one hundred and thirteen days."

"Yeah, well, the story is not all cheery, Urse. Hang on to your hat, we'll find a way to you soon, all right then?"

JANLIN CHECKED ANAYA again. The Gitane ship's medbay was clearly breathing for her, the pump wheezing in and out, whistling down the tube to the mask. Some sort of electrode seemed to be monitoring other life signs, and the equivalent to an IV continued to drip a grey fluid.

Gordon paced in and out of the medbay door. "We could sure use this ship," he said, staring at Anaya's inert form in earnest. As if he could somehow make her well out of sheer need. "If Diona and Stepper are going to fight over the *Hope*, we need to take what we can and get out of here. Stepper doesn't care about the Orbital populations anyway, and we sure as hell know Diona doesn't either."

"Can't be that hard."

Gordon stopped pacing to stare at her. "What, to bloody care about people?"

She scoffed. "No, apparently that's the hardest thing of all for some. What I meant was flying this thing. We're both pilots . . ."

Gordon actually laughed. "You always did believe you could fly anything, and you never got your chance with the Huantag shuttle, did ya?" He turned and stalked out of the medbay, which led into the central bridge area.

Janlin glanced at Anaya, not wanting to leave her. But if Stepper Jumped the *Hope* again, her friend would likely die. Janlin had to trust the machines monitoring Anaya and try and get them free.

She joined Gordon to find him experimenting with the ship's controls. "And you say I'm ambitious," she said, poking him. "You think you can hack anything with electrical components."

"That's because I bloody well can," he replied. "And will, if that's what it takes to go home."

She squeezed his arm. "We'll get there. Maybe we should join Steve's mutiny and take *Hope* from Stepper."

"And Diona?"

Stepper's sister, SpaceOp's CEO, was a whole other concern. Fear grew in her belly at the idea of being under arrest. "Maybe we could scare her off."

Gordon regarded her with a raised eyebrow.

"We might still be contagious, after all."

He nodded in appreciation of her idea, then quickly changed it to a shake. "Tell her that and we're quarantined as well as under arrest. She's not going to just let us fly off. And it's just a fat lot more ammunition against us, especially once we've been home. Spores *and* an alien virus? We'd be doomed to never, ever set foot on Mars."

"Who cares? With the Huantag tech, we can repair Earth and make a life there. We don't need Mars anymore."

Gordon still disagreed. "We don't have that tech yet, and now it seems aliens don't take the Jump well. Geesh, neither do we, for all that," he said, holding his head. "Huantag tech might not come soon enough."

"Hey, come on," Janlin said. "We can't solve all the problems in one go. If we can make this ship fly, we'll sneak out of here so we have a chance to sort it out later, all right?"

"We need to take food stores," he reminded her.

"On it. Keep an eye on her, would ya?"

Janlin ran down the short corridor to the open airlock. This was where she had once entered off the Imag slave ship to first meet Anaya, Yipho, and the rest of the Gitane ship's crew. Now it stood open to *Hope's* flightdeck. Bins of food stores, seeds, and all kinds of trade goods from Huantag were strapped against a nearby wall. The Gitane ship she had dubbed "Freedom" had been instrumental in shuttling most of it to the *Hope* before they left.

"Woulda been an idea to maybe leave some aboard," Janlin grumbled, turning back for the sled they had used to move the unconscious Gitane. The idea that Stepper had his proverbial finger on the Jump button made her skin itch. What was happening on the bridge right now? She tapped her earcell and sent a ping to Steve, only to hear a high-pitched whine of feedback that chattered out to silence.

"Dammit!"

Then the ship-wide alarm sounded to prepare to Jump. She immediately changed course back the way she'd come. Climbing into the Gitane ship, Janlin took a moment to lift one of the floor covers that led down to the ship's storage bay. There, to her relief, were a dozen bins. Food? Medicine? Gitane tax records? Who knew, but there wasn't time to check.

As she turned away, she caught sight of something familiar. Their Huantag flight suits lay piled atop the bins she hoped were full of food and seed stores. What she wouldn't give to try flying with those in zero-G.

She ran back to Gordon, happy to see the console lit up. "We're outta time," she said, "And while there are some bins down below, I don't know what's in them."

Gordon did not look up. "We need a password, I think. We have power, but no control."

Janlin felt her blood pressure rise. "Again? How do we keep getting ourselves in these situations?"

"I don't know. But if Stepper Jumps to Mars, I for one am not sure I'll make it."

She read the pain on his face in the way his mouth tightened and his eyes squinted. "That bad?"

He swallowed and nodded. "Sometimes I can't even see. Blackness creeps in from the sides, you know?"

She knew. Several times the pain got so bad she thought she might puke. "What about the people we leave behind? They could die, like Inaba."

"I can't care about them just now."

"Gordon!"

"What? You're worried about Anaya, aren't you? And we can't save everyone. We have to get food to Ursula."

"Of course we do, but not at the expense of our crew here. If we stop Stepper and ensure *everyone's* safety, they can create a diversion when we go." She couldn't believe they were having this conversation. Why couldn't he hear her reasoning?

But Gordon's stubbornness, and his understandable desire to just get food to Ursula, gave him tunnel vision. "He could Jump at any minute. Any second! And to effing Mars, Janlin."

"Fine, get this thing going then." She crossed her arms.

"You're just gonna bloody stand there?"

She considered. "No, I'm going to go help Steve stop Stepper from endangering *everyone's* lives," she said, a little heavy on the snark.

They glared at each other, gauging, angry, frustrated to suddenly be on opposing sides. He turned back to the board, and with a huff she left at a run.

CHAPTER FOUR

HOPE WAS BIG enough to have three levels, interconnecting corridors, bulkheads to seal off each section, and accommodations for three hundred and twenty people. Getting from the flight bay floor where the Gitane ship was parked all the way back to the bridge let her know just how awful she was still feeling from the Jump. The fear of ending up like Inaba made her take it slower than she'd like.

The viability of the whole Jump technology would now rest on making it safe for biological beings.

It was probably good that Gordon was focused on getting the Gitane ship away from *Hope*. Like he said, they *were* still under arrest.

Did she dare contact Diona and reveal their contagion? It would at least slow her takeover and buy them some time, wouldn't it? *Bah, smart lady like that already has us under quarantine, I'll bet.*

A larger crowd now filled the hall leading to the bridge, but people parted and let her through. Although she was pretty sure they understood the whole story behind the arrival of Anaya's team with a miracle cure, some crewmembers still looked at her askance, as if they also remembered the suspicions that Stepper had thrown around.

The bridge was equally packed, and Steve stood before a pinned-down Stepper, who was brilliantly red in the face. He turned his hot gaze on her, and Janlin cursed the twist of fear it brought in her gut. The guys holding him to his chair tightened their grip.

"We will not let you Jump again, Stepper," Steve said, arms folded. "You endanger everyone's lives, which gives us firm ground within SpaceOp's policies to refuse."

"Fuck SpaceOp and the whole lot of you," Stepper snarled. "You're gonna let that bitch take it all, own you all, even after she left us to die? Can't you see we'll never have a say on anything until she has some competition?"

"Maybe so, but we're not Jumping again and risking lives for you to start some corporate battle with your sister."

Time for diversion.

"We've contacted Spectra Orbital and spoken with Gordon's wife, Ursula," Janlin announced, and it produced just the effect she wanted. All eyes turned to her, and questions were called out.

"They are alive but hurting, Urse says. And there's been awful things happening on Mars." She tried to tell the story quickly, which only seemed to add to the horror. "My point is, Stepper is right. That ship out there does not have our best interests in mind. We need to buy some time so we don't have to Jump, and telling them we are carrying an alien virus might be the truth we need."

"What about the food we brought for the Orbitals?" Steve asked.

"I propose we sneak Anaya's ship off with some supplies."

This was met with general agreement. Stepper stared at her, a sneer on his face. "Trying for Captain, Jannilove?"

Janlin ignored him and turned to Steve. "As ranking officer under Captain Inaba, you are next in command, so that makes you Captain. I was wondering if you have any ideas for a diversion that will allow us to slip away? Oh . . . and how we might get past the Gitane ship passcodes? Gordon has power but no control, but we don't have a conscious Gitane to ask."

Steve unfolded his arms and blinked at Janlin. *Come on, Steve, I need you to take the lead here.*

"All of these things and more will need discussion," he said, standing straighter, even as he winced and rubbed his head. Janlin sagged with relief. "Clearly, we need more information."

Stepper began yelling, spewing profanities and rhetoric

against his sister, and then against Janlin, then against Steve. Steve indicated for him to be taken out. "Do we even have a brig?" he asked as Danal and another of the larger crewmembers hauled him out the door, Stepper still spitting profanities. "If we do, put him in it, and if we don't, make one up and post a guard."

Janlin tapped her earcell almost out of habit, and by some small miracle this time got through. "Mutiny accomplished," she said to Gordon despite still being miffed with him. "How is our patient?"

"No change, but . . . Janlin, I have to go."

"I know. Our new Captain is going to create a diversion for us, we just have to figure out how to fly it without its owner's permission."

She heard a humourless snort. "Hacking code is one thing . . . this is completely alien, literally. Maybe our attention would be better spent waking her up."

"And how?"

"I don't know." She heard the despair in his voice. "I just want to go home so Ursula can eat."

The fear of Diona taking everything and not letting them go to the Orbitals grew in Janlin's mind. Stopping Stepper was vital, sure, especially after what happened to Yasu Inaba. Then she wondered where they had put his body, and that just made her feel morbid. "We'll find a way to her soon," Janlin assured her friend.

Steve set people to tasks gathering info on their Jump home and searching for ideas to their problems. "In fact, Linder, you and I should take a look at how to Jump without it being so life-threatening."

Nano-biologist Dr. Linder Brown, another survivor from the first Jumpship, *Renegade*, shrugged. "I'm not sure there is anything to be done about the cognitive dissonance the brain suffers when we fold space. It's impossible to alleviate the discrepancy between traveling two vastly different distances at the same time."

"Keep thinking," Steve encouraged, waving Janlin aside. "What's going on?" he asked her in a low tone.

"Gordon can't fly without access codes, and our Gitane friend is still unconscious."

"And with SpaceOp? Here Stepper was stringing us along, and

when I think back on it, no one ever thought to ask him outright how he convinced Diona to let him do this. But you seem to know something."

Guilt wracked her. "I knew because I called him on it over my dad, in my initial briefing. He knew he wouldn't have everyone's support if he told them SpaceOp wasn't behind it."

"Geesh," Steve said. "Risky as shit."

"That's our Stepper," Janlin said. "But now I'm concerned Diona will commandeer these food and seed stores right along with the *Hope*, and the Orbitals will never see a morsel."

"That's our Diona," Steve countered, and they both gave a grim laugh. He considered. "Maybe we can make a deal."

"A deal? With CEO Diona Jordan?" Janlin grimaced. "Good luck with that. Our contagious state is really all you've got to work with."

Steve smiled. "No, we have something even better."

"Captain, we're being hailed again."

"Hologram, please."

CHAPTER FIVE

DIONA, IN HOLOGRAPHIC form, took one look at Steve and demanded, "Who are you?"

Steve politely gave his name and calmly stated the facts of the situation: they were carrying a deadly alien virus, Jumps appeared to be potentially lethal and had just killed one of their crew, and Stepper Jordan had been detained after endangering the lives of the crew.

"So you see, Commander, we are quite compromised," Steve said as he summed things up for Diona. "Might as well let us go home to the Orbitals. They're willing to take the chance on the virus, and I know you wouldn't want that on Mars. Meanwhile, I think I can offer you something in return for releasing us . . . something, or someone, shall I say?"

Diona Jordan, CEO of SpaceOp and Stepper's older sister, regarded Steve.

"You mutinied," she said, eyes narrowed, "and you're trying to bargain. Interesting." She tipped her head, an iconic pose of hers that everyone knew. "I gather you're offering me my brother? Why would I want him?"

Steve stood by the captain's chair, head high, back straight. Janlin stayed out of the line-of-sight for the hologram comm unit.

"Why? For the knowledge of Jumpships and how to build them, of course," Steve said. "Then you have no need of this contaminated one."

Now Diona crossed her arms. "You're telling me you actually went to another world and met aliens," she said.

"We did. We lost two hundred and eighty-seven crew members . . . sorry, two hundred and eighty-eight now, first to slavers known as Imag, then to an alien virus we were infected with by the Imag before being shipped dirtside to meet the Huantag. We can assure you Stepper's Jumpship tech works, even if it has some rather harsh side-effects that need ironed out."

Again Diona paused, considering. "So, Stepper would need to remain in quarantine indefinitely?"

Steve smiled. "That would be my recommendation, Commander."

Soon enough, Stepper had been handed over in a full EVA suit, having been previously gassed unconscious to make life easier for everyone. Janlin called Gordon up, and they watched Stepper's body being floated between airlocks.

"Danal, begin a slow burn to Earth orbit please," Steve said. There was a brief pause, then several of the crew broke out in a cheer. Janlin didn't have the heart to join them, and Gordon didn't seem ready to celebrate either. She put a hand on his arm and squeezed.

"We'll be home soon."

And sure enough, before too long they were making the final approach, slower by far than Gordon wanted, but nevertheless they were nearly home. They took the time to do a deep cleanse on the interior of the ship, everyone pitching in to sanitize everything they could. They might have anti-virals, but if they could avoid making anyone sick at all, that would be best.

Once her own cabin was shining with the stink of disinfectant, and she had checked on Anaya and found no difference in the alien's condition, Janlin climbed to the bridge. Real-time monitors and expansive windows teamed up to give detailed close-ups and stunning vistas of Earth and her Moon standing against the backdrop of blackest space.

It was something she had looked forward to doing with Anaya.

Views of Spectra, New Horizons, and Advent, their three orbital homes, were shown on the screens above the view window, offering a zoomed-in look at what was currently only small, distant specks speeding around Earth. Janlin studied the planet that filled the viewscreen, searching for pockets in the storm clouds. What was once known as the Blue Marble was now a churning dirty-white cotton ball. Wistful at first, her mood shifted when she thought of the desperate people there. Nightmares of that blue-eyed man waving a gun at her and urging her to run plagued her as much as dreams of Stepper ranting at her before slamming down on her knee. That thing still ached. Add her grief over her dad and the fact both her parents were gone now to everything else, and it was no wonder she still couldn't find any joy in their homecoming.

Gordon, on the other hand, might just climb outta his skin if they don't hurry up, she thought, watching her friend pace before the window.

"New Horizons and Advent populations all moved here recently," Ursula was telling Steve on the comm. "So there's no need for shuttling things to the other Orbitals. Our last count put us at 7,824."

Steve checked with Janlin, who gave an affirmative nod. "We have enough anti-viral meds for everyone, although we should not still be contagious," he assured Ursula. "And we brought grains, flours, dried fruits and tubers, and especially for you, seeds! All from an alien planet named Huantag."

Everyone grinned at the joyful whoop that came over the speaker. Janlin watched Gordon and knew that, if it were possible for a human to Jump or teleport or whatever you wanted to call it, he'd be on Spectra Orbital Station right now.

When the docking was finally complete, the air cycled, and the hatch opened, the surviving members of the *Renegade* and *Hope* crews filed impatiently through the UVC sterilization process, helping again to kill any viruses or bacteria they may be carrying on their hair or clothes. They flowed through to flood into the waiting room full of friends and family. Janlin used to hate the UVC scan, suspicious of it actually harming their cells, but now she was glad of it. Despite smart people like Linder telling her enough time had passed, and that they should not still be shedding the virus, Janlin was nervous. Memories of all too quiet shapes under blankets in Huantag huts was enough to have her worried.

Ursula was right by the door as she and Gordon emerged, and instantly they were in each other's arms. Suddenly, Janlin felt the joy, the relief, the success, that she hadn't been able to believe until this moment. She sagged against the nearby wall, weak in the knees.

"Okay, Janlin?" Steve paused by her elbow, facing the room full of people celebrating.

"Yes, I'm okay, thank you." She smiled her cheeriest smile at him and got a toothy response. "Are you okay?"

He took in the celebration. "I sure didn't mean to become Captain of a Jumpship." There was a fair amount of chagrin in his tone.

"Ursula," a woman called as she approached. She wore scrubs and the insignia of the orbital medical teams. "We are ready to begin scanning these supplies."

Janlin saw that Gordon would not let Ursula go, not for now anyway and not for a while, so she waved the woman over. "Here," Janlin said, pointing to the sled stacked with medi-kits. "This is the anti-viral. The packets are in groups of a hundred. We are to only use them on a patient that gets ill."

"Excellent, thanks." The woman grinned as she watched the long-separated couple.

"You have hair again," Ursula was saying to Gordon, still wrapped firmly in his embrace. Her cheeks shone with happy tears as she cupped his bearded face in her hands.

"What a great sight, eh?" the nurse said, staring wistfully at them.

Janlin couldn't agree more. "They deserve so much happiness, those two." She stuck out her hand. "I'm Janlin."

"Cassie," she replied with a firm nod and firmer handshake. "Cassie Milner. Is this anti-viral a subcutaneous injection?"

"A *who*?" Janlin asked, and Cassie laughed.

"Where was it injected?"

"Mine was injected here," she said, indicating her shoulder. "Anaya would know . . ." she started, glancing back down the airlock corridor.

"Tell me about these aliens," Cassie said.

"Well, Anaya is eight foot seven, average height for her race, and they have grey leathery skin kinda like an elephant's. They are rather frightful looking," Janlin admitted.

"Are we certain they are friendly?"

Janlin tried to be patient with the nurse's uncertainty. She hadn't lived with the Gitane like Janlin had. In fact, no one had, not like she did after her escape from the Imag.

"I can vouch for Anaya," Janlin said, meeting Cassie's gaze square-on. "You'll understand better once you've heard our story."

Cassie regarded her with frank curiosity. "I can't imagine. I see the evidence of wounds that are more than just physical."

Janlin nodded at her astute observation. "Do we have many therapists on board? I'm sure we'd all benefit." She tried to keep her voice light, almost joking, but Cassie saw through her bluster and pulled her into an abrupt and unexpected hug.

"Oomph," Janlin said. Then she just melted into it, like a surrender, and returned the hug. "Aw, man, thank you."

Cassie held her at arm's length. "You're welcome. Come on, let's get this inspection centre set up. How long do we have to wait for the all the juicy details? Can you tell me about the virus at least?"

Her chatter helped Janlin keep it together, and she gladly guided the sled to follow Cassie. The mood was high as people reunited all around them. She did see some people weeping, though. There were so many that weren't coming back.

"I'd rather ask you about my alien friend's health first, if that's okay," Janlin said, as much to keep her mind from her grief over her dad as anything.

The Gitane's condition nagged at her, begging for some answer, some solution. She explained the situation to Cassie. "They said Yasu Inaba had suffered a stroke due to a brain aneurism. I'm worried Anaya's brain could be struggling with the same thing."

"I'm sorry, that sounds horrible, and to lose someone . . ." She shook her head. "No wonder I'm reading such trauma in all of you."

"Here's the thing, we lost many, my dad one of them, but we haven't lost Anaya, and I'm really scared we might. Is there anything we can do to help her brain recover? Or at least scan her to find out what's . . . oh, who am I kidding, it's not like we'll know what looks right or wrong."

"An-a-ya. Yip-hoe." Cassie repeated the foreign names like she was tasting them.

Janlin chuckled. "Well, Yipho laughs at me every time I say

his name, so I'm pretty sure my accent sucks. Yip-yo, Yip-huoe, I don't know, something like that." She sobered and shook her head. "They are special to me, like family now, if that makes any sense."

Cassie nodded. "I get it. Sometimes special people become family very quickly. I'm in good with an excellent doctor," she said with a wink, pointing to her wedding ring. "Maybe we could examine Anaya once these supplies are unpacked."

Janlin nearly choked on her relief. "That sounds great."

CHAPTER SIX

Cassie called Janlin away from the hubbub of the welcome home party. "Come meet my guy, Dr. Li Wei," she said, waving Janlin down a medical arm of the pod. They entered a side office attached to a row of examination rooms. Dr. Wei looked up from an electron microscope.

"This anti-viral isn't biological," he said before introductions could begin.

"Hello to you too," Cassie said. "This is Janlin Kavanagh from the Jumpship. She could use your help."

He immediately set the sample aside and rose. "I have a room prepped if you would follow me," he said.

Cassie patted his arm. "No dear, it's not for her, it's her friend."

"Oh," Dr. Wei said, dropping back into his seat. "Are you sure? You don't look so good."

"Fair enough," Janlin said. "I don't feel so great either." Her head was splitting in two with a machete chop of pain, and every spike made her squint. Inaba's stroke was very top-of-mind. "What did you mean, not biological?" she asked, gesturing at the slide he pulled from the microscope.

"It looks an awful lot like nanite machines just like our NECS. What do you know of the virus it is to heal us from?"

Janlin stared at him, stricken with this news. "In that case, it was likely a nanite-driven illness, too." She was surprised Anaya hadn't told her, and a little hurt. "And I'm only just now questioning something else. They gave me a vaccine of sorts, before I went dirtside on Huantag. The others received this anti-viral because they were sick with the virus. I never came down with it. So, why didn't they send us what I received, which was obviously a vaccine, instead?"

"We'd better run some tests on these medicines," Cassie said.

Li was quick to agree, but Janlin worried it further. "We've already tested both the Imag virus, and the Gitane anti-viral that stopped it from killing people, in real time. Trust me, even if they're nanites, you want these Gitane meds just in case there's any more of those Imag ones still floating around."

Li fixed the slide and made a few notations. "Can't say as I like it. We're full of machines we don't fully understand, that we can't fix when they fail, and whose capabilities must be restricted because they could go AI and us take over," he muttered. "Feels like a risky game we're playing . . . and now we're going to add alien gear?"

Janlin sighed. "None of you received injections from the Imag, or spent time on their awful ship, and enough time has passed we shouldn't be contagious anymore, despite what we told Diona. Hopefully no one will fall ill at all."

"We can hope. I'm glad to hear you took the precautions with cleaning, in any case."

"Would it be better to have our whole system purged of nanites?" Janlin asked. "Is it possible to remove them?"

Li looked doubtful. "The process would require highly specialized nano-bots to clean the NECS out, and we don't have the tech or the parts to do that anymore. It died with civilization on Earth. Also, the NECS help us deal with a lot of physical ailments and stresses of life in orbit. We may not do well without them." Li gave a little bow of his head, then switched track. "What can you tell me about your friend?"

"Her name is Anaya, and she's alien. I can fill you in on the way."

Li blinked at her. "Alien?" he finally said.

Cassie chuckled and pulled him out of his chair to follow Janlin, who she waved out the door. "Yes, dear, she's in a bit of a way, this alien. The Jump seemed to do something nasty to her."

Janlin snorted. "Does something nasty to each and every one

of us, especially right afterward. That's why you thought I was your patient." She described the vertigo, spiking pain in the head, general inability to think straight, ongoing feeling of bugs on the skin, numb spots, memory loss, loss of balance, head spins. "And things just don't taste and smell right anymore, either," she complained.

"Definitely sounds neurological," Li said.

"Which would make sense," Janlin agreed. "Plus, there's all the problems with the earcells . . ."

"Oh, that's been happening here, too," Cassie said. "Lots of theories going around about the nanites starting to fail on us. One programmer I know wondered why there aren't any updates, and figures there should've been. You know, patching and upgraded drivers, like any software."

They entered Spectra's hangar bay. *Hope* sat there with her hatch open and a ramp projecting down to the floor. Within *Hope's* bay sat the Gitane shuttle, its airlock also open. Janlin led them inside.

Janlin held her arms out. "Welcome aboard. We can't seem to pronounce the name of this alien shuttle, so I call her *Freedom.*"

Cassie and Li both looked a little stunned at all the strangeness around them. Janlin forgot how weird it would seem to them. To her, it was a refuge, a sanctuary, the place she began to heal from the Imag torture.

"Good memories," she murmured to herself. Li went instinctively towards the soft glow of the medbay. They followed him inside.

"I hit that button," Janlin said, pointing. "And it seemed to do the right things." She smoothed Anaya's brow. The grey skin had no life to it, but it wasn't hot. That was a good thing, right? Did Gitane get fevers?

She looked up to see Li staring at her hands where they lay on alien skin. With a visible mental shake, he overcame his shock and began to examine Anaya, his training taking over.

"Clearly an IV," he murmured, tapping the line leading into Anaya's arm before peering at the other tubes. "Oxygen, good."

Cassie came up beside Janlin. "She is strangely beautiful," she said, laying a gentle hand on Anaya's arm. "You are good friends with her?"

Janlin had to swallow the lump in her throat. "Yeah. And she kept her promise. When everything seemed against it, she came through. She saved us all." She looked up at Cassie. "She didn't have to. She could've just stayed out of the way and protected her own. But she didn't. She risked her crew to save us."

"Well then, she deserves the best care we can give her. What do you think, Li?"

He straightened up from looking in Anaya's eyes and threw his hands up a bit. "I don't even know what I'm looking at. Do their pupils dilate? Do they have pupils? I couldn't tell! Palpitating the abdomen is standard, but I don't know what organs are beneath the skin nor their position, so that's useless. What about blood pressure? Do these beings get fevers? Is her temperature a good sign, or a bad one? I mean, I want to help, but there are so many unknowns."

Janlin chewed her lip. "I understand. Thanks for having a look at her anyway."

"Don't worry, this medbay seems like it's doing its job," he assured her. "Perhaps she only needs time to heal from the Jump trauma."

Janlin massaged her own skull, desperate for any relief. "I hope time heals us all."

"AND THAT'S MY version of the story."

Janlin stood on a raised platform in the largest gathering area Spectra had. Some eight thousand people listened in near-perfect silence, an eerie feeling. Steve, in his official role as Captain Netchkie, had already told the *Renegade*'s perspective in abbreviated and censured form, and had asked her to do much the same for *Hope*, as she had the unique perspective of her relationship with the Gitane.

Steve stepped up to Janlin's side and thanked her. "Please stand to take a moment to honour all those we lost."

Like a sighing wave, the crowd came to their feet. The entire front section held all the survivors of the two crews. Janlin couldn't look at Gordon and Ursula. They would either make her laugh or sob, neither of which would be appropriate.

She couldn't wait to be out of the public eye.

Dad, Teardrop, Tyrell, Yasu, Sandy, Fran, the list went on. Janlin swallowed hard, tears dripping down. She held on to the good, to knowing Gordon and Ursula were together again. Now she did look, and they both watched her, love and concern on their faces, tears too, their hands gripped tight.

As long as those two are all right, I'm all right, she told herself, giving them a weak, watery smile.

JANLIN QUICKLY LEARNED Cassie and Li were good friends of Ursula's now. They gathered after the ceremony and told everyone about examining Anaya.

"Li hopes the coma is needed to heal whatever trauma occurred in the brain, and that she might come out of it just fine," Cassie said. "The medbay seems to be keeping her going safely through it."

Li nodded. "There could be bleeding on the brain, but there's no way I would consider operating . . . I have no knowledge of Gitane brain structure, strangely enough . . ." His smile was friendly and sad.

"She'll pull through," Gordon said. "The reason Janlin and Anaya are such good friends is they're both tough as nails," he told the group. "Anaya has proved a good and loyal ally. We would not have survived the Imag virus without her and her next in command, Yipho."

"That's it!" Janlin cried. "You said it right. Do it again!"

"Yipho?"

"No, like before," she said, trying to understand and hear the difference so she could repeat it. "Yipho." Soon everyone was trying it, this way and that, to much laughter.

"Oh, I wish Anaya was here," Janlin said, sobering. "But if we thought we had problems being allowed on Mars before, now that we told Diona about our alien cooties, there's no hope at all."

"Not long after you left, Diona released a statement saying there was little anyone could do to help the Orbitals, but Mars was safe, and people needed to stay calm. As if staying calm was going to fill our bellies," Cassie said.

The helpless anger was palpable. "Bloody hell, we have to become self-sufficient," Gordon said, pounding a fist into his palm.

Janlin couldn't agree more. To be dependent on Diona and by extension Stepper made her feel ill. "That's why the Jumpships are so important. We need a new planet," she said, gearing up to tell the others more about Huantag.

"I don't agree," Gordon said, cutting her off. "We need to be like the Huantag we met and take care of what we have, not go trying to find it somewhere else."

This started a heated debate that turned sour quick.

"Look, the Jumpships were supposed to be our saving grace," Janlin said to Li, on her feet now.

"But they aren't safe," Gordon said. She turned to him.

"That doesn't mean we shouldn't work towards possible ways to make them safe. *Hope* is a damn fine ship, and if we can solve the dissonance at the very least we can move between here and Mars quicker, and without so much radiation risk." She looked to Steve, who nodded in support. "What if we made it back there, and as a result, could rejuvenate Earth with help from the Huantag?" she asked Gordon. "They successfully bioengineered a way of living in harmony with their planet after almost losing it the way we did," she explained to the others.

She saw the doubt. Both Cassie and Li frowned.

"How do you calm the relentless storm cycles?" Cassie asked.

"Or cure the plagues?" Li said. "Polio, covid, and anthrax could still be in the water."

"Plus the earthquakes are still frequent now the weight of sheet ice is lifted," Steve added helpfully.

Li nodded. "Add to all that the acidified oceans, the water tables that are spoiled or dry, the soil depleted of minerals, animal populations decimated, seventy-eight percent of mammal species extinct . . . are these aliens that good?" Li's questions were legitimate ones, and Janlin didn't have the answers.

"I guess it all remains to be seen. We need more information on how they repaired their own planet." She turned to ask Li more about the anti-virals being nanite tech.

"I have an idea for Luna Base," Gordon said before she could. All eyes turned to him. "Vent it, blow it clean through, and start fresh with the seed we brought. And," he said, holding up a hand at Ursula's attempt to interrupt, "those who go in do a cleanse, cold rinse, crack on in there naked if we have to, whatever it bloody well takes. Worth a try, luv, don't you think?" Some laughed at his "naked" suggestion.

"Maybe," Ursula allowed. "Although we must be sparing with our experiments. As Janlin noted, more help is not coming any time soon if we cannot safely Jump."

They made plans in general agreement, and Janlin saw that taking action, any kind of action, was the best medicine of all. But Luna wasn't a final answer, it was never meant to be. They needed a planet, and for that they needed to Jump.

Why did it feel like everyone was against her on that?

CHAPTER SEVEN

JANLIN SAT BENT over seed trays, the smell of soil and water rich in her nose. She wrote tiny codes on each section of tiny plants. Gordon and Ursula were each making piles as they unpacked crates. Ursula would put half in each pile, then Gordon would pick from the "stay" pile and sneak it into the "Luna" pile. He saw her looking and winked, putting a finger to his lips. Janlin just shook her head and snorted a laugh. Ursula would notice, reprimand him, and re-sort it. It was what they did, and it was magic that she could watch them together like this again.

The spore seemed contained, so they planned a trial garden of Earth crops in with the Huantag ones as well. Once done with the labelling, Janlin's next mundane job was to set seeds to germinate.

"Are you sure we shouldn't test a small Jump?" Janlin said as Gordon brought in another crate.

Gordon rolled his eyes. "If you could fly that bloody ship alone, you'd have done it by now, wouldn'tcha?" His voice had some of the old joking, but there was a new edge of frustration. Janlin did her best to keep her own edge tamped down.

"We will find a way to safely Jump eventually, or we're doomed as a species," Janlin insisted. "And it might be the only way to get Anaya some help, to say nothing of getting her home." She thought the last point made it all very much worth it.

"If we have food, we will bloody well survive," Gordon

countered. "The Earth will repair itself eventually, we only have to hold on."

"For what? And why wait for that 'eventually' if the Huantag can help us now?"

"Why risk dying for the slight chance they will actually help? Do you remember how they left the Gitane and Imag with no planet? And how little they like leaving their planet? What's to say they don't lock up their borders once again and refuse to talk to us even if we do manage to get back there?"

Ursula sighed, got up, and left the room where they were sorting seeds. Janlin let her hair fall over her work, hiding how close to tears she was. Gordon maintained the silence.

Ursula returned, carrying more trays, just as Steve appeared at the main pod entrance. His expression was grim. "Our head of Orbital Navigation, Aarav Najeev, just suffered a stroke."

Gordon turned on Janlin. "See, Kavanagh?" he cried, tapping his own head. "There's no safe way to Jump. I'll have me teeth pulled with pliers before I'll risk another Jump."

Janlin raised an eyebrow at him. "I'll pull them for you if you hold me back from trying," she said, only half-joking.

Ursula tsked at both of them before turning to Steve. "I am so sorry to hear this; Aarav was an excellent cook and great conversationalist. Who will cover him?" she asked.

"One of his teammates, either Pravin Parmar or Najiib Farah. Problem is, we don't have anyone else trained in Orbital Navigation. Their backups were both on *Renegade* and didn't return with us. There is one Orbital-born teenager that's shown an interest, but he's nowhere near being of help, and they are adamant they need at least three on their team."

Janlin blinked. "Wasn't Aarav with us on *Hope*? What have they been doing in our absence?"

Ursula gave her a bland look. "Working overtime."

"A lot of overtime, from what they tell me," Steve said, running a hand through already frazzled hair. The straight black spikes made him look comical, at a time when nothing was funny. "They decided to share Aarav's duties while we were away, thinking we'd be back sooner, of course. Now they're both threatening to quit if they can't get some help."

Cassie and Li arrived at the door. "Did you hear about Aarav?"

"The stroke?" Janlin said.

Cassie shook her head, her eyes filling with tears. Li pulled her close and spoke for her. "He passed. Another brain aneurism, like Inaba."

Steve groaned. "We have no future," he blurted out, pacing around a bit only to throw himself down into a chair. "We've got no backup, and with Mars out of the picture, no ability to even try and manufacture our own replacement parts. We have no one to take Inaba's place, or Aarav's, or the other two hundred and eighty-six people we lost on that trip. We can't go forward, we can't go back . . ."

Ursula came up behind where he sat and put her hands on his shoulders, giving a few gentle squeezes, her pale hands in stark contrast to his brown skin. "If we can grow these seeds, the plants will give us more. If we can sterilize Luna Base again, we will have more room, too. And perhaps then we can look to help from these alien friends of yours someday, see about repairing our planet. But listen," she said as she waved a finger at Steve and then at all of them. "All we have is this moment, right here, right now." She waved her arms to encompass them, the room, the pod, the whole orbital station. "We have food, air, water, shelter, and each other. We have now. It's all we've got."

Ah, that's where the line of thought had come from in Gordon. Janlin felt tension drain out of everyone. Steve rose and gave Ursula a grateful hug. "You always do know just the right thing to say," he told her.

"Bloody rights she does, and good thing too, 'cause I never say the right thing," Gordon exclaimed, to sympathetic laughter.

Everyone got into the mood that Ursula had set and sat to enjoy the strange meal laid before them. Those that had Jumped helped those that were new to Huantag food decide what to try and how to combine things. The blue tubes brought Janlin back to their first night on Huantag, when the fresh grief of her dad's death made her uninterested in the strange food and Gordon had done his best to comfort her in the face of his own loss and grief.

But even as they strove to live in the moment and keep the conversation light, troublesome subjects kept popping up, and Diona's misdeeds became the topic yet again amongst heated debate on whether or not they had any responsibility to help those being ostracized.

"There's also the Mars families and next-of-kin of those we

lost," Janlin pointed out.

Steve's eye widened. "Ah, yeah, they need contacted. Would you work on that, Janlin?"

"If we can find a way to connect," she replied. "We've been cut off from Mars comm link for a while now, but I think I know someone who could help," she said, thinking of Jessie Brighton, the IT specialist.

"I can't believe they just cut us loose like that," came the old refrain, and the discussion got going all over again.

"I guess it's just all top-of-mind, Luv," Gordon said to Ursula when she pointed it out. "Got ourselves some wee problems, and if we don't talk 'em out, we won't solve them, will we?"

JANLIN TAPPED HER earcell and subvocalized "Gordon" as she had a thousand times before, but all she got was feedback that pierced her already unhappy head.

"End call, geez, *end call!*" The noise stopped. Janlin thought about trying Urse, but she felt a little raw from the bombardment of noise, like she'd just been dressed down by a drill sergeant.

She was in *Freedom*, was that blocking the signal? She left the alien ship and wandered out into the expansive shuttle bay. From here, *Hope* was magnificent, a shiny Biocrete structure perched on the gleaming bay floor like some giant bird of prey ready to soar. In comparison, Anaya's shuttle was dull metal, dark and brooding.

She tapped again, and this time connected with a ping, although still a bit garbled. Then static started and wouldn't stop, and there was no response on the other end. She sighed, cut the call, and made her way from the bay to find him. As usual, he was helping his wife with her crops. Janlin complained about her earcell.

Gordon rolled his eyes. "Oh yeah, I got a line of feedback that near wrecked me skull yesterday. It's brutal, left me completely knackered, yeah? So I put myself on 'away' setting."

Janlin nodded in empathy. "I should, too. The pain is a little over-the-top. Have Ursula and the rest been having this much trouble, or is it just us?"

"Nah, it's got them too. Urse and I have given up using it, really."

"Damn. So, those that *didn't* Jump are having head pain

troubles too?"

Gordon's eyes widened. "Bloody hell. No, they're not, but Urse mentioned feedback, static, and dropped calls. Not so piercingly awful like us idiots that Jumped, but they are buggered too, and that's right shitty news."

"So it's not just Jumps, the NECS are failing. We have to find a way to purge our systems of these screwed-up machines!" Janlin said, pounding the table for emphasis.

"Kavanagh, that is one thing you and I can agree on. Once Luna is growing . . ."

"Can we wait?" she asked, interrupting him. Another spike hit her brain, and she hissed, her eyes scrunching closed.

Gordon waved her off, his own squint belying his nonchalance. "Steve said the programming would take time . . ."

"And Steve admitted we don't actually have the replacement parts or the tech required. We need Mars, Gordon. Mars has parts, Mars has the specialists, Mars has answers."

Gordon slammed his own hands down on the table, making her flinch in surprise. "Mars is not *our* answer," he growled. He glared at her as if daring her to push the issue. "Have you forgotten how they cut us off? Did you even hear Ursula's story about what happened there?"

"Yes, I heard," she replied, with perhaps a bit too much snark. "Doesn't mean I can't slip in there and . . ."

"Good Lord, Kavanagh. Give. It. Up. We are here, we have food, we have hope. Stop chasing adventure like a child." He turned and walked off, not even letting her respond. "I'm going to help my wife."

CHAPTER EIGHT

DIONA BROUGHT UP the lights inside Stepper's cell. He came to his feet immediately, his face twisted in anger.

"Why did you let them go?" Stepper raged. He banged the thick window, fully aware that the cell was impenetrable, completely sealed, cut off from communications and contaminations, and even safe from radiation and EMP blasts. A "Faraday cage" for emergencies. Another idea her father had. Diona thought it also made a great quarantine room, especially since the louder her brother got, the more she turned the volume down. He sputtered and ranted, cursing her even being born. "That's my fucking ship, you had no right to let them just fly off with it like that."

She laughed at him, knowing how much it would drive him mad. He spit at her, the juices running down the glass between them. She just shook her head.

"I did it to watch you blow your stack, dear brother, and you've complied as hoped. That ship will still be there when we need it." Stepper flipped the bird at her with both hands, then threw himself about the room, swiping each surface clear of the few items she'd allowed and kicking the chair over. Sometimes she wondered if they were really siblings. He had no control over his emotions at all. "Next time maybe you won't fuck off doing your own stupid projects when I'm trying to keep us alive here." Couldn't he see how much she needed him to be stronger? To have her back like a brother should? But no, she had to do it all on her own, and then *he* had the nerve to be mad at *her*. Made her want to rage, but she was better than that. She stuck to the facts and gave him the dressing down he deserved. "Besides, Jumps only degrade the nanites faster. You knew that and still put over six hundred people through it? And only returned with three hundred and some?"

"Stop pretending you care. They were Orbitals peeps, every one of them, and you plainly don't give a fuck about them."

"Your reasoning is skewed," she came back. "What of all those NECS you've wasted? I told you not to try the Jump . . ."

"To be fair, some stayed on Huantag . . ."

Diona slapped her hand against the glass in frustration. He smirked, enjoying his small win. But his face fell quickly enough. After all, she was the one walking free, and he was the one in a cell. "You always focus on the wrong thing, brother," she said, turning to go. "That's why you're going to stay in here a very long time."

Diona flicked the holo control that cut the mic and lowered the lights in the control room until she stood in darkness. He stood bathed in the lights of the cell, unable to see her at all. She watched with some small pleasure as Stepper threw a magnificent temper tantrum that ended with him curled on the floor sobbing. She turned to leave but, as an afterthought, called up the holo to dim the lights inside the cell as well.

Stepper's head shot up. He was shouting at her, waving a hand, clearly crying out, begging her not to leave him in the dark, so desperate it was delicious. Those aliens really had done a number on her poor brother. Good thing he was safely tucked away from causing any harm.

THE MOMENT DIONA emerged from the secure bunker, her earcell chimed several times. She frowned at the static marring the line. Making her way through the list of messages, one stopped her heart.

"Thea has taken a turn for the worse."

She turned away from the door leading back into the colony and instead entered the airlock that most would assume opened onto the raw Mars landscape. It cycled shut behind her, but she did not engage the outer door. Diona turned to a side panel and pressed her thumbs in two different places at once, and a hidden door opened with a hiss.

She could protect Thea from the Orbital spore. Or an incoming solar storm. Or even a potential riot of the Mars colony. She could feed her daughter, mine clean water for her, and keep her sheltered despite the extreme conditions on Mars. But the one thing she could not do is fix the blood disease pulsing through the girl's veins.

Other calls continued to buzz through, but she ignored them. The concerned citizens full of their everyday complaints could leave a message. Wasn't that what her assistant was for?

She hurried along the passageway, aware her absence would be noted and scorned by the colonists. Again. And it fuelled talk of her forest dome . . . or a garden burgeoning with life, an urban myth making the rounds that made the forest dome seem like just another tall tale. Her favourite rumour was the idea she was testing a secret Jump system that would set them free, elaborated further to surmise she had already travelled to distant planets to prepare a place. That came from her supporters, along with calls to be kind to the poor mother that lost her only child.

The haters said she stockpiled goods in the hidden bunkers, and demanded she reveal the location of all of them to the Mars public. They had no idea about the truth. They had no idea that there were no goods to stockpile. No idea that their brave leader's sick daughter actually survived her disease, or that it was her brother that tried the Jumpships and nearly died for it, now a PTSD wreck in quarantine inside one of those hidden bunkers.

When Thea's rare blood disease became apparent, Diona wanted to use experimental nanites to fight it. She knew she would face opposition. Knew they had a right to be concerned. But it wasn't their only child that lay dying.

So Diona took her to the one place no one would find Thea, hired a doctor who agreed to full nondisclosure and a life apart, under threat of his wife and kid being removed from the colony, and reported the tragic loss of her daughter in hopes that her grief would offer some excuse for her frequent absence from the public eye.

This all worked in her favour. If there was anywhere she might be free to do as she pleased, it would be here. She climbed the stairs, opened the heavy hatchway door, and stepped into her paradise. A small meadow cut by the water canal held a cosy domicile, a stick-built structure more like the old homes of Earth than anything you would expect to see on Mars, with wooden siding and open beam timber framing extending out over a front porch. What made it different was that it backed into the rock cliff at the edge of the dome, and the back of the house seemed melded to the regolith behind it.

When Diona first gave Thea the standard micro-dose of NECS for children, it caused a secondary blood infection that left the child dangerously anaemic. Her body refused to accept the flood of foreign machines in her system, no matter how tiny. Penicillin worked for a time, but Thea's blood refused to settle and allow the NECS to do their job, and antibiotics were running thin despite efforts to create more on-site.

So she brought her child here, away from the masses, and put her in a clean room bunker much like the one Stepper was in. Diona could control and monitor everything from here. The doctor was still an essential nuisance, but Diona shooed him away as she approached. The man was always complacent, and simply nodded and walked off. Probably glad for a break.

Thea lay propped up on her bed, an oxygen tube hooked into her nose. Her daughter smiled a pale smile, but her head fell back again before Diona could even cross the room. Every breath seemed a struggle.

"I'm tired, Mommy," Thea said. Diona smoothed the hair back from her pale forehead.

"It's okay, you are allowed to rest," Diona said. She wrapped her fingers around Thea's wrist. The child's heartrate was still too high, and she was pale as anything. Rising desperation left Diona shaking. "Does your tummy still hurt here?" She poked just under the ribcage on the left side, and the girl winced, a move she tried to turn into a wiggle.

"Not so much anymore," Thea said, lying.

"It won't help me to lie," Diona scolded. Thea turned her face away.

"Sorry," she whispered.

"Computer, report," Diona subvocalized, and the digital doc that sourced the medical databases, ran labs, and monitored Thea's situation replied through her earcell.

"Elevated heartrate, fatigue, muscle weakness, dizziness. Loss of mental capacity. Pain in left side under ribcage. Diagnosis: Hypersplenism, or overactive spleen. The spleen helps filter old and damaged cells from your bloodstream, but if overactive, it removes the blood cells too early and too quickly. Treatment options include: growth factors to stimulate healthy blood cell production, using nubots to send the appropriate signals. Steroids to suppress the immune system. Chemotherapy to destroy abnormal cells; caution, the nano-electrochemical systems could be damaged by this option. Transfusions to support healthy blood cells; you are a good candidate for a blood match."

Ah, yes, she was, if she didn't also carry NECS in her system. That would only worsen the problem. She had run out of steroids and the plant crops to make more had failed. Chemo was out of the question.

Now, sending a message to the NECS to promote healthy blood cell production, that was worth a try. It meant injecting nubots, of which they had very few left, that would mount themselves into the ports on the back of the NECS and load the instructions. But anything like this could cause a whole new rejection response.

It would be better to get the NECS to a point of self-repair. There were some foreboding restrictions against networking nanites, no matter what end the means seemed to justify. But with the help of solid programming by her best nano-technician, it should be possible to keep it well within control.

She knew what to do to prevent an AI. There wasn't enough processing power to create one, in any case, but she would protect against the possibility of it even if it couldn't happen. The upgrade would have a shut-off routine written in, a fail-safe. A simple code would work, it could even be designed to be spoken. At any rate, the NECS were single-purpose and would never have the power to connect up and form intelligence. The idea was absurd, and all the heavy restrictions around it were overkill.

"Mommy?"

She realized Thea had called her several times.

"Yes, darling?"

"Am I going to die?"

Diona met her gaze straight, tubes and patches and all, and squeezed her hand tight. "Not on my watch."

CHAPTER NINE

JANLIN SEARCHED THE databases for some relief from her frustration, finding terms like dichotomy, dissonance, discord. Beyond the painful headaches and loss of coordination, she was always of two minds. It seemed she was always questioning, doubting, and always seeing both sides of things.

Case in point, she both understood Gordon's stubbornness and couldn't believe he could be so pigheaded, all at the same time. It gave her no firm footing to stand on, and nothing certain to stand up for.

She read a few interesting articles, but one in particular stood out.

"Carl Jung called the paradox one of our most valued spiritual possessions and a great witness to the truth. He wrote, 'Only the paradox comes anywhere near to comprehending the fullness of life. Sometimes beautiful. Sometimes terrible. Always deeply human.'"

While not solving anything, the passage offered some comfort. Janlin quit the holo screen and wandered the corridors of the orbital station. She tried to play some favourite music on her earcell, but the static was intolerable.

She both wanted the NECS fixed so she could Jump, and at the same time wanted them purged. "I know now I am deeply human," she laughed, noting that the philosophical article left her both comforted and scornful, again at the same time. "I am nothing but a paradox," she decided.

Janlin sought out Linder to ask about the possibilities they had. But that wasn't what came out when she got there.

"Am I acting like a child, Linder?"

Linder's eyes widened. She was only a few years younger than Janlin's mom would be, and Janlin found her a great listener. It wasn't just her greying hair that gave away her age, it was the kindness, and how calm she could be in the face of chaos. Janlin hoped she could be half so wise someday.

"You and Gordon still fighting?"

Janlin rolled her eyes and let out a puff of exasperation. "Yes, and while I understand why he's acting the way he is, it doesn't make it any easier to tolerate, especially when he's shutting me down all the time. I don't think investigating all our options is acting like a child."

"So he digs at your shame points to get you to focus on that instead of the matter at hand, simply because he's afraid of you pursuing something other than what he wants, especially without him?"

Without him . . . Janlin gaped. "Uh, wow," she said once she got her jaw off the floor. "You sure know how to see right to the root of things."

Linder smiled, but there were acres of pain behind it. "I was in a passionate, volatile relationship with a controlling narcissist once. I learned a lot in recovery."

"I'm sorry."

Linder nodded. "Now, Gordon is no narcissist," she said with a new grin, "but the thought of having you go off without him is torture, yet the thought of leaving Ursula again is impossible."

"Geez, and I thought I was struggling with the 'being of two minds' thing," Janlin said. "I'm so torn between having the NECS work so I can Jump, and having all nanites purged from my system for good, I'm not sure what action to take next."

Linder frowned. "We are not likely to survive a purge. Those things are keeping us alive up here. We need some way to repair the NECS instead. Then a home planet with a stable habitat, *then* maybe we can think about purges. Food is not our only problem."

"Gordon doesn't seem to realize that."

"Or he doesn't want to hear it," Linder said in her gentle, sad way. "We haven't much recourse, you know it too. Our food supply is always threatened, and Earth won't recover in time for us to repopulate or grow crops there. There's a chance we aren't well enough anymore to even have children."

"Okay, stop," Janlin said, hugging herself. "Please don't share that with Gordon and Urse?"

Linder's sadness only grew. "Ursula likely understands and would never consider pregnancy without a more certain food supply in place anyway."

"We need better options." Janlin threw herself out of her chair and began to pace, ticking things off her fingers. "If we can't find a way to safely purge them and start again, then we need those repair bots, upgraded software and drivers, perhaps even new NECS built specifically to repair the original ones."

Linder cautioned her. "New NECS would be great, yes, but how do we get the parts for it? You know full well that going to Mars is a bad idea, and so is attempting another Jump. You aren't considering looking back on Earth, are you?"

Janlin couldn't stop shaking her head. She had nothing to say, nothing to offer, and no clue how to help, because she wasn't going back there anytime soon either. The nightmares from her last trip still haunted her. Linder gave her arm a squeeze.

"In any case, Janlin, you are not acting like a child any more or less than the rest of us, including Gordon. We've been through a lot, these are hard times, and we face many challenges. We are all doing the best we can."

Janlin left Linder to her work and made her way back to *Hope*. Anaya looked an unhealthy hue of grey. Janlin ran her fingers over each console button. One called up a holo full of indecipherable markings. "There's probably a ton of information here I need," Janlin muttered. "Oh, Anaya, why did you have to come alone? I know you and Yipho argued over it. He wanted to come, wanted to be at your side. What if he'd been okay enough to help you?"

Ah, but what if he hadn't been okay?

Janlin sliced through the holo, effectively shutting it down. She paced out of the small medbay, then back. She stared at Anaya. What would help? What thing was she not thinking of? Could she reroute enough systems to the captain's chair to fly *Hope* alone? Did she dare Jump back to get Yipho's help?

Then something sunk in. She called the holo up again. There, one indicator was now yellowish instead of green.

Why is green always go? she wondered, just as she had when she first approached this Gitane ship's airlock. The yellow made her feel a little sick. *She's getting worse,* she thought, turning to her friend. *What do you need, Anaya?*

Then she had it. She tapped her earcell, waiting for the chime to speak, and cursing when it sent a squeal of torturous feedback. She took off at a run, snaking her way through foot traffic and bouncing off walls as she took corners too quickly.

She burst into the science lab. "We have special NECS that do internal surgeries, right? For accidents, right?"

Linder looked up from her datapad, wide-eyed. "Sure, minor ones, but we tried it on the earcells and they're not powerful enough . . ."

Janlin leaned on her knees, panting, waving off Linder's explanation as unimportant in the moment. "How quickly could you program some to look inside an alien brain and maybe repair an aneurism?"

The nano-biologist looked intrigued. "That's actually a workable idea, even if we don't know her physiology."

"It's urgent. One of *Freedom's* medbay lights has gone from green to yellow."

Linder stood from her desk. "I'll start right away." She was already stacking holograms in the air. One began running calculations. "Have you seen Brendan?"

BRENDAN BROUGHT IN a pair of young programmers Janlin recognized immediately. "You were on Huantag!"

"Yeah," one said, the other offering a haunted smile. "What a place, eh?"

Janlin had a memory of something Tyrell had said. "Are you really called Huey and Duey?"

"Howard and Donald," Howard said, pointing first at himself and then at Donald. "Huey and Duey was Tyrell's thing, and it stuck. Some ancient cartoon he was always going on about. Now it's a way to honour his memory."

"I like it," Janlin said. "I'm sure Tyrell would, too."

"I remember some hulking alien sticking me with a needle," Huey said. "At that point I was hallucinating pretty bad, and

Duey was unconscious." Huey gave Janlin a shy smile. "Thanks for saving our lives."

Janlin patted his arm. "I couldn't have done it without Anaya's friendship, so I'm here to help you help her, any way I can."

They settled into it. Linder stared into a microscope. Huey and Duey typed endless lines of code, conferring occasionally in terms that Janlin could make no sense of. Janlin paced and watched and checked the live cam feed she had set up to watch Anaya.

Despite a lack of better options, Janlin wondered if she was wrong to be putting these things inside Anaya.

"Linder, if she has an adverse reaction, can we stop the NECS? Turn them off, somehow? Take them back out?"

The nanoscientist regarded her. "Turning off the programming would not interrupt any toxic reaction to the nanites themselves, which does occur in a small percentage of humans. In that instance, removal is only possible within the first while, and it's an unpleasant process."

"But we could remove them if Anaya had some bad reaction?"

Linder nodded. "I would say her chances are good to survive our NECS because we survived their meds, which Li noted appear nanite-driven as well. I know you're worried, but you have a solid idea here. These NECS should help Anaya recover from whatever damage the Jump caused. It's actually something we need to consider with everyone."

"Adding more NECS? Will these ones screw up on us, too? We could be adding even more problems for later, potentially."

Linder took a deep breath and let it out slow. "One problem at a time? It's up to you if you want to try this with Anaya. It might be a short-term solution and all we do is buy her more time."

Janlin nodded in appreciation of this logic. "Guess that's all we are ever doing, eh? Trying to buy more time." She weighed the options and wished it wasn't on her head. "Let's give it a try. And with the way I've been feeling," she said, rubbing her temples, "I would be willing to try them too."

Linder turned to the programmers. "Are you having headaches?"

Huey nodded, and Duey threw his hands up in the air. "Good grief, yes," he said. "Sometimes my brain feels loose in my skull. I keep getting headspins that make me feel like puking."

"Me, too," Linder admitted. She held up the vial of nanite solution ready for Anaya. "Why don't you lads go talk to Steve about setting up a little NECS surgery hack like this one to stabilize everyone's head while we attend the Gitane captain."

The young men headed off, while Linder gathered up what she needed for the injection. They headed for the Gitane ship, each step taking longer than it should to Janlin. They entered *Hope's* bay through the open airlock and climbed into the alien shuttle.

Janlin stopped in her tracks at the doorway to the medbay.

"You okay?" Linder asked.

She wasn't. "If this works, I have to tell her that she can't Jump home."

Linder regarded the bulk of grey flesh before turning back to Janlin. "As a scientist, I want to help a living being in need. If you like, I will stay with her and explain what has happened."

Janlin smiled at Linder. "You're kind, but that's okay. The least I can do is be here if . . . *when* she comes to."

Linder sunk the hypodermic into Anaya's bloodstream and stood back to wait. About twenty minutes in, Janlin found a seat. Linder used a scanner to get a read on the NECS. Having only rudimentary networking software in the nanites, they couldn't monitor them digitally, they had to watch from outside. The scanner would read the behaviour and messages from the NECS.

Another twenty passed. Janlin wondered at the damage she was doing to her lip, chewing it the way she was.

Linder spoke, startling her out of the prolonged silence. "We programmed the NECS to seek damage and send a repair request, and they are asking to do repairs in the skull region on what appears to be an aneurism. It took them much longer than usual to report a prognosis, and nothing I'm seeing is familiar. Should I proceed?"

Janlin held her head. "Yes, do it." If it could stop Anaya's brain from doing what Inaba's did, whatever happened after would be worth it.

Linder took a deep breath and sent the command. "I hope we can create a similar injection for each of us that Jumped, too." Janlin noticed the line between Linder's brows had deepened in the time she'd known her, and her salt-and-pepper ponytail had far more salt these days.

Another twenty minutes passed, and then another.

"Janlin?" Steve stood in the hatchway. "Got a minute?"

She gave a weak smile. "Yeah, sure, got all the minutes." Both of them looked to Anaya. Linder waved them off, indicating she would stay and keep watch.

"Did Huey and Duey find you?" Janlin asked as she rose.

Steve sighed. "Yeah, I took a look, and the programming is a little ragged. Don't get me wrong, those youngsters hacked up a decent version of NECS brain scan diagnostics and surgeries, but it might take a long while to run the repair." He tipped his chin at the comatose Gitane captain. "Don't give up."

Janlin nodded. "Okay. It's not really my schtick anyway," she said, trying to lighten the mood.

They moved out into the bay. It felt good to get some air, have a little space.

"I actually came by for a different reason. Remember before the sickness, when the Birdfolk wanted to attempt reprogramming the contraceptive portion of the NECS code?"

She remembered Stepper wanting to live there forever, no matter what it cost anyone else. "Sure."

"I think I understand what they were proposing, now that I compare it to what Linder's crew just did. We could try it with a couple like Gordon and Ursula."

Janlin straightened right up. "Linder thought that might be the best we have to hope for, and it would mean everything to them . . ."

"I wanted to talk to you first. You *are* my second-in-command."

Now Janlin's heart really did stop. Then it kick-started double time and extra hard. "Command?" she asked stupidly. She rubbed the back of her neck, willing the faint dizziness away. Sometimes that seemed to work. Mind over matter?

"Whether it follows the strictest chain of command or not, you have proven yourself as a valuable leader. Can I count on you?"

"I don't know, Steve. I'm not comfortable with authority, why would I want to be it?"

Steve chuckled and shrugged off her doubt. "Not like it should be much of an issue," he said, waving at the docked and stationary ship. "The thing is, right now the role of programmer and nano-biologist are our best hope. If I wanted to chase that, would you step into this position if needed?"

She took a deep breath and let it out slow. "Seriously, I don't know. Give me some time to think about it, okay?"

"Of course."

"Meanwhile, I think your idea, even just the proposal of its possibility, would go a long way to offering hope to everyone . . . although, until we have secured a few rounds of food crops, Urse won't have it."

Steve agreed. "The alien crops are doing well, though."

"What about Jumps? Do we dare try that again? Is there a way to use the Jumpship NECS to help it be less deadly?"

"The NECS designed for the Jumpship materials are for non-organics, and aren't meant for biological use like the surgical, contraceptive, and vaccine ones. They're for manufacturing, and they're a bit toxic."

"So, hack the ones we already have," she suggested. "Make it work. We need to be able to Jump, for us, for the Gitane, for the help the Huantag can bring, for all the planets available to us out there, all the resources—" She smacked one hand into the other for each point.

"Okay, okay, I get it," Steve said, palms out. He seemed uncomfortable and made to go, and she realized she'd gotten too intense, too passionate.

"Sorry. I guess I feel guilty for bringing Anaya here. And a little panicked about how to tell her she can't go home, if she survives."

Steve gave her a sad smile. "I'm sorry too. The NECS are an engineering marvel, sure, but I'm at a loss how to make them correct our brains' disconnect over Jumping. That's just not what they're designed for. So, having babies here, now, with what we have, might just be all we've got to live for."

Janlin nodded, still embarrassed. She fought back hot tears. This was why she didn't want a leadership position. No people skills. It was so much easier to go it alone. Her ideas were always considered too dangerous, and her manner too blunt. Who would ever have babies with her?

"Listen, have you contacted any of the Mars families yet?"

Janlin had to admit she hadn't. "Between Anaya and helping in the greenhouses and . . ."

"Maybe we should team up on it. It wasn't fair to give it to you alone."

Janlin appreciated that, but it wasn't right. "No, you should be focused on the NECS, just like you said, and I'm not busy with anything important."

"Nothing important? Hey, you figured out how to help Anaya, that's been your focus," Steven said.

Janlin took a deep breath. "Thanks. But you're right. The families deserve to know, and it shouldn't be left any longer."

CHAPTER TEN

DIONA STARED AT the woman. What was her name again?

"Explain."

The nanite tech bit her lip. "The nanites should've protected this person," she repeated, gesturing at the blood sample slide still locked under the electron microscope apparatus.

"But they didn't?" Diona said through gritted teeth, angry she even had to prod the woman.

"No." She swallowed, and Diona noticed dark circles under her eyes.

Would she have to ask for more again? The woman seemed overcome.

But the tech straightened and answered properly. "No, the NECS are failing. The upgrades aren't enough, they need repair programs or replacement . . ."

"We don't have those options."

The woman swallowed again, then nodded. "Correct." She wouldn't meet Diona's gaze.

The blood sample was from a child Thea's age that died recently. It brought all her fears to a vivid forefront, and made them impossible to ignore any longer.

"And the other samples?"

"Same trajectories. Except for that one special one I pointed out. Those NECS are also fouling exponentially, much worse than any other I've seen, and there are new nanite particles that I can find no current records for, or their implant date, or any process logs, or even exe files. I have no idea where they came from. If I could get more info . . ."

"You know they are voluntary samples under the promise of anonymity."

"Yes, of course," came the meek reply. The tech bent over her microscope once again. Diona sighed.

"Focus on it, despite the lack of information. See if you can slow the deterioration."

"Yes, ma'am."

Diona hated it when she called her ma'am, but she ignored it for the moment.

"How do we get the NECS to do their job again?" she said with a slap of her hand on the stainless-steel lab bench. The tech jumped, giving her a wide-eyed stare of helplessness. Diona snorted and waved her off.

"Never mind. I'll figure it out."

DIONA WATCHED STEPPER through the hermetically sealed encasement. He was lit by lamps he had no control over, while she stood in darkness, watching her brother unseen. It was exactly the type of situation she liked best.

She could've taken them all, and the Jumpship too, but it was far more of a drain on resources than the colony could take. *Can't believe they managed to lose an entire Jumpship and get infected on the first outing.* If she had been in charge, instead of her inept brother, Mars would have a working Jumpship right now, maybe even two.

Stepper paced back and forth, muttering. She'd been listening for some time, and little of it made sense. Foreign words, apparent daydreams of having wings and flying like a bird, rants at various people but most especially Janlin, Gordon, and Steve. Oh, and Fran, who was apparently a dead hero now. Diona had been proud of hooking her brother up with Fran. Ridiculous that Stepper let Janlin get in the way of that, too.

There was one thing he didn't rant on about that only came up when he dreamed, and those nightmares left him sullen and silent. The alien race that had tortured them was clearly brutal, and she needed more information on their potential threat.

More urgently, she needed information on the disease Stepper carried.

"Is the contagion really so deadly? The alien nanites seem inert."

She got some small satisfaction watching him flinch and then flush with anger. "Knew someone was there, shouldn't doubt, knew it, knew it." He cast furtive glances full of venom into the darkness surrounding him before continuing his pacing.

"Come on, Stepper, I need information if I'm to ever let you out of here."

His step faltered to a stop, his head hung low. "It's deadly," he confirmed. "Dozens of people died within days of contracting it, hallucinating with fever and drowning in their own phlegm. I'm only alive because of the hulking alien Janlin befriended."

"So, it's biological," she said, voicing a conclusion that could be wrong . . . Stepper couldn't resist correcting her, or anyone, so this should reveal what he thought was the truth. Turned out he wasn't actually sure.

"Yes, well maybe, but it was planted in us, engineered by the Imag." He twitched away, his face turning grey and his body tensing, some primeval protection mode kicking in. The trauma went deep. He shot the darkness another hard look, still uncertain of where she stood. Her voice emitted from speakers inside his cage, giving him no echolocation clues. "It is more likely nanite-driven, just like yours."

Her gaze flickered over the controls to be sure all recordings were off and comm channels closed. When she looked back, he was smirking at random darkness.

"They may even conflict, who knows. Or yours might be made inert. Oh, or maybe they'll team up and have mutant nano-virus babies!"

"You are such an ass." She grit her teeth, chest tight with anger and adrenaline. "You know it's not a virus, it's an upgrade."

"Upgrade?" He laughed, a crazed laugh. "Upgrade to what? Your slave? You better rethink this, sister mine."

No one would take this man's advice, in his state. Why should she? And why let him work her up? She dumped the tray of now-cold food in the airlock chamber and sealed it off. Stepper just leered at her, paying no attention to the food.

Diona turned the lights off on him again, fed up with trying for information. For now, she had more important things to do. Maybe after a few days he'd be less jerk and more family team player.

CHAPTER ELEVEN

THE SOLDERING IRON slipped, and Janlin burnt her left index finger for the third time. Cursing, she set the iron on its stand, disconnected the power, and sucked on her finger. The control panels of Anaya's ship lay gutted before her, wires jutting out every which way, some of them connected haphazardly to human datapads and control interfaces.

If she could just understand the controls, she could make sure Anaya had what she needed.

A powerful shuttle like this would be useful, and Janlin had it in her mind to talk to Steve about making it Jump capable. Even without, it would help to have another ship, what with all the travel back and forth between Luna Base and Spectra. And that would give her a vital role in this new society. There was room within for plenty of people and gear, and it was tough enough for re-entry if needed.

If she also wondered at its capabilities to handle Earth's storms, she didn't let the thoughts surface for long. There were still too many other problems with resettling there, and she had her own traumatic memories to face from her last visit too. She occasionally woke gasping from nightmares of men eating babies, and blue eyes telling her to *run* . . . when it wasn't the Imag torture chamber, usually with Fran lecturing her with great disdain, or Stepper screaming at her as he destroyed her knee.

She shuddered and tried to box those thoughts up and stuff

them away.

Sucking on her tripled-layered blisters, she reviewed her progress. The only screen she had been able to get to communicate was a micro datapad meant for mechanical diagnostics. She had gathered it from the recycling centre along with all the other electronic oddities scattered around her, hoping to find something that would interpret *Freedom's* systems and allow her to operate them. But all it showed was the tank levels of the ship, letting her know that water and fuel tanks were low, while the waste tanks were full and ready for a flush.

"How useful," she muttered.

Gordon would be a lot of help, if he cared at all. Was it just jealousy talking? She certainly didn't feel like they were very good friends lately.

Attempting the next connection left her boot dribbled with solder and strange symbols running across the screen. "Gordon would know what to do," she said, frowning at her disaster. Surely he could spare her an hour or so?

She climbed to her feet a bit too fast and lightning pain shot through her skull. Groaning, she leaned against the wall, staggering along the passage with one eye shut.

"Ugh, make it stop," she complained, but it just kept coming, shock after shock of searing pain through the left side of her head. Blackness closed in, and she dropped to her knees in case she passed out. Fear made her gasp. Was she dying?

"Janlin?"

It was Cassie. "Yeah?"

"Is it the head again?"

"Yeah."

"Here, try this." A sharp poke told her Cassie was giving her an injection. "We found some stores of old-fashioned painkillers that were used before the NECS took care of those things. It's been shown to help improve the headaches."

Janlin opened one eye. Cassie crouched beside her, watching with a sad smile. "I think I can feel it working already. Where am I?"

"Corridor D near the shuttle bay hangar."

"Huh, made it farther than I realized."

Cassie chuckled, though she looked a little worried. Janlin pushed up into a sitting position. "Still feel a little nauseated."

"Well, the painkiller won't help with that, but the NECS should. Except . . . well, looks like they're crapping out on us?"

"Yeah, I've heard."

"Maybe you should get some help with that shuttle?" Cassie said, ever so gently, as she helped Janlin up and caught sight of her burnt fingers.

Janlin shrugged. "Was thinking of doing just that," she admitted. "Gordon's just been so busy, though . . ."

"Yeah, he has. You feeling better now?"

"Well enough, thanks." They wandered along the corridor. "I'm mad we can't purge the NECS out of our bodies," Janlin said, her tone changing. "They aren't doing their job, and chances are that's what is screwing us up when we Jump."

They walked into the nearest junction node. "Be careful of false correlation, Janlin," Cassie said, waving to indicate she was going left to Janlin's right. "The NECS truly are the only thing keeping us alive out here. We need a lot more information before we start laying blame for the Jump dissonance."

Janlin sighed. "You're a voice of reason," she said, grinning. Cassie grinned back. "Still, I'd volunteer as a test subject if Linder wants one!"

Janlin blessed Cassie and her lovely injection of relief as she moved through two more nodes and headed down corridor A-13. Here, larger containers were joined and opened up within to create "fields" for the crops. Row after row of lights ran above, while hundreds of meters of water pipe ran below. Everything was hydroponic, a plan that was intended to reduce the risk of soil-borne diseases. Unfortunately, fungal spores loved moisture and didn't need soil at all, so now Ursula had brought in the soil from all the parks and container trees around the orbital, something they created compost for regularly.

In the back corner of one of the massive areas, Ursula had set up isolated beds of seedlings, sealing them off and working with them only through robotic means. The open-air crops had more volunteers every day. Which meant that there wasn't a whole lot Gordon could do but watch plants grow, in Janlin's opinion, although as she strode up, he was washing trays in a big steel sink while Ursula entered data on a pad.

"Hey, how's your babies?" she called out. Urse smiled, clearly happy with the results she was seeing. Gordon gave her a nod of greeting.

"Look here, Janlin," Ursula called, waving her over to the second enclosure. Janlin peered in through the condensation on the window. Purplish plants were glowing in proud rows.

"I saw these on Huantag!" Janlin cried, recognizing them. "I remember these getting flowers that were used to create the glow-lights."

Gordon dried his hands, nodding in agreement. "Would be nice if we'd gotten some bloody instructions with this lot, though," he grumbled. "How're we supposed to know what's food and what's . . . ah . . ." He waved at the vivid plants. "A torch?" He rolled his eyes with great exaggeration.

Janlin caught Ursula's eye and gave her a "what's up with him" look. The German scientist just shrugged and shook her head in warning. Asking for Gordon's help might not go over well right now, by the look of things. Maybe if she could find just the right leverage . . .

"I did get one screen to interpret Anaya's controls," she casually mentioned.

"Nice. What did you learn?"

"That we need a Gitane sani-dump station."

That got the laugh she was hoping for. "Anything else?"

"Not really. I can't figure out why the interface of that datapad will communicate with the dashboard, but the others I connected won't." She looked up at her friend, tempted to beg a little. "With your help I'm sure we could figure it out."

But this reminder worked against her. "How many times have we gone over this? You have decided that's the best place for your time and energy to be spent. I disagree. Here is where I'm needed, here is where we'll survive or die trying, not flying an alien ship!"

Janlin was sure someone had just sucked all the oxygen out of the room. Unable to process her hurt, she just kept nodding like some stupid broken toy. Of course, he was right. Why was she putting so much into making the Gitane shuttle fly? To run away from things, like usual, just like Gordon had said. But wasn't it just as vital to try and understand the medbay instructions too? Anaya was in trouble!

Steve appeared in the distant doorway. He jogged over, slowing as he assessed the mood. "Everything okay?"

"Never mind those two," Ursula said, kicking out a chair for

Steve to join them. "You have a look, what have you learned?"

"Been studying the NECS," he started, pausing dramatically. Everyone leaned in. "They're emitting a signal," he finally revealed.

"Like, as in they could talk and go AI?" Janlin asked.

"No, this is different. This is a long-range pulse, like a locator beacon."

Something clicked. "*That's* how Diona knew when we were back. Dammit!" The whole idea of Diona monitoring them, studying them, spying on them made her skin crawl. Janlin jumped up and started pacing. She wanted to hit something. Diona's face would work just fine.

"Can you shut it off?" she demanded over everyone else's inane comments of dismay.

Steve shook his head. "It's not that simple. None of this is. They were designed to be resistant to hacking, reprogramming, and manipulating them."

Janlin swore again. "What about trying Jumps again?" She wanted to go personally wrap her fingers around Diona's neck.

"It's impossible to differentiate the NECS signal from our own cells'," he explained. "Plus, there exists a hierarchy of complexity, where antibody and enzyme nanites are specific, one-note machines built for one job only. It would be beyond difficult to upgrade the antiviral and contraception nanites to do other more complicated things, and they may be completely unable to handle the job. We would need a more complex whole-cell and tissue effect, and entire physiological effect, to change what the Jumps do to us, which is a whole new level of programming. And the only way to get what we want is to actually hack and reprogram them ourselves, which as I said, they are designed to resist. But we will only be able to sync better with the Jump nano-tech if we can accomplish this task." Steve didn't look confident. "And there is one further obstacle."

"Of course, there is," Gordon muttered. Ursula shushed him.

"They used a polypyrrole electro-polymerization on electroplated AU on flexible substrate . . ."

"Whoa, smarty-pants, plain Greek, please."

Even Ursula seemed to agree.

Steve blinked a few times as he processed their request. "Okay, try this: the electrode a nanite rides on is wrapped around the nerve to both send and receive signals, so we're trying to discern between what the NECS are signalling and what our own cells are doing naturally." He paused, they waited. He got a pained look.

Janlin got a hunch. "Why are you reluctant to go on?"

Steve winced. She was right, something was wrong that meant trouble right now, not just for Jumpships or making babies in the future.

"Scar tissue forms," he admitted, "and the electrode kinda gets, I don't know, enwrapped." One of his hands encircled the other. "This causes the problems like instability in the signals, low frequency noise, static in our earcells, even some leakage."

"Leakage?" Janlin felt a bit ill.

"Our bodies are absorbing the NECS into our cellular structure even as they are breaking down. We need to create and inject new NECS to repair both the scarring and the old NECS' physical states. We can measure some electrochemical processes to see which tissue is okay and which isn't . . ."

"No," Janlin said, cutting him off. "I want them out. No more SpaceOp rules, no more screwing up our Jumps, no more signalling Diona our every move." She stared hard at Steve, who gave her a stunned look back. "Please tell me you can take them out."

Steve shook his head, helpless. "No, that's what I'm saying . . . it's called bio-fouling. Our cells have grown around the NECS, enveloping them in scar tissue. Removing them would likely kill the host, if it's possible at all."

Gordon said something impolite. Ursula glanced at her husband as she asked, "The removal, you are saying it is completely impossible?"

"I am ninety percent sure. We . . . they are too grown over . . . we are one with them on a cellular level now. And we have no way of knowing how it will affect us as they degrade."

CHAPTER TWELVE

THE NEXT TIME, Stepper got right to business when Diona brought up the lights.

"You have to understand, these aliens have tech we need if we're to reclaim Earth," he said, rising and approaching the glass as soon as she engaged the lights.

Diona came close enough to the glass to let him see her. Then she stared as if he spoke gibberish. It always unnerved him as a kid, and the tactic didn't fail her now.

"Come on, stop that and talk to me. You're being a child."

"Can the engineered virus be turned off?"

Stepper relaxed a fraction. "You need to talk to the aliens that cured us. Janlin's friends. Start there." Again, he smirked. He was keeping something back, aware that she could tell and was powerless to get it out of him. His only bargaining chip, really. Or it was a bluff, and he had nothing at all.

"Janlin and her entire crew are a threat, now for two reasons, and you've proven Jumpships unsafe. How am I to access this tech? Sounds useless to me, or too dangerous."

Stepper acknowledged her point, yet still, the knowing quirk of the lips lingered. She could get it out of him if she could reach him physically. But this alien virus . . . she simply didn't know if it was viral, or nanotech, or whether her NECS could handle it either way.

Send in a test subject?

Seemed overly cruel, and no one came to mind that wouldn't be missed. Thankfully, her brother had already been injected with nanites she could control. She brought up the holo and ran the file.

"Have you told anyone?"

Those dark brown eyes, so deep as to appear black sometimes, and so very much like the ones in the mirror. "No, I haven't."

Okay, that should be truth. He would have no choice. Now it was time to get what she wanted.

"What are you holding back from me?"

He should be spilling his guts to her right now, falling over himself to comply, but instead he tipped his head in mockery of her famous move and taunted her.

"Wouldn't you like to know."

DIONA SLAMMED THE datapad down in front of the tech, making the woman flinch.

"It didn't work. Why didn't it work?"

The tech was already accessing the data, her fingers darting over the datapad and calling up holos. "There's too much noise," she murmured, pointing at three stacked signals. "Multiple programs involved, somehow, and they're interfering with each other. I can pull them apart, see if one isn't ours?"

"Dammit, speak like you know something about this, would you?" She ran frustrated fingers through her long straight hair. One thing Thea inherited from her, lucky girl. "Strip it out and analyse what each one is doing."

All the tech could confirm was the presence of a variety of nano-tech, a large percentage of which were in much better shape than the SpaceOp NECS.

"This blood has new nano-tech installed, some experimental stuff," the tech concluded. "I've never seen anything like it." She was the same one paid off to test Thea's blood and keep the findings to herself, so it only made sense to have her look at Stepper's blood. After all, she would come at it without any preconceived notions. "It looks to be along the same lines as your newest NECS, working at a viral level rather than cellular. They are created with one sole purpose and go defunct once that's complete. Normally they are purged from the body naturally, but these ones have stayed in the bloodstream as if waiting new commands, much like your upgrades prepare the NECS for . . ."

"That's fine, thank you," Diona said, talking over her so the woman wouldn't say things out loud that were better left unsaid. She had no way to confirm it was alien without revealing the possibility to the tech, so that would have to wait.

"Can you hack them?" That alone could lead the tech to a discovery she would have to cover up, but Diona thought it worth the risk. Most people would automatically dismiss the idea of anything being alien anyway. She herself was still a little stunned to discover aliens and their worlds actually did exist, and suffered moments of doubt about the whole story . . . until she thought about those blips all disappearing as one, only to return all scarred and traumatized and filled with new nanite technology.

Father was right to set things up so she could track the signals. He thought to track the NECS for recovery in emergencies, whether the host survived or not, since they gave off a residual pulse energy for a while afterwards. And he'd been right to think that way, too, since now they were desperate for new materials and programming. Now, however, she was dealing with foreign substances that could change everything, hardware that she had no way of knowing how to utilize and control.

"I've been trying to break in on the coding," the tech said, clearly uncomfortable. "I can't get it to talk. I may need to try old programming languages before I can hack . . ."

Diona walked out, making her way back to the hidden bunker where Stepper was kept. The tech wouldn't find a language that worked, of course, and that suited Diona fine. *What was her name again?* Whatever, the tech didn't know "Imag" or whatever language it was. Imag, the aliens that broke Stepper screaming from sleep. Whoever had the power to make him a PTSD mess like that was dangerous, and she needed more information about what was now inside of those who had Jumped.

"Use Janlin."

Diona wasn't used to Stepper making sense, so she did a double take. "What?"

"Use Janlin," Stepper said, not looking up from the food in front of him. "She's got something different in her. She was immune to the virus while the rest of us dropped like flies, so she had a vaccine instead of an anti-viral . . . and they brought back bucketloads of the second, but none of the first that I could see. Make her come to you and use her to test on."

Diona studied her brother. "You just want to see her," she taunted. Again, he shrugged. Then he looked up with the coldest, emptiest eyes, so devoid of any caring that her skin goosed. "If she Jumps, it could kill her," she added, unable to hold silent.

"Good." He was focused on his food again.

"No, that doesn't jive. She's your 'Jannilove', there's no way . . ."

He moved lightning fast and slammed into the glass with force. She rocked back on her heels, barely holding her ground, despite being safe outside his hermetically sealed box. His face muscles jumped as he ground his teeth, and his lip curled. "She shamed me, in front of everyone. She turned them all against me." He banged the glass again, a dull thud on her side, his rage tinny in the speakers. "There's no love there."

This was different than before. She tipped her head and considered. "The idea may have merit. Any ideas how to lure her here, as you suggest?"

Stepper began to snicker, then chuckle, then laugh out right, head thrown back. "Oh, damn, that's right, I haven't told you yet." He laughed some more, shaking his head as if he couldn't believe his restraint. When he met her gaze, the glee he felt was as obvious as a child's.

"Janlin brought an alien back with her."

He wagged his eyebrows at her as she stood stunned, her breath misting the glass.

"An Imag?"

He snarled. "Looks the same, but claims to be different."

Fascinating.

"She's probably dead by now, she didn't take the Jump well, unless that fully-loaded alien shuttle they also brought with them is handy enough to keep the freak going." He gave her a soulless smile. "All yours for the taking, and all yours for the testing on, yes? Tell Janlin you can save her pet alien, and she won't be able to help herself. Two-for-one."

Diona considered. "The virus is purely nanite-driven," she said. "If we can hack the code, we can turn it off. So, I need to know how this new hardware works and whether it's going to affect ours. Like you said, they could conflict, and we can't have that during a Jump."

"The alien can help, I'm sure."

"Why did you keep that from me until now?" she asked, frustrated. "I wouldn't have let this go on so long if you'd told me."

"Look, I kept your secrets because I know you're right: we can't survive without functioning NECS. But there's no telling how these alien injections are affecting us, or what all they are meant to do. And the NECS weren't enough to brace us against Jumps." He tapped his head with a wince. "I could still die on you, sis, based on the way this feels." He gave Diona a long stare. "But what you're thinking of doing, that's risky as hell, beyond all the rest. How is Thea?"

Without pause she lied. "She's better. The procedure was successful. I did the right thing."

Stepper shook his head. "Poor kid."

And with that he wouldn't look at her or answer her questions. And the hack the tech had made for her still hadn't worked, hadn't got Stepper talking as it should've, so now she doubted everything. Had these alien nanites completely ruined her plans? Were they going to make it both impossible to Jump, and screw up her plans to cure Thea?

CHAPTER THIRTEEN

COMMUNICATIONS CONTINUED TO be cut off between Earth orbit and Mars. Janlin wondered how she was going to contact the bereaved Mars families and deliver the horrible news, but if she was honest with herself, she'd been letting the conflict between colonies be her excuse to not even try.

It did occur to her, however, that once done, she would have contacts . . . a way to get information . . . perhaps a safe place to go if she were to risk it . . . and help gathering the needed tech. Maybe she could convince someone like Tyrell's sister to send a Seekersend bot to deliver the much-needed parts, no contact needed. That would be the safest route for everyone.

Janlin called up the list of deceased that had family on Mars.

Tyrell Richard Gregory
Emergency Contact/Next of Kin: Lauren Muriel Gamble (nee Gregory) (sister)

Janlin needed Jessie Brighton, the tech that inadvertently let her take a shunter dirtside. *Was that really only a few months ago?* Before she could ping him, she noticed another name: Fran Delou, emergency contact, Isa and Jerril Delou (parents).

That ought to be a fun conversation.

Could she just send some official-looking notices? No, that wasn't right and she knew it, and there certainly wasn't a post service anymore. The fact that this news wasn't delivered in person was horrid enough already. Maybe Cassie had or knew of a procedure for these sorts of things? Janlin shook her head. This wasn't a Spectra Station thing. This was about those that didn't come back from the first Jumps humanity ever made. The families deserved respect. They deserved to know how brave their loved ones were. But should she reveal where they'd been?

She scanned the list, wondering which of the names was the white-haired man in the end bunk of the Imag ship, the one with the nerve damage in his arm. She saw Teardrop's listing, and was devastated anew to see no next of kin or emergency contact listed. If they had survived, Tyrell would've brought Teardrop into his own family and made her a part of it. She and Lauren would've been sisters-in-law. Now instead, they would never meet.

Janlin wondered how to carry the grief of it all.

Sandy and Ron were both Orbital residents, and their contacts were aboard and had received the news. Same with Brendan, and many more Janlin hadn't known personally.

Yasu Inaba. That one really hurt, and his contact was a brother on Mars. Again, Janlin knew that as hard as it would be, these siblings deserved to hear the news from a crewmember directly, not by some e-notice that may never be allowed through.

She touched her ear, sub-vocalizing the name to connect . . . then cursed as garbled static was her only result. It was such a habit to use them, she had taken it for granted. Being without them made everything even harder.

With a huge sigh, she made her way to Brighton's pod and hit the door chime.

Brighton's door slid away, and he was shaking his head. "I forgot the door had that function, to be honest," he said. "We usually knew people were coming beforehand because of the earcells. Bet you tried to buzz before you came over."

She had to laugh at that. "I did, it's true."

He grinned, happy to be right. "What can I do for you, Kavanagh?"

She explained the obligation she faced to the young IT wizard. "Is there some way to get a private two-way punched through? These families deserve a proper call."

"Oh, sure, I can help with that. A few others have asked the same, trying to keep in touch with family or friends out there. I just have to boost a handheld signal for you."

"Wow, that can reach?"

He chuckled. "Only with some help. Unfortunately, we are short of NDBs, since we're using a bunch in the new gardens for extra ventilation and filtration."

"NDBs?"

"Nano-diamond batteries? You know we run on nuclear, right?"

"Sure."

"Well, where do you think all the toxic waste goes?"

"Oh." Janlin shrugged. "Guess I never thought about it."

Brighton sighed. "Tsk. That's more than half our problem, not thinking about the fallout of our actions, or how we dispose of our waste . . ."

Janlin lifted an eyebrow. "Because we have so much leisure time these days, you know, to think."

Brighton ducked his head, and Janlin realized she was being abrasive again. He gestured at one holo hanging in the air. "Anyway, we can pull NDBs from systems, but that might upset some people."

Janlin pursed her lips. "Some people as in Gordon?"

"Well, to be fair, Urse would be upset, too, if her pumps fail or the filtration goes down or . . ."

"Okay, I get it!" Janlin's blood boiled as she noticed him flinch. She took a deep breath, and then another. Hell, why not three?

"What was your point, Brighton?" she asked, suddenly weary beyond belief.

"Point?"

"These NDB things?"

"Ah, yes, well, NDBs can boost the old handhelds. That's how we received Gordon's call when you first got back, actually. I'd powered one up as an experiment and gave it to Ursula. For hope."

"Nice work! Reminds me of Anaya's favourite comm units. They're all handheld, no 'gear in the ear' like us."

"Maybe there's a cautionary tale for us there."

She put a hand to her forehead, massaging out the latest shot of pain. "Maybe."

"The problem is, the handhelds need even more boost for a Mars call, and we aren't creating the waste as fast as we need the batteries," Brighton said. "We have to keep a close monitor on Urse's needs . . ."

"Can you set up these calls for me or not?" Janlin asked. "It is by order of my captain."

"Uh, sure, Kavanagh, I can do it."

"Get that done, then, I'll come by again later." She sighed. "Not looking forward to this."

On her way out the door, she paused. "Oh, and Brighton?"

"Yeah?" He looked as tired as she felt.

"Sorry I'm so grumpy."

ONCE BRIGHTON DID his magic, Janlin put the first call through, and a female voice answered.

"Is this Lauren Gregory?"

"It is," the voice answered hesitantly. "Who is this? Why are you calling on the emergency handheld instead of my earcell?"

"This is Janlin Kavanagh of Spectra Station. Our earcells are malfunctioning, so we boosted a handheld to reach you."

Lauren's voice came back clear. "Hmmm, you guys aren't getting the upgrades, I bet . . . according to my tech friend, the NECS are designed to fail out if not upgraded regularly."

"Upgrades?" Janlin echoed. "Wait, what? Back up, there's a few things we need . . ."

"Why are you calling me, though?" Lauren demanded. "I'm no one special."

That derailed the questions she had. There was nothing for it but to get straight to business. "I am very sorry to inform you . . ." Janlin choked up a bit, unable to continue with the strong voice she had promised herself she would use.

"God, no . . . Tyrell?"

"I'm sorry," Janlin managed, and a wail of anguish filled her ears. She cried right along with her, then forced herself to pull it together.

"What happened?"

Janlin delivered it as kindly as she could. "Your brother was taken by a severe illness that also killed his new partner."

This brought a gasp. "I didn't even know he'd met someone," Lauren said, deep grief filling her voice.

"You couldn't have known," Janlin said, wanting to offer some comfort. "But I hoped it would bring you some peace to know how happy they were together.”

Lauren’s voice hitched. “And this girl, what was her name?”

“Iphimedeia Junta.” Janlin struggled to speak past the lump in her throat. “We called her ‘Teardrop’ for a small scar on her cheek.”

There was a silence, and then a blast Janlin never saw coming. “It’s no wonder SpaceOp tells us we shouldn’t reach out to you! You’re all infected, you, your food, everything! I shouldn’t even be talking to you right now! Diona made a public announcement telling us to beware of strange calls.” Lauren’s voice climbed an octave. “She said a digital virus could come across a comm link.”

Janlin reeled back in her seat. “What?” There were so many things wrong with what she just heard. “Wait, no, first off, I have no clue how anyone could send a virus over the comm link, and secondly, this didn’t happen here . . .”

There was a long silence. She had said more than she should’ve, and Lauren picked up on that. “Tyrell is . . . *was* stationed on Spectra. And you said that’s where you’re calling from. If this didn’t happen there, where did it?”

Janlin had to give the young woman credit. She asked incisive questions and expected an answer, although the bit about how they were all contaminated was off-putting.

Janlin sighed and debated how truthful to be. “We were dirtside.”

Lauren gasped.

“Listen, it’s not at all what you think. We were part of a very specialized exploration team.”

“I don’t know, I don’t believe Tyrell would go on such a dangerous mission.”

Oh goodness, girl, if only you knew how brave he’d been. Janlin sighed. “Look, I don’t know how to prove it to you. Can I contact you later? We could talk more. I’m curious what the official word is there on Spectra, because we’re beating the spore and starting new food crops.”

“Really?”

“Really. And for what it’s worth, I was devastated to lose Tyrell and Teardrop. They were amazing people. I’m still hurting.”

This seemed to reach Lauren in a way little else would. “I can hear it in your voice. Okay, Janlin, you can contact me again. I still have a few questions of my own. But you won’t send a virus through the line, will you?"

"I won't, promise."

ANAYA STABILIZED, BEARING a healthier shade of yellowish grey than before, but she remained unconscious. Janlin watched the display on the Gitane medbay screens, understanding nothing, but worrying over little things. Like the fluids being fed intravenously. What if they ran out? She wanted to take control of *Hope*, fly for help even if it meant a Jump, but she realized if she unplugged *Freedom* from *Hope*, she had no idea how long it would run.

Plans were flying along to reopen Luna Base with new crops. A small team had gone in and blown the place clean, and then each other, and then the place again, and then each other, until every test done on the surrounding surfaces was clear of the spore. It now sat unpressurized and without atmosphere, ready for one more complete wipe down before they brought in new crops.

"We'll still seal them in the grow tents," Ursula had told her over breakfast. "There's a really good chance we'll have sustaining crops again."

Ursula was a ray of sunshine, but Gordon never seemed able to join them anymore, and Janlin was okay with that for now. She didn't know how to face him.

Now it was after shift and she didn't want to meet with Gordon and Ursula, not as a third wheel, not with Gordon being such a pissant. That was probably the most useful British word he'd taught her, and seemed perfect for the moment.

She wandered the halls, avoiding areas of congestion and keeping as far away from corridor A-13 as possible. Instead, she headed for the opposite end of Spectra, far from the greenhouses, to a large, twisting common room that had window seats, recliners, vid-screens and holos of the known universe, and a currently-closed drinks bar along an outer edge of the station. This area was especially popular when this side of Spectra faced Earth, but in this part of the orbit there was only open, empty, pinpricked darkness. She would stare out the window for a while before facing up to stuff and people and her own worries.

Janlin rounded a bend to find Steve staring out her window.

"Hey, great minds think alike," she said as she approached.

Steve smiled. "Was this your idea, too?"

She nodded. "It's a great view, and usually quiet." She tipped her head. "Wanna catch a drink, see who's around? After enjoying the view, of course."

"I would, but . . ." Steve turned a deep shade of red. "I, uh, met someone cool and we have plans. We're meeting here, actually."

"Wow, that's great! What's their name?"

"Mark." Steve's face practically glowed, and Janlin felt joy for him. "Mark Nkosi. Don't know how we've never run into each other before, we both love science and playing Ten Thousand."

Janlin laughed. "We should have a game sometime, I'd love that." She clasped Steve's arm, gave it a squeeze. "I'm really happy for you."

"Thanks."

"I guess I'll find a different viewpoint then," she said, giving him a wink and finding great pleasure in watching him blush even harder. That, and a little envy. She turned to go but stopped a few steps away.

"I've got your back on the *Hope*, Captain, but you know I don't want it, right?"

Steve gave her a puzzled look. "I know, but I don't get it. You could take the *Hope* and do what you want if you were captain. Gordon couldn't say a thing."

Janlin laughed. "Well, that doesn't always work. Look what we did to Stepper."

"Fair enough."

Janlin sobered and shook her head. "Everyone seems against me and what I think is best, so I have to step back and listen to that, take a good look at myself, not just bull my way onwards. That way a good captain does not make."

"Just don't forget to be okay with yourself the way you are, all right? Be the you that forged an alliance with an alien. Who cares what other people think? You do you. If that means taking off to Mars to try and get some answers about the NECS, then do it. And, yes," he said to her raised eyebrows, "that is your captain speaking."

She got thoughtful. "Yes, sir, Captain, sir." She saw someone who could only be Mark rounding the bend and gave Steve another wink before heading off on her own.

CHAPTER FOURTEEN

Linder and her new team worked around the clock to create repair bots that could go in and hopefully negate the damage a little bit, but everyone was also watching to see how it would work on Anaya first.

Janlin found if she kept busy and didn't turn her head too fast, or look up too long, the loosey-goosey brain was tolerable. The post-trauma stuff, though, that wasn't so easy to fix.

Janlin entered the greenhouse to find about a dozen people wandering about, some alone, some in groups chatting and smiling. She took a deep breath. *The air tastes alive in here.*

Ursula came out from her office area, Gordon in tow as always. "I'm guessing there's a pure psychological benefit of just seeing things grow?" Janlin said, indicating all the guests.

Ursula nodded. "Cassie proposed it, said that it might do everyone some good. I suggested she study to become our psychologist. She has a natural ability to sense what is needed for our hearts."

Janlin couldn't agree more.

Gordon bent over the newest seed trays, poking one of the tiny sprouts. Ursula poked him in admonishment, but then bent over the tray and did practically the same thing. They babied each new batch like children, and it made Janlin so happy to see them this way.

A little jealous, too, if she was being honest.

She wished Anaya was here beside her, and they were planning their next adventures around the universe instead of fighting for the next breath, or the next meal. *It was supposed to be humanity's greatest achievement, our evolution to space-faring colonists,* she thought. *I wish . . .* She practically heard her father's voice in her ear.

"If wishes were horses, beggars would ride."

The thought of him buried millions of light years away, in a place she may never see again, brought another round of grief. She wandered the rows of trays set in their nutria-water baths and did her best to breathe through it, but the if-onlys kept piling up.

If only he could've met Anaya. He would've understood my need to do whatever it took to help her now. And he also would've fully supported improving the Jump technology, and probably woulda known how to fix it too. Like father, like daughter, he would've longed for the freedom to travel anywhere, anytime, in an instant. It would be worth any risk.

If only me and Stepper had worked out like Gordon and Ursula.

"If only Anaya were okay," she completed, not even really meaning to speak out loud.

Gordon just growled. "Bloody hell, I told you she shouldn't have come."

All of Janlin's grief became fury in an instant. "What? You said no such thing."

"I did, and you were having none of it. Never will listen to a word when you've got an idea in your head."

Ursula's eyes widened at Janlin's face, and she jumped in. "Gordon, whatever the case may be, Janlin's friend is unwell," she gently reminded.

It hit Janlin once again, no one else got to know Anaya the way she did. Anaya had been her friend, not Gordon's or anyone else's. Now she was sick, and it didn't matter the same to Gordon or Ursula or Cassie or Steve or anyone.

And it *was* all her fault, even if the Gitane came along of her own free will, it was still Janlin's fault she was here and none other's.

Janlin choked on her grief. She'd known Anaya just long enough to learn to love her, even if she was an ugly brutish-looking creature. Janlin needed to find some way to help, needed to ask Gordon for help, for getting Anaya's medbay comms figured out, needed him and he didn't need her, didn't want to help, didn't care . . .

Ursula was at her side. "Here, here, sit down before you're on the floor." Gordon got her some vitatea. Janlin blinked and blinked, sucking air, her throat closing on her words, trying to figure out if Gordon would help, and if she should even ask him. There was Ursula, they just got to be together again and they couldn't leave the crops . . .

Ursula knelt before her and took her hands. "Whatever you need, we're here for you."

Janlin shook her head. She couldn't speak, couldn't ask, couldn't ever watch Gordon go through that again. No, she couldn't ask him, wouldn't, shouldn't.

Won't.

CHAPTER FIFTEEN

JANLIN TRIED A smile for the fellow serving that day's breakfast vitatea and rations, and got nothing but a scowl for her efforts. Doing her best to let it slide like water off a duck, she scanned the cafeteria to see Cassie, Li, Steve, and Mark all just headed out the far door, each probably off to their respective labs to solve their most pressing problems. Not seeing any other familiar faces, she gathered her food and made her way back to *Freedom*.

Munching on the bar-shaped block of unnamed nutrition, Janlin considered the strange reaction Lauren had, expecting digital virus sabotage able to travel over a comm link. How was that even possible? And why would anyone do that? To what gain? The other folks she had relayed condolences to had taken her news stoically and ended the call quickly. Did they feel the same? Janlin couldn't imagine asking after delivering such devastating news.

She always did think it was a bit creepy having these little robots inside of you, but mostly she didn't think of them at all. She just blindly relied on them to do what SpaceOp and her parents promised they would do.

SpaceOp was just Diona now, and all their parents were dead. The remnants of humanity were spread around the inner solar system and reliant on this woman. Did Diona care? Janlin couldn't help but think how creating rumours like this could be a cover-up for Diona's own actions. Maybe going to Mars was as much about checking in on the Jordan siblings as much as anything else.

"Manipulating popular opinion, spying on us, holding out on food and seeds while we face famine, and now holding out on NECS upgrades . . . what else?" Diona was capable of anything to get her way, but what was it she wanted? She wouldn't send digital viruses through the population, would she?

A bolt of pain lanced through her skull, and Janlin knew what *she* wanted: a way to take control of her NECS, if she couldn't have them out. Wasn't so much to ask, was it? But even without that, there had to be a way to shut off that signal, and she was going to find it.

Earth was no longer viable, and wouldn't be for a long time to come. Mars and Luna both had their problems. They needed Huantag. She longed for the warmth of the breeze there, the taste of those special tubers, and Huantag's sun shining out of that beautiful green sky.

Thinking to ask Li to drop by and see Anaya today, Janlin changed her course to take her by his and Cassie's pod. She stopped short outside the doorway when she heard Gordon's voice within.

"She's too reckless, too wild, too bullheaded . . ." Gordon, clearly fuming about *her*. How dare he vent to Cassie? Was she so horrible that he couldn't talk to her about it?

"You mean brave, fun, and determined?" Cassie said, her blasé tone carrying the barest hint of threat. Janlin warmed to it, her black mood lightening as she heard her new friend support her. "Isn't that what makes her great?"

Wow, Cassie was really standing up for her. "You Jump survivors need to give each other a break," Cassie continued. *Thank you.* "I would professionally declare you all suffering PTSD symptoms if I were in a position to."

"No surprise, really," Gordon mumbled. "Not a bad idea, either."

"Maybe you should talk to her?"

"Right, the one that won't listen to me at all? She looks daggers at me all the time, and I can't say nothing right."

"That's because you always shoot down my ideas."

Gordon froze in mid-step of his pacing, and Cassie stared at the floor, looking mighty uncomfortable.

"I'm trying to be patient," Janlin continued. "I get that I do jump in too quick. But I have different priorities than you, and all I'm looking for is a bit of help to get me on my way."

Gordon chewed on this for a moment as they took measure of each other. Then he pushed past her and left without saying a word.

"I'm not against you, Gordon," she called, but he was gone. Janlin realized she was shaking, and it was hard to catch her breath. "Why won't he just talk to me?" she wailed.

Cassie placed a hot vitatea in her hands and guided her into a seat. "Deep breaths, you're almost hyperventilating there, chica, and this is getting to be a habit."

Janlin did her best to think of nothing but sucking in air and letting it out again. Cassie was chatting on about inane things and unrelated topics as she made a second mug for herself. She sat down across from Janlin and peered into her face.

"Better?"

Janlin was sipping the hot liquid and relishing its descent into her gut. She didn't want to think about anything else but breathing and sipping her drink.

"You know, a trauma-scarred brain often misinterprets gestures of concern as outright attacks," Cassie said. She blushed a little. "I've been studying. Steve wants me to help counsel everyone who Jumped."

"So, what you're saying is, I blew things out of proportion again? I don't seem to know how to *not*."

"In this case, no, because Gordon's brain is damaged just the same, yeah?" A small smile crept in as she saw Janlin get it. "See? I wasn't pointing at you, I meant him, but you immediately took it on."

"Wow."

"Right?"

"But it just seems like another version of blowing things out of proportion," Janlin pointed out.

Cassie sighed. "Y'all are gonna need an extraordinary amount of patience with yourselves and each other."

Janlin snorted. "We should make posters saying as much. Public service announcement," she spread her hands over an imagined wall hanging, "Jump folk require extraordinary patience."

Cassie laughed. "Janlin, you have a wonderful, wry sense of humour. I think it's your superpower!"

Janlin shook her head. "Thanks, Cassie. Most people seem to think I'm just a smartass. Wry, sarcastic, it's a fine line, yeah?"

"But only if you're walking it!"

Their laughter died too quick, and inevitably they had to face the issues at hand once again.

"If Jumping her home could get Anaya the care she needs to survive, I'd take the risk," Janlin explained when Cassie asked after the alien. "I just need help getting it set up."

Cassie was shaking her head. "That would pull a lot of people off their current responsibilities."

"Yeah, I know, I just want to make her life a priority and no one else here does." Janlin banged the table, and Cassie winced. Seeing that, Janlin felt anger sweep over her as if she'd been doused in fire, only to have it abruptly die and become the heaviest grief she'd ever felt. "Never mind. I'm sorry. I shouldn't be unloading on you any more than Gordon should've."

"Look, Janlin, it's okay. Did you hear what I said about you all suffering PTSD?"

Janlin nodded.

"It's not my area of expertise, but I know enough that y'all are acting a bit crazy and it's only to be expected."

"So, you think I'm crazy? That I shouldn't be trying to save this alien's life either? That I'm insane to even think of Jumping to try?" Janlin was on her feet. Cassie looked a little scared, and that really got Janlin. She had to get out of there. "Look, I get it, I'm crazy, and humanity's survival should come before one lousy alien's life, I get it. But no one here knew her like I did. No one. No one understands how important she is. And I'm not giving up on her." She marched out, forgetting all about asking Li to visit Anaya.

Cassie called after her, but Janlin couldn't face her. Or anyone. They all thought she was making foolish, harmful decisions, but they didn't value Anaya's life one bit, and Janlin couldn't help but take that a little personally.

She banged her way through Spectra's hallways, praying with each turn to not be accosted by anyone requiring polite conversation. Back in the hangar bay, she climbed into *Hope* and headed for her quarters there. She'd spent more time in this bunk than in her Spectra one, wanting to stay close to her friend.

Once there, however, it was too small, too much the same same same, and she marched back out into the hangar bay and stood with her hands on her hips, wondering what to do with all the pent-up rage and hurt and indecision she carried with her all the time.

The irony of her walking out and not turning back when Cassie called was huge. Hadn't she just been pissed and hurt by Gordon doing the very same thing? Cassie was right. They all had problems, and the aftermath of their trauma was making it harder than ever to endure the problems they faced.

Then an idea lit her up. A quick jog back to *Freedom* and she had her Huantag flight gear. Laying it out, tears filled her eyes at the memories that flooded her: teaching others how to fly, flying over the village, landing on the ledges of the towering Huantag city buildings, soaring over the forests with Huantag flying on all sides of her . . .

She shoved down the horrid guilt and pain. So many Huantag had died because of the humans. It was the same old colonist story of bringing sickness that seemed to plague humanity, even if this time the Imag were the ones to blame.

Then there was the memory of Stepper, and that kiss that made them lovers again. That certainly didn't turn out well either. And despite being more than done with him, she was feeling awfully alone right now, and a little touch deprived.

Shaking it all off, she focused on the current moment. It was all she had to work with, this, right here, right now. Gathering up the flight gear, she made her way back out into Spectra's huge hangar bay. Piece by piece she donned the harnesses, tightened the straps, and finally flexed the wings.

She launched from the floor, relishing in the relatively stable air currents of the bay and the light gravity. With each pump of her arms, she felt more and more right.

With enough height she was able to stretch out and soar, actually catching the current from the station's air filtration systems. From up here she could see the patch on the bay doors, and again guilt plagued her. She was the one that had punched a hole in the side of the Jumpship.

Maybe she did have a wonderful, wry sense of humour, like Cassie had said. Maybe she was impatient and just craved adventure, like Gordon said. And maybe they were all suffering from the trauma induced by the Imag's treatment, the Jumps, and the failing NECS. But why did that make her the bad guy? Was she making a mountain out of a mole hill?

Lifting above *Hope*, she drifted in lazy circles, letting all the remorse and confusion fall away with each turn until her mind felt clear.

LATER, AS SHE removed her Huantag flight gear, Janlin found herself staring at Gordon's Seraph sitting idly by. Hers, of course, was wrecked in her unsuccessful attempt to escape the Imag, and was later dismantled by the same, but this ship those wretched aliens had left alone. She walked alongside, running her fingers over the exterior.

Stepper built these things fast and tough. Would it get her to Mars and back? She climbed in and opened one of the compartments to find standard survival gear: extra rebreathers, carbon scrubbers, filters. Janlin glanced around. The bay was quiet. She carefully refolded her Huantag flight suit and stowed it in a pack. She added a couple extra rebreathers and extra filters. She left it alongside the other gear before closing the hatch.

If she needed to go somewhere, it would be nice to be prepared.

A sound began to echo through the flight bay. It was clear, but distant.

Freedom's medbay!

Janlin ran. Cassie appeared at the hangar bay airlock. She saw Janlin running, heard the alarm, and began to run as well. They met at the ramp, and Cassie waved her in first.

Anaya looked the same, but the medbay was lit up with messages and warnings and alarms that neither of them could read.

"What's happening?" Cassie cried.

"I don't know. I thought she was getting better," Janlin said, checking the one screen she had managed to get some info from. "All it says is 'running program'."

Cassie gave a little shriek, and Janlin spun around to see the slab Anaya was on being wrapped in a transparent bioplaz sheet with a big mechanical arm, Anaya within. The sheet made it look like a body bag. Then a panel opened up and the whole slab bed began to slide away into the wall.

"No, no, no, no," Janlin said, trying to grab the slab, the sheet, Anaya. Her fingers slid away, the slab was swallowed whole, and the wall closed back up again.

Cassie moaned.

Various beeps and hums came from the machine, and then it all fell silent. A yellow light started to flash on the console, blink, blink, blink, slow and steady like a heartbeat.

"What the hell?" Janlin cried. "Is she dead? Is that button meant to eject her into space or something?"

Cassie bit her lip. "What if it was something that needed pushed?" she asked, not being helpful. "Or it's a suspended animation chamber to keep her alive until better help is at hand?"

Sadly, better help was not coming. Janlin's mind went one way, then the other. "How can we possibly know what's the right thing to do?"

CHAPTER SIXTEEN

Diona marched into the lab gunning for the tech. The others steered clear, and one even flinched when she looked his way.

Peons, weakness embodied.

The tech . . . what was her name? . . . was nowhere to be found. She pinned down one of the others.

"Where is this one?" she asked, gesturing at the woman's office.

"I don't know, Commander. She's been having headaches from the nanite degradation."

Diona ground her teeth. "The NECS are fine," she said, knowing it was a lie, knowing this monkey in a lab coat knew it, too, thanks to where he worked. "Who is completing her work?"

"She wasn't sharing it with anyone," the lab monkey said. "Was actually really secretive about it."

Good. Exactly the answer I'd better hear.

Her father tried to get her into nano-tech programming, told her again and again that they needed to understand them to use them well, but Diona was far too much like him for that. He had the ideas and paid others to do the work. She followed in his footsteps in that way.

She had done her homework, however, and was able to create rudimentary code. But she would have to find another tech with a spotty history, need, or weakness she could use against them if this one didn't hold up to the strain.

Diona marched through the corridors of what was once considered humanity's finest nano-biology department ever. Now, it was the only one, and their only hope of survival. She tapped her earcell.

"Computer; private domicile for . . ." *Dammit, what was her name?* ". . . lead tech on my private nanite research." Hopefully that would be enough.

"Eliza Moran is your current lead tech. She resides at 2514 Platform D, in the Newton Domicile."

The smart database gave her directions as she went. It wasn't often she travelled amongst the colonists, and even though she was still within the corporate science area she was pulling some looks. She stepped a little quicker, and a little taller. While she had a good handle on the population as a whole, there were always those with dreams of grandeur and a plot to takeover.

She entered the habitat as directed, grateful once more for her social standing ensuring she did not have to live cheek by jowl like these bric-a-brac. The lift was crammed, and they all stared at her open-mouthed. Worse, instead of exiting the lift as they should've, she had to step in with them.

This woman was going to pay.

Diona marched to the correct door and ordered it opened. Within was the standard single apartment, but to Diona's astonishment, it was a riot of colour. Tapestries and shawls hung everywhere, covering every possible glimpse of metal, woven together into this strange pattern. The standard chairs were missing, and instead pillows lay piled atop a thick rug.

"Ugh, she's like a child," Diona said, picking her way through. In the bedroom, a form lay under the covers.

"Miss Morid!"

The woman gasped and rolled to face her, lifting a black-rimmed gaze. Despite enjoying the stark surprise she had induced, Diona felt a cold rod of fear travel through her as if the woman's obvious fear was contagious.

The woman's shock drained away quickly. "Moran," the tech corrected before curling back into her bedding.

"Whatever. Are you ill? I need your results. I want to run some tests."

Moran sat back up, twisting around with a look of abject horror. "Don't. No, no tests," she said, winding the bedsheets into a knot. "It's too dangerous."

Diona watched this overdramatic display. "Oh?"

Moran looked ready to beg. What was the problem? Unless . . .

"I can't cure the blood disease," Moran blurted out. "Not without unmitigated risk to us all." Now she was shaking violently, clearly terrified at having to deliver this news.

Diona took a deep breath and let it out slowly through her nose. She shifted a chair around and sat, then tipped her head at the brilliant but terrified woman.

"AI," was all she said.

The woman gave several quick, sharp nods. "Those new nanites are beautiful, a perfect function of repair and rebuild . . . but each time I let more than a few work together, chain reactions begin, and it was all I could do to shut it down in time." She eyed Diona for her reaction. "It was very close," she said in a whisper.

Her desperation was starting to wear on Diona. Did the woman really think her such a monster?

"You've done well," she said, and Moran relaxed a fraction. "Keep retracting the networking processes to see if we can find a functional, safe, and perhaps slower way to accomplish the repairs."

The tech nodded. The advice was obvious and probably already processing. But there was more. Diona could read it in her face; the tech had something to say. She even opened and closed her mouth a few times, each one a false start.

"Space me, would you spit it out already?"

Moran took a fresh grip on the bedding and actually shook her head. Diona raised an eyebrow. The threat couldn't be any clearer.

Still, the woman hesitated.

"Tell me!"

Moran squeaked, shuddered, and finally gave over.

"There isn't enough time for whoever belongs to sample two."

DIONA FOUND HERSELF back in her office, unclear exactly what path she'd took or who she'd met along the way. All she remembered was the tech's horrible words . . . and then she was here.

If she couldn't find a solution, her daughter would die.

Likely they would all die, even if she ran a restricted upgrade.

Nanite degradation. Bio-fouling. Purge options that were risky as hell. And even riskier upgrades that pushed the AI envelope. What would plague her next? And Thea . . .

How far was she willing to push it?

And was there a way she could safely test it?

"THINGS GOT WORSE, Stepper. It's not just Thea's blood disease anymore . . . I'm working to save us all."

"How dramatic."

Diona ground her teeth. How was he so good at pushing every single button she had? Made her more than willing to experiment on his sorry ass.

"So, is my alien nano-tech messing with your programs? You still don't know all my secrets." He grinned like a maniac. "I bet that pisses you off."

Diona reminded herself which side of the glass she was on. "Yes," she allowed, "your blood has quite a mess of foreign components in it, turns out, and it did mess with my usual programs." She watched him gloat. It made up her mind. "So why not play a little more, see what happens?"

His eyes narrowed, and she saw his Adam's apple bob.

"My update is ready, and I want to try it on Thea, but my tech is a little terrified, seems to think I'm pushing some boundaries."

He stepped up to the glass, new interest in his eyes. "I always was one for breaking some rules, especially those set by our own parents." Then he sobered. "But what if things go wrong? Do you really think you can contain me in here?"

He spoke her fears so easily. "I will take extraordinary precautions," she informed him. "Even as far as to disconnect this bunker from the rest until we're sure."

Stepper looked skeptical. "And how will you be sure? An AI could easily hide until . . . oh, no, sister darling, no, no, no, you're not really thinking of keeping me in here forever, are you? Even you aren't that cruel."

She brought up holo images between them, flipping some to face him. They showed the nanite structures in his blood. The enlarged image could be a deep-sea creature, an alien, or a bacteriophage, only it was the Imag virus. Riding on its back was a smaller version locked into an upgrade port. "Whether the first one is natural, engineered, or a mutant alien we don't understand, it behaves exactly like a virus in the human body. Replicates like one, destroys like one, and travels easily between beings, as you've experienced. The one riding its back is what's protecting you, blocking the first from fulfilling its function. I don't know that they're all blocked, or that these talented nanites couldn't leave your body and travel like all good viruses do. Allowing any contact with the population is out of the question. I'm sorry, brother. It does make you a perfect test subject."

Now it was his turn to grind his teeth. She knew that bunching knot of muscle in his cheek all too well. "And if this upgrade fixes things without going AI, as far as you can tell, you're really going to try it on the populace? That could go horribly wrong. And you're supposed to get consent."

"After all the rubbish I've filled their heads with?"

"Yeah, that's a problem. I can just imagine how much fun you've been having with your social media experiment."

"It's not true social media, just message boards to help us stay connected," she countered. Social media had been banned since they were children, and for good reason. "Besides, if I didn't guide their thinking, they would never allow me to go ahead with the upgrade, even though it's for their own good."

"Is it?" Stepper gave her the same tipped head move that she was famous for, and she snarled at him.

"I'll be by later with your new upgrade," she said, killing the lights both inside and outside the chamber. She also killed the sound feed just as he began to shout, and, guided by the illumination of a datapad, left him to stew.

Thea's organs would shut down, eventually, and stop supporting her.

The thought was agony.

There was no choice but to proceed.

CHAPTER SEVENTEEN

Brighton cleared up the signal best he could for Janlin to connect with Lauren again. Wondering what sort of reception she would get, she grabbed a big lungful of air before connecting.

"Janlin?"

"Yes, hi Lauren, are you okay?"

"For the moment, yes," she replied, her voice low and distant. A constant crackle undermined the connection. "But I'm scared."

"Why? What's happening?"

"We've been 'outcast', as they call it," she said. Janlin heard choked tears in her voice. "There are a few who claim the issues we've been having lately are due to the spore, and because we came on the last transport, we are suspect. They say the only way to fix things is to cull all the carriers."

"That's absurd," Janlin said. "It won't help anything."

"Well, you and I both know that, but these people won't hear reason. I'm terrified. We are hunted now, no matter that I've never set foot on Luna Base, no matter that we passed every test, every quarantine, and been here for nearly a year, no matter that I bring my skills as a nurse, I can't even walk down the street, or buy food in the market. I may even have to take Tyson into hiding if these nuts find out where I live. Without a sympathetic friend, we would simply starve . . . and most here would cheer."

Janlin wanted to assure Lauren that it was probably the NECS malfunctioning. Then she realized that was no reassurance at all, and kept her mouth shut.

There was another question she didn't want to ask, but it needed done. "And Tyson's father?"

"I was told he died in an accident while administering first aid at the Hawking Mine, but . . ." She paused, and Janlin's heart broke at the sounds of Lauren's struggle to maintain her composure. "Ah, yeah, sorry," she sniffled. "Anyway, his body was never presented to me for identification, and be damned if I feel like he isn't really dead. Is that crazy of me, Janlin?"

"No, always trust your heart, Sweetie."

A gaping pit of horror was growing in her gut. Seemed Diona wanted to be sure no one questioned her decision to not send help, so she created propaganda to make the general population afraid of "outsiders". The saddest part was how well it worked. People were capable of terrible things when they were scared.

"I'll bring hope," she said, hearing the double meaning and wishing she could take the chance. She shouldn't Jump. How fast could she fly in the Seraph? "I'll get you both safely away, but I need you to bring whatever nanite materials or upgrades you can."

"When?" Lauren's voice sounded so distant, as if she was too tired to hope. Her little Tyson was crying in the background.

"The first possible moment. Right now, the most important thing is getting you out of there. Hang tight, I'll be there as soon as I can."

Did she dare Jump? Would Lauren and Tyson survive the time she needed to traverse to Mars more slowly?

"It's not just the witch hunt," Lauren murmured, her voice calm as if she mentioned watching the stars or something. "If you don't upgrade, things start to disable. It's in the programming. If you don't stay connected to SpaceOp, they will eventually take your NECS down completely. That's what they say."

Janlin doubted the woman knew what she was talking about. After all the other propaganda she'd been fed, what could Janlin believe? "I've never heard of upgrades to the NECS. Wouldn't that require networking abilities? Maybe it's physical deterioration, not a lack of upgrading."

"I have a tech friend, she works for . . . you know . . ." Lauren's voice dwindled more as she spoke kindly to Tyson in the background. In that same voice, just barely enough for Janlin to catch, she added, "So I know about the bio-fouling. The upgrades are supposed to help, but my friend confirmed they do have scary stuff in them, like networking software." Her whispers ceased as Janlin took that in, then her voice came clear and strong again. "Still there, Janlin? Sorry, had to take care of the kid."

"Yes, I'm here," Janlin replied, keeping up the ruse. At this point, she was glad Brighton wasn't recording these calls. "Thank you for chatting, I'd better let you go tend to Tyson." Then, in a quick undertone, "I'll get there somehow."

JANLIN EXPLAINED LAUREN'S situation to her friends. She ended with the news of upgrades, both the ones they had already missed, and the ones in production.

"What makes AI so terrifying anyway?" Janlin asked once her report was delivered. She knew there was plenty of fear instilled in the population over it, but she'd realized she didn't actually know why.

"Can't control them," Steve said. "Simple as that."

Linder added, "Theory is, humans would quickly be seen for the destructive beings we are, and therefore we expect we'd be punished or destroyed for it. Karma might be a thing after all, eh?"

Ursula set a steaming pot of root tea in the centre of the table while Gordon handed out cups. "There is historical evidence that allowing a technological singularity to occur creates uncontrollable growth that could, and did, create unforeseeable changes to human civilization," Ursula said.

"What happened, exactly? I only remember some history lesson as a kid instilling fear of AI, but not why," Cassie said.

Ursula nodded. "While WWIII on the surface rose out of disagreement on how to handle pandemics, the underlying conflicts began years before, and were unknowingly aggravated by AI development in social media platforms that created echo chambers of belief, causing a divide between ideologies unlike any ever seen before in humanity's history."

"Wow, really?" Janlin said. "Is that why social media was outlawed? I always thought it was about wealth inequality because the owners of those platforms hoarded billions while others starved."

"That was part of it, to be sure. But the real problem with

social media was the algorithms that began to have negative impacts on our society as a whole . . . and those algorithms were AI based. In short, we can't be sure that an artificial intelligence can be made to understand the nuances of what we want and need as humans."

"It's true," Li said. "The machines were just feeding us more of what people wanted without understanding the consequences."

Linder jumped in. "In bionanoculture, we had to find ways around the issue, which is why we create an individual nanite for each task and never allow them to network or communicate. Everything we were taught said the NECS must be kept at the first level of AI, reactive machines, nothing more."

"There's more than one kind of AI?" Janlin asked.

Steve jumped in on this one. "Yes, there are four types of AI: reactive machines, limited memory, theory of mind, and self-awareness. If we allow NECS to evolve and become self-aware, they begin to base decisions on past experiences, to theorize, and thus, to postulate," Steve said. "If Diona really is feeding the colony upgrades with networking capabilities, she could be far more desperate than we realized."

"Desperate for what, exactly?" Gordon asked.

There was a silence while each speculated. "My fear is she wants to build one huge AI running off everyone," Cassie said, "like that old show, you know, with the hive mind alien robots?" Everyone gave her blank looks, but the idea tickled Janlin's memories. Her dad watched that old show, raved about it.

"Space Trekking or something like that," she said, and Cassie lit up.

"Yes! They had an enemy in the storyline where all beings captured were connected and controlled by one mind, like a queen bee in a hive."

Mark piped up, with Steve's encouragement. "Maybe things with the NECS are going bad on Mars, despite their upgrades, and it's all she's got to try and fix it."

Steve agreed. "And I bet if that were true, even the colony population wouldn't know the full extent of it."

"Of course not," Janlin said. "She would never admit to any wrongdoing. That's a Jordan thing."

Cassie piped up. "Well, being ever the optimist, maybe a

superintelligence would analyse and repair not just the NECS, but the human genetic code . . . at great speed, no less. Maybe we'll find eternal youth, or at least a way to stop the bio-fouling and Jump safely."

Li smiled at Cassie, but was shaking his head. "AI that is superintelligent is really unlikely, I hate to say," he said. "Artificial neural networks can learn for themselves, yes, but they have severe limitations. Any thinking machine can be thrown off by situations not encountered before. It would be like a teenager, defined as an 'inexperienced adult', which is why teenagers often make really dumb choices."

Steve agreed. "A machine has no volition either, no human insight, no concept of emotion, no conscience. I've read that intelligence does not necessarily lead to sentience."

"And yet, are we not machines?" Janlin asked. "Humans are just complicated chemical processing factories, when it comes right down to it, and we somehow got smart."

Everyone laughed. Mark piped up, "I read an old book from the early twenty-first century about AI in that time, his name was . . . something Russell . . . he said it was like fusion. If you want unlimited energy, you'd better contain the reaction. Same with unlimited intelligence. You'd better figure out how to align that intelligence with human needs, or 'contain' it in case it doesn't agree with us. He said we're basically teaching a god how we'd like to be treated."

"Whoa," Cassie said, to general agreement.

"Apparently the greats of that time, like Hawking, Bostrom, and other computer scientists all warned of the potential hazards," Linder said. "So, in my mind, it's worth proceeding *only* with the most stringent 'containment' in place. Then the question becomes, in what form? I don't want an AI inside of me."

For a few moments they passed the tea around and filled their cups. Janlin wished they had something to celebrate. Thankfully, Cassie and Ursula had it covered.

"Here's to renewed good health," Cassie said, ever the optimist.

"And strong, nutritious food crops," Ursula added, and they clinked mugs.

"So," Janlin started after everyone sipped. "I'd like to go get Lauren and Tyson. She's going to try and secure some nanite gear, too, maybe even this new upgrade so we can see what that's all about. I'm just trying to figure out how to pilot *Hope* alone and Jump . . ."

General pandemonium broke out as shouts of "hell no" and "what?" mixed with disbelief.

"You can't be serious," Linder asked, "the way you've been feeling?"

"But they could be killed . . ."

"You're blowing it out of proportion . . ."

"Not your problem . . ."

"*You* could be killed . . ."

And the worst, from Gordon . . . "Why would we help them when they were happy to leave us in the lurch?"

Janlin stood. "Because this is Tyrell's sister, Lauren Gregory, and her child. She came from here, from the Orbitals, and Tyrell agreed to keep Stepper's secrets and risk everything to fly the first Jumpship just to get her a spot in the colony. Only now they're ostracizing her and her little one, threatening to let them starve, or outright kill them. We can't just let that happen!"

No one would meet her eye. She couldn't believe the response.

"It is what it is," Gordon said, looking to Ursula for her support. "Anyone who signed up for the colonies knew what they were getting into . . ."

"No. Not like this. Plus, we need more information about these upgrades we were supposed to be getting. And we need nanite gear."

Linder squeezed her arm. "It's just not safe." The others nodded.

"So, even though Diona is trying to form an AI *on purpose*, and people we should care about are in trouble, you guys want to do *nothing*?"

"Janlin. Enough with the conspiracy theories!" Gordon cried. Cassie and Li both stood, readying to go. Linder joined them. Everyone looked uncomfortable.

Janlin thought steam might come out of her ears any second.

Gordon wasn't done. "Look, it's a month to fly there under top speed, and you have no crew, and no right to ask for one either. You can't Jump, or you'll probably die. I'm sorry, we simply can't help them. And we can't let you just take the Jumpship . . . why would you do that to us?"

"Look, *Hope* isn't yours, nor is *Freedom* or anything or anyone aboard it. And if we can't help Lauren and Tyson in a moment like this, then we're just as bad as Diona."

"If you go, don't come back," Gordon said.

Painful silence filled the room as his words struck Janlin to the bone. Everyone shuffled their feet, staring at the floor.

"You'll be compromised," he tried, but the damage was done. She turned to go.

"We can't allow it," Gordon continued. With every word he spoke she felt heavier, like he added a stone to her gut each time.

She couldn't believe Gordon would send her away forever. She was an outcast, for wanting to help people. For caring. And her NECS continued to make her feel awful, so she probably wouldn't be any help anyway. She was broken. Useless. A burden and an annoyance. She thought about Cassie's suggestion they go easy on each other. Well, no one was going easy on her.

Janlin was appalled that everyone brushed off Lauren's appeal for help so easily. How dare they ever complain now about Diona's decision to leave them hanging, when they could so easily write off Lauren as not their problem?

"Fine," she said to the empty corridor as she made her way back to the shuttle. "You guys stay here and focus on food production. That's great. I'll take the Seraph and go to Mars. Those shuttles got some umph. Get there faster than they realize."

She banged around the bay, tossing cables aside in a pile to clear the shuttle, not wanting to wait and see if anyone would try and stop her.

It was going to take ages longer in the Seraph than it would in *Hope*, and it sure as hell wasn't going to be all that comfortable. Instead of weeks, how sweet would it be to Jump there? She would be gone and back again before Gordon would even say "blimey hell" if the risk weren't so high.

As if on cue, her skull was pierced by another stab of pain so intense, she couldn't keep her left eye open. The agony shot down through her ear and neck before radiating through her ribcage, feeling all too much like a heart attack. What did a stroke even feel like, she wondered, as she arched her back in agony.

As far as she could see it, Lauren and Tyson didn't have any other options. And going to Mars could gain them the tech needed to repair the NECS. Maybe that's why it hadn't helped Anaya. Maybe even the lab NECS were degrading.

She didn't know, she didn't have the answers, but she had to try something. Everyone else could worry about food production, she was going to get to the bottom of these bio-fouling, signal-tracing, head-tormenting NECS, Diona's upgrades, and help Tyrell's sister and nephew in the meantime.

Janlin dumped her flight gear in the cockpit, grumbling under her breath. Her jerky movements and shaking hands revealed how angry and hurt she was. *No time for that.* She would need a calm, steady hand for piloting. She sucked air, drawing it in as deep as she could, struggling to lower her heartrate and blood pressure.

If she had to do this alone, then she would.

CHAPTER EIGHTEEN

JANLIN SHOVED THE last gear into a storage locker and slammed it shut. She grabbed her pack, climbed into the small cockpit, and began the rundown to takeoff.

With gentle nudges and careful flying, she settled the Seraph into the loading airlock, then climbed out, set the airlock to cycle in five and to reset after she was clear.

Soon the door opened to the blackness of space, and she was able to guide the Seraph out, free of Spectra. She got up to secure things and check the auto co-pilot settings.

A sound, a feeling, a shift in the way the air sat in the tight cockpit . . . she wasn't sure what made her turn, but she did . . . only to find a guy behind her. She let out a yelp of surprise.

The surge of adrenaline made her head pound, and she groaned and closed her eyes, gripping the pilot's chair as her knees went weak.

"Thank you, Ms. Kavanagh," the man said. She peeled one eye open and tried to focus. All she registered was piercing blue eyes. "You've provided me the opportunity I've been waiting for."

She peeled the other eyelid open. Something about the guy. Dark hair framed his face, filled by an equally dark beard—the facial hair itself wasn't common in orbit so she should be able to place him—average build, and those blue eyes . . . "Do I know you?"

He got a funny look. "You don't remember?"

Janlin's head settled and she took a better look. "I . . . am I supposed to? You do look familiar, but there's a lot of people on Spectra."

And then it all came rushing back. The girl, the storm, the lashing winds, the guy with the knife, and this guy, waving his gun. This guy of her nightmares telling her to run before he couldn't hold the other guy back anymore. It was those eyes, those blue eyes.

He was opening his mouth to reply when she cut in. "How the hell are you *here*?"

Then, of all things, he grinned, and she was a little taken aback by how it changed his looks. "Stowaway."

She stared, stunned beyond words.

He was still grinning, but it faded. "You tore outta there so fast for that meeting with Stepper, and then you were busy with the Jumpship mission . . ." He shrugged. "I stayed outta sight, waited for you to be gone. But then I couldn't steal a ride or find a pilot to take food back home as planned, and, well, there wasn't any food to take after all anyway." He looked sheepish. "Guess you weren't lying about that."

She could feel the Seraph's jets maintaining their position in orbit, awaiting her flight plan input. "What are you doing here *now*?" she asked.

He hesitated. "Look, I heard the stories about you," he started, and Janlin felt her eyebrows climb.

"Me?"

"Yeah, you, the one who convinced an alien leader to save both your human crew and a different alien race they were fighting with. Word is you did that, and that's the kind of person I need right now." He looked earnest, but the set of his jaw also spoke of determination.

Janlin crossed her arms. "Okay, enough with the flattery, what is it you want?"

He regarded her with those same blue eyes that had haunted her. *Go now, before I can't hold him back.* Only it was sometimes an Imag killing the pregnant girl, not this guy's buddy. "There's food now, and seeds," he said, squaring his shoulders. "I want to take some home."

"I can't, I'm trying . . ."

He shot her an apologetic look as he drew a taser gun from

under his coveralls. "I'm not taking no for an answer."

HAD HE POINTED anything else at her, she might've laughed. After all she had been through? But the taser . . . it would feel so reminiscent of the Imag nerve whips. Far too reminiscent. She hurt just thinking of it, and realized her PTSD was hampering her in this moment.

"Look, people need help on Mars, too," she stammered. "No one is immune to trouble. You can't just go commandeering a shuttle on your own. I mean, well, I did it once, as you know, but I'm a pilot, it's what I do, I fly good." She realized she was babbling, even as her brain scrambled for a way out of this.

She also knew the set of this guy's mouth. She'd seen it before. Stepper could get the same look, and it always meant bullheaded determination.

"Exactly," he agreed. "You can't just commandeer a shunter . . . I've tried. Can't undock with the station without the right release codes." He narrowed his eyes. "Makes me wonder how you managed it, to say nothing of how you piloted off planet through that weather. But it suits me fine that you can."

He eased closer, and she had nowhere to go, backed up against the pilot's seat. He had an intensity to him that promised a pulled trigger if she gave him reason. Her brain continued to spin out the implications of this man's presence on Spectra.

All of it her fault, of course.

"You know that might kill me?" she said, pointing her chin at the taser.

His eyes narrowed. "You would say that."

If she hadn't gone dirtside, this wouldn't be happening right now. Her heart thudded too hard in her chest. She did not want to pilot back down there now, especially not with *him*.

She kept remembering that pregnant girl.

"Did you really eat people?"

He grimaced. "No. I never did. Tanner did. And the girl he killed, she did, just like he told you that day." He bit down on the words, clearly as sickened as she was. "Now go on, sit down. Just a bit more of that fancy flying of yours, and then you can do whatever you want."

Janlin set her feet. "I don't think so. That itty-bitty gap in the weather I got through is rare, according to Gordon . . . and he tracks it, has been for years. You can't just fly in there all willy-nilly and expect just because I'm a good pilot we'll make it."

Gawd, she still sounded like an idiot, and there didn't seem to be enough air in the room. Could she psych him out somehow? Meh, who was she kidding. Could she tolerate the taser long enough to fling herself on him, thus taking him down too? And what good would that do?

Her mind couldn't grapple with anything properly, and no weapon of any kind presented itself within reach, and damn it she was just so *tired* of the struggle. But she could not simply let this guy take her on what could be a suicide mission. To be honest, she could not let him take her prisoner. It made her insides scream, and her headache was spiking ever worse with the strain.

She dodged left and went right. When the taser hit, her mind exploded into thousands of tiny, excruciating shards of pain, her body arced and stiffened, and the ground rose up to smack her in the face.

By some mercy, unconsciousness quickly took over.

CHAPTER NINETEEN

DIONA STOOD HIDDEN in darkness and listened to her brother's voice over the speakers.

"The Imag, they can't all be dead, that would be too easy. There must've been more of them. Hasn't anyone thought about that? We never did see where *Renegade* went. Did it blow, too? Damn it all, they are my ships, I built them, I gathered the right people, I did it, not her, not her, should be mine . . ."

She took out a vial and dumped it thoughtfully into the cage's drinking water supply. She then gently rose the lights, leaving them on a muted setting. He was easier to deal with if she allowed small measures like this. The PTSD was rather apparent, and quite bothersome.

He sat with his back against the glass, staring maniacally out into the darkness. "I'm a lost cause, sis," he said, rolling his head this way and that like an idiot, not even looking for her. "I'm not worth the canned air I'm breathing. Go ahead and experiment on me, open me up and get these alien NECS working for you. Ours are buggered up anyway." He gave a guttural laugh. "Extraction never was an option, was it?"

Gosh, no, she thought. Their parents quickly noticed how cellular tissue tended to grow to encompass the nanites. That's why she was working so hard to improve them . . . or work better with the integration. Their very survival depended on it, on them. No one realized how vital her work was, no one.

"Everyone was right to shame me like they did, you know," he continued.

Great, still on the self-pity kick, I see.

"I was a complete ass. You really should just use me up."

"No, I want to save you for later."

Stepper flinched, cursed, and curled in on himself, hissing words the speakers couldn't deliver.

"You are still of value to me alive, brother," she continued. "And I'm fascinated by these evolved nanites and how they can travel between beings like a virus. It's guiding my work."

Stepper stared out at the darkness with a gaunt look that reminded her of their father in his last days. "As cruel as they were, Imag are no dummies," he admitted, attempting bravery. "They nearly wiped out an entire planet of aliens using a handful of us humans just so they could move in and claim the place for themselves without damaging it one bit."

Talkative today. Good. He's lonely. Malleable.

"If there's more out there, they would be a formidable enemy. We need to know how the Jump affected Anaya. She went down at first, but some of the crew did too. We even lost one. But if Jumps take the aliens out, then good, good, we're safe. If not, we could still have trouble coming."

Diona brought up a console. Stepper immediately zeroed in on where she stood, her face now partially illuminated by the hologram's light. She tapped and slid until she had what she wanted.

"The upload is nearly ready," she lied to him. No need for him to be aware of what he was about to drink. "If you do well with it, I will try it on Thea."

She went to leave, dimming the lights only a touch and lifting her finger away when he cried out.

"Bitch," he said.

"Oh, one last thing. Janlin has moved off from the last functioning orbital station, so my guess is she's on her way here. Do you think she'll have this alien on board?"

"Oh, likely, they're besties, you know," he snarled.

"Good. It's nearly time to, as you said, take what I want. Jordans are famous for that, after all."

AFTER A FEW days, Stepper showed no signs of disrepair from the new NECS. Most of his SpaceOp nanites seemed unaffected, although small repairs were underway in some areas.

"It looks promising," the tech assured her. The woman had made some turn-around and seemed to support Diona's efforts now. Which worried Diona.

"What about all those warnings you were spouting off about AI?" she asked, leaning in.

The tech re-checked her data. "The repair programs can only work if they can talk to the old NECS. They appear to be doing so without causing any other problems." The woman looked up at her from her station. "That could change," she added bluntly.

"But they look fine."

The woman smiled. "Yes. They look fine." Was it fake? Meant only to indulge Diona?

Didn't matter. "Excellent, you can begin production. And I need a second dose prepared immediately. Just make sure of that fail-safe shut-off option. Build in an optional voice command to initiate."

CHAPTER TWENTY

Janlin grabbed for consciousness, thrashing and gasping. New enemy number one was in the pilot's seat bent over the ship's controls, his dark head close enough to the vent fans that he didn't hear her. She could feel the thrusters adjusting and the deep throb of the hydrogen core.

They were underway.

Janlin surged up, only to fall forward. Her feet were tied together. Her hands too. The fall was less than elegant.

Adrenaline roared, and panic tightened her chest. *Live free or die*, had been the motto once upon a time, and right now her traumatized brain could see no other alternative than to fight her way free, no matter the cost. She would not be this asshole's captive. She was not returning to Earth. And she was tired of people not caring about what she was trying to do!

With sheer determination, she regained her feet and shuffled her way towards her abductor. He wasn't that much taller than her, and certainly just as skinny if not more. She could win this.

As soon as he set his course and leaned back, she slipped closer and thrust her tied hands over his head.

He bucked and twisted, but she held on, feeling a bloodlust rise that made her sick. So much loss already. So much pain. How dare he add to it all? How dare he tie her like some farm animal awaiting slaughter, like some*thing* to control?

With a frightening chill, she wondered if he planned to eat her.

He found some unknown leverage and pushed her backwards to the wall, knocking the wind out of her. She held on. He was clawing her arms now, desperate, weakening, and the thought of victory made her roar.

Then another roar caught her attention. It was the sound of re-entry beginning.

Damn, they were further along than she realized.

"You jerk," she cried, tightening up even more as he began to go limp. "You stupid asshole, I don't want to go dirtside, I don't want to be your pilot, I don't want to be eaten, *I don't want to be tied up!*"

She held on longer than she should, worried that he would fake her out. She didn't want to kill him. She saw a glint in his pocket. Carefully she lifted her tied hands back over the guy's head, suddenly aware of the smell of him and the feel of his hair on her arms. His head fell and bounced on the floor as she pulled away a bit too quick.

"Sorry," she muttered. Pain spiked through her head, and she wondered if she might have an aneurysm like Yasu did. What if she'd killed the guy, and then she died, and they crashed? No one would ever be the wiser to what really happened.

Gordon would hate her forever.

She blinked away that morbid thought train and gently snagged the silver, sliding out a nice folding knife. With a snick, it opened to reveal a honed and polished blade sharpened to a fine edge. On the side of the handle was etched a tiny image of an axe. She propped it between her knees.

Three swipes and she was hands free. Feet came next, and then she crouched over her captor with two handfuls of rope and little desire to touch the guy.

Where was that taser he shot her with? The ship rocked, and the pressure was building. She cast about but couldn't see the telltale black and yellow. Would suit her fine if the cartridge was spent. She'd had enough nerve damage to last a few lifetimes.

Re-entry made every move ridiculous, between the roar and the heat and the g-forces, and her own body's complaints from all the neurological abuse, but he could regain consciousness any second. She needed to pilot the ship out of re-entry and into atmospheric flying, not be worried about him. With a grimace, she began tying his booted feet together.

As an afterthought, she looped the rope over a frame beam and tied that off too. She pocketed the knife with a twinge of guilt. It was hard to find steel like that in orbit. Seemed a fair trade for her trouble.

Now that she was in control again, Janlin's over-stimulated system settled down, and the fight or flight instincts quieted. Since they were already underway, she would dump this guy dirtside as asked and get back to orbit. It still irked her to be delayed from helping Lauren, especially forcibly, but she was calming down now and could have some small respect for the guts this guy had.

The idea of Lauren and her little boy shoved out an airlock onto the red plains of Mars haunted her. She felt a ton of responsibility for Tyrell's little sister. Now that he was gone, who else would watch out for them if she didn't? Hopefully she could still get there in time.

Her last memories of Tyrell and Teardrop filled her mind, unbidden, as they settled out into atmospheric flight. Bad timing. Her throat closed, her eyes welling up with tears she couldn't afford as she piloted the Seraph. Janlin swiped her arm over her eyes and sucked in deep breaths, willing herself to get it under control. She saw a clear spot in the storm clouds before her, and this asshole's private mission would only cause a brief delay. It would be okay.

A glance at the flight plan revealed coordinates that seemed awfully familiar. Of course. It was near her dad's cabin. She knew that would only make sense and felt dumb for not thinking of it sooner. The storms were too vicious and too frequent for any unprotected humans to be wandering far, so this guy and his crew must have a place close by her old childhood cabin.

Thoughts of her dad made grief well up again. Would it ever end? Would there ever be a day when couples like Gordon and Ursula would be safe and at peace, well-fed, healthy, and able to reproduce? As mad as she was at Gordon, she also understood where he was coming from. She couldn't really fault him for it either.

A small sound alerted her, and she ducked aside in time to see the stunner miss her and hit the console. Sparks flew. She kicked her knee up, driving his hand and wrist into the console and knocking the gun free.

He must have a drive stun, she thought. Any touch of that activated tase would work as well as the wired tines he shot her with earlier. Despite the gun cartridge being empty, the drive stun had the capacity to inflict multiple and prolonged shocks . . . *not* something she was willing to take.

Janlin shoved at the controls, and the Seraph responded with just the g-forces she needed. Dude, bent to reach for the gun, was sent flying sideways. She saw that his feet were still tied, but his hands were free. Clearly, she was no knot master.

Alarms screamed their warnings. Ignoring that for the moment, Janlin used the momentum of her piloting to launch herself on top of her assailant while he was down. A well-placed elbow just *there* . . .

He somehow twisted aside, and her blow hit a corner beam where it met the floor. Pain lanced up her arm, the not-so-hilarious funny bone exploding in agony.

"Argh," she cried out as he slugged her with a closed fist. "You. Ass. Hole." With each word, she punched him back. Her other hand got a good grip of his collar, offering leverage and a way to bang his head on the floor.

A different, more urgent claxon sounded. She used his face as leverage to push herself up, and gripped the pilot's chair. It could be fatal if they landed too far from shelter.

Of course, it could be fatal to crash, too, even in a hull as strong as this one.

As she flew, some background part of her exulting in the experience alone, she was aware of her hijacker pulling himself up with a groan. All she wanted was to dump him and his stolen bin of food near his coordinates and get gone before the storms made it impossible. But what she didn't want was to have to deal with this jerk once landed. Chances were he'd be happy to keep a working shuttle with a full power bank onboard, to say nothing of the NDB batteries, the rebreathers and filters, and so on. Then there was the risk of being added to the menu. She had to make sure he was down-and-out for the count.

Just one little tip, at the right moment, should throw him hard enough to knock him out. She braced for it, and kicked the Seraph nearly sideways.

He flew exactly as she envisioned.

His head struck the hull and he sunk to the floor, and she

refocused on getting them safely landed at the coordinates.

Except things weren't responding.

A fire warning appeared in the holo controls. She punched at the controls, taking over manually in a desperate attempt to still fly despite the damage already done. But the fire spread relentlessly, she could feel the heat now.

"No," she whispered.

They were going down, and they were going down *hard*.

She fought the elements with little control, redirecting systems wherever possible, as quickly as possible. But they were in a nosedive and she could not get the controls to respond.

"Have to get the nose up," she cried through gritted teeth. The ground rushed closer. They were not levelling out fast enough. "Come on, baby, come on." She risked letting go with one hand and slapped a few manual switches over, then pulled harder again.

There was no more time left.

CHAPTER TWENTY-ONE

Diona made her way through quiet passages and took convoluted routes in hopes no one would notice how often she visited this particular area. She slipped down the hall to the airlock, through the airlock's hidden door, and up the tunnel to the forest dome.

If she let the colonists in there, she mused, they would wreck it. Always was that way, too many people meant problems. And the new tech running it all, creating such a wonderful Earth look, was far too expensive to install in the first domes, where the colony lived now. So, her father built this as a retirement place, a hidden dome of the best and newest tech of the day, while Earth was still supplying it. He then planted two million trees, adding bushes, groundcovers, grasses, fungi, and all the rest. When he died, they buried him there instead of in the humanure compost pits that were only out-sized by the food scrap and gardening compost dome beside it.

It had been his plan to create a fear in the colonists of the Martian dust to prevent exploration. He always did want to keep an iron hold on his employees, and his ownership of the valley.

Diona took a deep breath and shook out her arms. Her parents were brilliant, but she never asked for all this weight of responsibility, and she found herself feeling a little angry at them for dying. Weren't the NECS supposed to conquer that, too?

She snorted at her own derision. The NECS made it possible

to survive out here, despite the junk germs everyone packed around all the time, despite the lower gravity, despite the solar radiation, despite all the usual health complications that plague the human race. But death was the ultimate levelling machine, and the NECS couldn't stop that.

She entered her tracking centre and, with practiced movements, brought up the holos and scanned the numbers. The total human population in space stood at 17,296.

One missing.

Feeling a little flushed, Diona tapped at the flashing icon, then let out an exasperated sigh. Janlin's profile stared back at her.

"Of course," Diona mocked. "Who else would it be?" Funny, though, she thought for sure that Janlin would outlast them all purely out of spite.

Had Janlin Jumped? Alone? And why? Didn't seem like a smart move after the problems Stepper described. The other question was, where had she Jumped *to*? Was she in orbit above Mars already? But a quick check of her live feed of Spectra's hangar bay showed *Hope* still berthed there.

It seemed Janlin was dead. This gave Diona pause. Would her NECS be worth retrieving? And was the alien with her? Had it died, too? There was no way to know, and it drove her mad.

She would do anything for Thea. The question came down to whether or not the upgrade would meet her needs. If it didn't, then tracking Janlin down would be her highest priority. If the upgrade worked, then chasing Janlin would be a grand waste of time.

She decided to put her faith in her upgrade.

CHAPTER TWENTY-TWO

JANLIN BECAME AWARE. Her fingers trailed over dirt and stones. Wind-blown sand scoured her skin. She was being dragged backwards by the collar of her jacket.

Dirt?

And what was that smell?

She peeled sticky eyelids open. Adrenaline coursed through her and she thrashed about. She was released abruptly and came down on her elbows, wanting to protest, but the sound died in her throat at the sight of the Seraph burning fifty-odd meters off. Dark smoke swirled up, borne on heat waves spilling off the already charred metal and whipped away by the wind. The Seraph lay pushed up against a fresh pile of dead, and now broken, trees, which were on fire.

Beyond the shuttle stood a line of mountains that she knew all too well. Janlin twisted around. Marching away, every line of his body marked with fury, was her captor. He had her pack on, the one that held her Huantag flight suit. It also had a first aid kit and rebreathers, but little else.

"Hey!" The ever-present wind snatched her call from her lips. If he heard, he didn't turn, or even hesitate. "Hey! Wait!"

She glanced back at the Seraph, feeling pretty guilty. The food and seeds he had stolen to bring here were probably toast. *Maybe he should have thought about asking instead of just taking.*

Worse, though, was the thought of having to call Gordon for

help. Gusts tore at her hair and clothing, and she squinted against the grit flying through the air. The combination of the burning shuttle and the ominously dark storm front bearing down on her position made her anxiety soar. She couldn't ask anyone to come down here. Not with so few shuttles left. She would tell Gordon to wait, and she'd survive somehow.

"Better get it over with, then." She tapped her earcell, fully expecting the chime that initiated a call . . . but her finger slipped on wetness, and the chime never sounded.

Her hand came away bloody. "Well, that explains the sticky eyes, then," she muttered. It shouldn't affect her earcell, though. That was bio-nano gear just like the NECS but simpler, made to perform one simple task: communicate. The fact it was not working at all was really bad.

A glance at her abductor revealed he had already put significant distance between them. She scrambled to her feet, and groaned as she anticipated pain lancing through her head.

It didn't come.

Well, that's an unexpected relief.

The guy kept going, eating up the miles. She watched as he dipped out of sight over a ridge.

What now?

At a loss as to where else to go, she followed cautiously. She would need some kind of help, tools, or a comm unit to talk to Spectra. Down here, he was the only people she knew. How terrifying was that? But the fact remained he had an obvious destination.

Clouds scuttled by overhead, moving astoundingly fast and roiling with ugly grey blue and green. Hail pelted her, quit for a few paces, and started again with a vengeance. Little whirlwinds of dirt and dead leaves swept up into her face, and she staggered along wondering if she had already lost the guy she was following. Gravity pulled harder down here than she was used to, and every step was an effort.

She could very well die down here.

A huge crack was followed by repeated flashes of lightning, and thunder rolled with incredible volume, going on for an extended time. She heard another kind of crack splitting the air, a sound she hadn't heard in decades.

A tree breaking.

The sound of a tree being struck and cracking, falling in the forest, it's something you never forget, and it happened once when they were out at the cabin for a family trip. If a tree falls in the forest, it does make a sound, a huge one.

There also seemed to be a rumble in the ground, unless the ongoing thunder was so loud it vibrated the very earth. It wasn't an earthquake-kind of shifting, it was more like . . .

Then a shout cut through all the noise, and a cry of pain.

She ran.

Over the ridge, she found the land had slid, taking dead tree trunks and tons of rock and releasing it down into the little valley basin. Way down at the bottom of the slide she could see the form of a man half buried under a large tree trunk wedged in place by boulders.

He was a lot farther away than she first thought, and it took her a while to scramble down. As she neared, after climbing over yet another downed tree trunk, she saw that he was unconscious, and breathed a sigh of relief. She glanced back at the slope she just descended, the burnt and dead logs all a jumble sticking out of the rock rubble. The trees were decayed, the remaining straggling bushes and grasses too few and weak to hold the slope in place.

Rain began pelting down, and the winds that accompanied it combined with the immense wet made it difficult to breathe. Gasping, opening her mouth wide to try and catch some oxygen, she glanced at where the man lay. The pack he lay on had rebreathers. All this toxic Earth air was probably doing immeasurable damage to her lungs. She had to get to him.

She looked up at the slope once again. The ground sagged across the lip. The weight of the rain made it a hazard waiting to happen. They needed to get out from under it.

"They?" she considered aloud, still fighting for every breath. She continued to make her way through the scree towards him, despite the question. What else was she to do?

She stopped and took a long look as she sucked air for a moment. His chest rose and fell. Was he broken, pinned, or just knocked out? She climbed down through the ankle-twisting debris of the landslide. Rain made everything slick. She slipped again, bashing her shin and scraping her palms. She cursed the rain even as it cooled her aching skin.

Inconceivably, the rain intensified. God, if *she* couldn't breathe, he would drown laying face-up in it. She managed the last few feet and leaned over to shelter him from the worst of it. He coughed and groaned, and his eyes fluttered but did not open.

"I'm worried the slope is going to let go more," she said near his ear, thunder cracking and rolling on and on as the rain slashed them. "Are you injured, or just pinned?"

He didn't respond. She tried digging at the loose shale to free him while a vicious torrent fell like a river flowing out of the sky. Rivulets began to flow. She managed to free him enough to roll him, and took out two rebreathers, slapping one over her mouth and nose before strapping his on.

The storm was so bad, she knew they could both die on this rocky slope. She dug and dug, shifting boulders and tossing rocks, her hands bleeding, rebreather clogging, and she could see the man's lips turning blue. By then she was sobbing, sure they would die, but she still cleared his rebreather and tried again to free him.

Then the slope gave way under them, and they were sliding. Janlin cried out, grasping at the man to try and keep them together. They slid towards the largest boulder on the slope, a massive thing the size of a small shuttle. If they were pinned against that, there would be no hope.

But the shift worked in their favour, clearing a small place of shelter from the deluge under the massive boulder. It was enough at least to pull him free and under, out of the worst of the downpour.

His lips were very blue. He wasn't breathing. "Dammit, dammit, dammit," she muttered, tears and rain from her hair still pouring down her face. She removed her rebreather and looked down at the dude. "Okay, mystery abductor, sure hope you brushed your teeth."

Five mouth-to-mouth blows and he vomited water, then promptly passed out again. At least his colour returned, and his breathing steadied out. She refixed his rebreather, and her own, and slumped back.

Trapped in a tiny hole under a giant rock, Janlin sat for what seemed like hours, battered, soaked, pinned down in place by a sheet of water pouring over the edge of the boulder while the storm raged on, beside her unconscious abductor.

EVENTUALLY, HE MOANED and blinked up at her, then wriggled . . . and winced. He touched the rebreather, then glanced at her again.

She watched, tense as anything and afraid to even breathe.

He studied the small piece of sky they could see through the sheeting rain, then started to climb.

What were her choices? Stay here and die, or follow him, that was all she had, so she climbed after him.

He climbed over boulders, but awkwardly, obviously hurting. Janlin pushed at a baby boulder, and the small stuff ran out from under and it rolled, nearly taking her down with it. She backpedalled, grabbing at air that became a solid hand. He pulled her up on the big boulder as more debris shifted and slid away further downslope. Even the massive thing they stood on threatened to slide, and they scrambled away to one side to get out of the path of it all.

Once they made it to the solid valley floor they could walk more normally. Still the storm raged, and the guy looked as angry as the weather. He ripped off the rebreather to yell at her. "Why did you save me?" he shouted, gasping and limping and appearing more mad than grateful.

"I don't know," she screamed over the wind, "maybe because you're the only human I know down here and I thought you were my best bet, even if you're going to eat me."

"I'm not going to eat you, swear to God!"

They stared hard at each other, saving their breath. Rain slicked over them, pouring off her nose and creating little rivulets under her shirt. She didn't know if she should stick with him or turn back. With this rain, was the Seraph still burning? Could she salvage stuff from it? Could she shelter within? Her mind twisted around, and nothing made sense.

She turned away from his intense stare to see a new viewpoint way down the valley: submerged Calgary skyscrapers. The West Alliance had dammed the Bow and many other smaller rivers downstream to sell water in an effort to hold some power in the years of WWIV. But trying to control and store the water brought on water-borne diseases that, in combination with the endless storms savaging the landscape, killed billions. Then, as so many humans and animals died, the sheer magnitude of corpses of all kinds mixed with the debris of modern civilization to make it all exponentially worse. Temperatures climbed, and the dammed rivers rose to flood the by-then empty city.

The rain lightened up, and the roar of wind tempered. She turned back to see him rifling through her flight gear bag before tossing it aside with a comment about "useless junk" and marching off, clearly still angry, but also with a decided limp.

Janlin grabbed her pack and swung it over her shoulders. While Earth may not be a good place to fly, the suit was too valuable to be left behind.

"Wait!" she called. He slowed but didn't look back. "Shouldn't we look to see what's salvageable back there? Or at least put any internal fires out?"

"Can't," he said, still marching on as she scrambled to keep up. "After the rain stops, the wind lifts the dead soil and it becomes a sandblasting machine that will shred your skin."

"Great," she muttered. "You should put the rebreather back on."

He did pause at that. The extra gravity was pulling at her, and she struggled up to where he stood. He looked at the rebreather with a strange expression.

"Thanks."

"So, you won't eat me, then?" she said.

"Promise," he said again, serious still, but the anger seemed to ebb. They scrambled on.

The sky brightened somewhat, but one glance to the west showed much more violence to come. He led her up another gulley, following the natural way of the land. They pushed through a thicket of dogwood and willows and jumped a creek. She was thirsty, but it stunk, and the water was rust brown.

"What do we drink?"

He closed his eyes a moment. "Nothing. Not here."

"But . . ."

His eyes popped open. "But nothing! *You* crashed the shuttle, leaving us miles from help. *You* made sure to do such a good job of it, it burned, probably ruining all the stores of food, seeds, gear, and oh yeah, water. *You* will have to wait until we get where we can purify some."

She thought of the flames, how they were spewing right from the food locker area. "*You* kidnapped and tased me, and hijacked a SpaceOp shuttle," she countered. He growled and waved off her argument, but she wasn't ready to let it go. "We haven't had it all easy as pie up there, you know."

"No, you haven't had it easy *lately*," he sneered. "It only gets harder and harder down here, and it was *never* easy." There was a great deal of disdain in his voice.

Smarting a little, she cupped her hand as they marched on, hoping to get a bit of rain.

"Rain isn't a great idea either, without filtering," he called back, "given all the airborne toxins."

She let the dribble fall with a sigh. The wind gusted harder, pushing her into a stagger. Judging by the sky, there would be even worse weather again within the hour. She wanted to ask how many miles away help was, but the weight of her guilt and her dry mouth kept her quiet.

They turned onto an old road, the paving cracked and buckled with tree roots, and filled with a forest of weeds. The sky brightened up a bit more and the rain quit. A quick glance showed the next wave of rain marching across the landscape towards them like a wall of water, currently engulfing an overgrown farm.

Her head echoed with a strange emptiness. For all the struggle through the weather, the previously-constant pain remained quiet . . . and her suspicions grew loud. It was as if some background noise had abruptly ended, and the silence left her reeling.

She caught up to him and grabbed his arm, pulling him around. "What have you done to me?" she demanded, pointing at her head.

He scowled. "I wiped 'em," he said as if her question was a pretty dumb one. "Gotta know those things are tracked, yeah?" He marched on. "Don't need that noise." Bitterness gave his words ice.

"Just like that? Some flip of a switch?" she cried, incredulous. "How?" *How was it even possible, and if it was, why hadn't she known? Why hadn't they all known, all along?* Just another thing the Jordans did to them without full disclosure. Rage twisted her stomach into a knot.

"Just machines after all," he said, looking thoughtful. "You have to remember *we* control *them,* not the other way 'round, yeah?"

Full impact of this struck her, and she stopped short, rocking on her feet. "I could Jump safely!" she cried.

He turned back and faced her full on. In the calm lull, his words carried clear and struck her like a slap.

"No, those things made it possible. And now, you'll never survive space long-term anymore, let alone a Jump . . . not without a new injection of NECS. They aren't just off, they need repaired or replaced. If you were to Jump, you would die."

CHAPTER TWENTY-THREE

"HOW . . ." SHE DEMANDED, but the lull was over and the storm bearing down on their location. Trees long dead from forest fires stabbed the sky with their blackened trunks, and the winds whipped up branches and twigs in a barrage of debris. The guy took off, and Janlin wondered where he would take them even as she made haste to follow.

Several times she lost track of him, stumbling along blindly. She held her hands up, palms out, to protect her face and the valuable rebreather, but it only made it harder to see. Her mind funnelled down to nothing but placing one foot after the next in the direction she occasionally saw his dark shape ahead. They climbed, and the trees became sparse, the rocks under her feet sliding, and she had lost track of any sense of direction, any sense of where he'd gone . . .

"Here," he called. She couldn't see properly, especially through her right eye, but he reached back and grabbed her hand, pulling her along through jagged rocks. She staggered, skinning her other shin, but he held tight, inching forward.

Then he dropped to his knees, let go, and crawled into a small crevice, quickly disappearing from sight.

Janlin's heart, already pounding as she struggled the last few steps, clenched at the idea of crawling in after him.

The wind shrieked, shoving her down, and hail started to pelt her, quickly becoming a beating. She couldn't get enough air, the winds sucked it away from her despite the rebreather, and the icy wetness on her skin burned like bleach.

"Come." His calm, deep voice cut through everything to reach her.

She peered into the cave to see his hard face within, blue eyes huge as they peered up at her. The rain kept running into her right eye despite her wiping it, and she looked down in a daze to see her hands were red, slick with rainwater and blood, but for some reason burning . . .

"Come out of the rain," he said again, firmer, but not yelling at her. It sunk in, she unfroze, and squeezed into the opening.

"That's it, you're okay." He had a cloth that he gave her, guiding her hands to her forehead. "Bit of a gash there, leaking again, but head wounds will do that." He let go.

She took a step and wobbled. "Sitting down now," she announced, and he broke her fall to settle her on something soft. His sweater. "It'll get bloody," she protested weakly.

"Not the first time," he assured her. His voice was still clipped with anger despite his helpfulness.

She was able to clear her vision as he moved around the small natural cave. It had a musty smell to it that suggested it might've once been an animal's den, when wildlife still roamed these hills.

He rolled away a couple of strategically placed boulders and revealed a store of clothing, bedding, first aid gear, and very empty food containers. He held up a stitching kit.

"If it doesn't stop," he said, gesturing at her head. She dabbed the wound with a fresh corner of the rag he'd given her and it came away disturbingly red.

"Might be a plan," she admitted. And if he was focused enough, distracted enough, maybe she could use the knife of his that still rode in her pocket. He continued to inventory the cache. "Ah," he said with satisfaction. He held up a box. "Butterfly bandages. Much kinder than stitches."

Then, "Thank all the gods," as he rolled out a five-gallon water jug. Then, "Even better!"

He held up two packages of vacuum-sealed dried food. "This cache is so far out, we haven't visited in a long while. Luckily no one else found it in the meantime. However, I'm going to need my knife back if you want these open," he said with a smirk.

She debated her options as she held her head in hopes of

staunching the bleeding. Which was unlikely with a head wound. Which meant she needed him to dress it for her with those butterflies. And they were clearly stuck here for a bit anyway, did she really think the knife would do her any good?

"Please tell me you have it."

Janlin couldn't decide, her brain had frozen up on her again.

"I won't eat you," he declared, rolling his eyes. "Look, let me get that taken care of so you have two hands." He put down the food and grabbed the bandages. He turned away, rummaging again, and came up with some disinfectant. "I'll pour a basin of water to wash up in."

She let down the cloth and he wet another to clean the gash. Janlin noticed he had little scars on his face around the eyes and down one cheek. Had it been wind-driven debris?

Once the bandages were in place and covered, and they were all cleaned up, she took out the pocket knife and held it out.

"Nice piece of steel."

He nodded and took it. "Hungry?"

"Always."

He nodded again and set about heating water on a small camp stove that was retrofitted to burn biofuel. Janlin poked through the supplies and found bowls and utensils.

They ate in silence, and he cleaned the bowls in the last of the wash water. She noticed he was careful to use the water sparingly, and many times over. He set the dishwater aside as if there were still more uses for the now-grey water.

She noticed he still limped.

"You all right?" she asked, indicating the hurting leg.

He shrugged it off. "Just a bruise." With a hesitant touch to his ear, he said, "It's doing better than the head."

She remembered him flying through the air thanks to her manoeuvres. "Sorry."

He shrugged and gestured at a small tunnel that led further back under the mountain. "That's the toilet. This is gonna be a bad blow, you can smell it. Might as well get comfy."

He then turned and lay down facing the wall, putting his back to her. "Turn the lantern off when you are ready to sleep, please."

She stared at his back, somewhat dazed and not thinking much at all for a long while. The storm raged on, nearly matching her fury. The tenseness of his whole body indicated he wasn't sleeping.

The light outside dimmed by degrees, so she clicked the lantern off. Eventually his breathing settled, and her mind thawed and went off chasing memories.

In the 2090s, a company named Negative Emissions Tech made a huge breakthrough in the field. It offered the promise to fix what past generations had broken, to harvest the emissions out of the air so the planet could heal. But emissions weren't the sole problem anymore. There was so much fallout from those times, that now the Earth still suffered acidified oceans, toxic watersheds, and dead soils. Wave after wave of pandemics, droughts, and storms had already destroyed extensive populations, human and animal, causing new issues of waste that could not decompose fast enough. There had even been marches for SpaceOp to open cemeteries on the moon, which had been denied due to, as the familiar phrase went, the "safety of those already in place". It should be SpaceOp's damned slogan.

When several wars over plague protocols, waste disposal, water rights, and food grew and merged into World War IV, civilized behaviour crumbled away forever down here. Humanity had never properly recovered from WWIII, also known as the Human Rights War, only two dozen years before.

She had joined her father on Spectra Orbital Station when she was fourteen, old enough to understand just how awful things really were on Earth, and young enough to believe her dad could rescue her from it all. Still reeling from her mother's horrible death, it seemed the new beginning they both needed.

Not long after she got settled, five shuttles were lost as people desperately made last-ditch efforts to save their loved ones still dirtside. SpaceOp declared Earth a no-fly zone, citing the Shunter crashes. After that it was forbidden to perform scouting runs for survivors or supplies of any kind, and it became more difficult to get flight clearance at all. Her and Gordon's positions as pilots were created to give them jobs as they matured, and to ensure limited access to the shuttles.

The official word from SpaceOp headquarters on Mars said Earth no longer had anything to offer, and SpaceOp facilities would survive fine. Speculation back then was that the storms needed time to blow out, and then the planet would recover. A few decades at most. But Janlin overheard her dad talking in hushed tones. A new disease ripped through the last pockets of people that was carried in the worst possible way . . . water.

"I mean, the place was already a mess, so there's little we can do to help," he said, "a water-borne disease up here would end life in space very quickly."

There was a silence while he listened, then he replied, "Which is why Jordan is right to cut off contact immediately."

She remembered learning about it later, when the stories got out . . . back when they still picked up comms and broadcasts from dirtside. She remembered the horror of watching it all going down on people's recordings and live streams. And she remembered everyone being scared of any water brought to space . . . including urine, spit, and sweat.

Special-op teams were created for rescue missions. The refugees were given their own orbital station. Visits to any other SpaceOp facility meant a full mandatory quarantine, and the deep clean of yourself and all your belongings was intense—heat, air, dry dry dry until it was a fire hazard. But that was the only way to stop the spread. At that point, they were already mining water on Luna's poles and from asteroids, so Earth water was banned completely.

Shortly after her first year in orbit, Earth was put under a full quarantine. Some vlogs were still streaming from dirtside, and she watched with fascinated horror, a teenager wrapped in grief over her mother's loss and still adjusting to her new life in space. Graphic footage of bodies piled in the streets, of people in the final throes of the sickness, their eyes weeping blood, their veins all standing out under the skin. Some people tried to help, she saw that. Then she followed those same helpers as they too sickened and died, looking at the camera lens to the very end.

She was so helpless to do anything for these people, and every time she thought about bringing it up with her dad, she remembered his words.

Jordan is right to close off contact.

Helpless, overwhelmed, and distraught, she simply stopped watching. Life on Spectra was busy with her school studies, new friends, and a promising future. There seemed nothing she could do to help those below, so she did like everyone did and ignored it. Whoever and whatever survived, well, it was out of her hands.

Thinking about it now, it gave her some perspective on how

the Mars Colonists felt about them and their crop-killing spore.

Within the year or so, all they got from below was radio silence, when they bothered to check. The assumption was that the storms made it difficult to communicate. Meanwhile, life carried on in the Orbitals, Luna Base, and the burgeoning Mars Colony. Children were born on Mars, parks thrived and matured, crops turned over and biomass was recycled wisely in a closed system that seemed to be working.

As a self-absorbed teenager, Earth simply became the view out the window. She graduated, got her pilot's training, earned her stripes, and never thought twice about the survivors down here.

No wonder he hated her and everything she stood for.

THE STORM RAGED on, which did little for her temper. She sipped at the water, thirsty as fuck, but also terrified. Was this water still infected? Was she going to die a horrible death, like some karma for her privilege?

Then there were bigger issues, if she survived this place. Could she ever safely return to orbit? Were Lauren and her boy already dead, driven out an airlock on Mars? How was Anaya doing? The vision of her being wrapped and sucked into the wall made her cringe, and she drove the thought down.

Darkness came on, and she let herself slide down and rest her cheek on the hard stone. She could no longer make out the shape of her abductor in the gloom.

Gordon would think she ran off to Mars. To be fair, that had been the plan, but if he pinged her and she didn't reply, he would assume she was ignoring him, or worse, she'd blocked him. Cassie and all the rest, they might think the same. They would never consider her actual current situation as an option—her reality was too outlandish a story to be believed.

There was no help coming. No help to be called upon, really. Janlin was on her own. Lauren was on her own. Anaya . . . well, Cassie, Li, and Linder would watch over her.

These thoughts and worse tortured her as she lay on the cold earth and tried to make sense of the ridiculous turn of events. Sheer fatigue took over at some point, and she faded into sleep.

SHE WOKE FULLY dressed and completely uneaten. Small noises beneath the muffled roar of the storm made her sit up. Buddy stood by one of the storage crates nurturing the tiny flame lit under a dented metal pot. With no shirt on.

Well, that's not hard on the eyes at all.

He'd lit the lantern, and now clicked a few more on and set them around the cave. He had a lean and lanky look that only accented the wiry muscles rolling under the skin, and dark black hair on his chest to match his head and chin. She pulled her blanketed knees up under her chin and watched him. He either didn't know she was awake or was trying to give her some morning privacy.

He moved with a certain grace.

"You've trained in martial arts."

He glanced over, blue eyes reflecting the light he held. He gave a nod and placed the light on a rocky outcrop. "As a kid."

The water boiled, and he added it to a basin of cold. "There, have first wash up." He stalked off to the "back room" to do his morning business.

Janlin scrambled up and washed best she could without undressing. Did she have two minutes? Five? Thirty seconds? Plus, the water made her need to pee. She wanted to be ready the moment he returned, even if it meant having to pee in his stink! She peered up at the dim patch of daylight being slashed constantly with rain-hail mix and flying debris. No spot to pee there.

He returned cautiously, calling out.

"I'm good, need my turn back there, please."

He hurried out, his head ducked low, face an interesting shade of red. "Sorry," he growled.

She didn't have time to think, or she'd need another wash and fresh pants. But as she squatted in the tiny dirt space and sighed with relief, she wondered at it. Was he that angry, or just embarrassed? She didn't know whether to be terrified or try and make friends, and her decision-making abilities seemed offline.

She returned to the main cave. He had put a shirt on, and was heating a second kettle full. His head hung low where he sat, hair falling forward to hide his face. He sat so still, and yet so full of tension. She cleared her throat, and he looked up. Instead of the expected scowl, he wore an empty, hollowed-out look.

"I'm sorry I wrecked the ship and supplies," she said. More sorry if she couldn't go home, but that was beside the point right now. "Why didn't you turn people's NECS off when we were all hurting after the Jump?"

"And give myself away?" He shook his head. "You know how strict the quarantines are . . . or were. I think you guys kinda forgot we exist, yeah? Plus, I meant what I said. The NECS truly are keeping y'all alive up there."

She snorted. "Well, that thought's terrifying."

"Yes, it is, especially because the bio-fouling that Steve discovered continues in you despite the fact I've shut them down."

"No clue how to remove them?"

He hung his head low again. "No. I do have some ideas on how to change them, heal them, using vibration . . . but it's just ideas, no substance yet."

"Vibration?" That sounded too simple.

"Resonant frequency science," he replied, but did not elaborate.

The wind blew, howling out the pain of living. The kettle boiled. He dug around in the storage crates and brought out two clay mugs. "I found a few old tea bags," he said, waving one before dropping it in one of the mugs. He poured the water and handed her hot, black, steaming liquid.

"Heaven."

"Better than nothing," he grudgingly admitted. "Bit of a miracle, too. I haven't seen a tea bag in years."

"I haven't either," she mused. "We drink that vitatea made from one of the few plants that survived the spore, but it's all looseleaf."

He wrinkled his nose. "That stuff is a bit nasty."

She could only agree.

The silence stretched out as they sipped. The storm roared on, becoming a background white noise like the pounding surf on a shoreline.

At one point, the smell of wildfire drifted in. "Hopefully we don't survive the sandblaster only to get smoked out," he said.

She raised her eyebrows.

He shrugged. "I'm not too worried, we haven't had a burn through this part in, I don't know, five, six years. Besides," he said with another shrug, "you can almost always smell smoke. There's never been a time when something wasn't burning nearby for as long as I can remember. We're also above the treeline a bit. That said, it is always a possibility smoke could overwhelm this cave and we wouldn't have a chance."

Lovely.

CHAPTER TWENTY-FOUR

"How did you turn the NECS off?"

He regarded her as if measuring how much to say. "That vibrational science I was talking about."

She waited, but it was pretty obvious he wasn't going to continue. "Which tells me nothing," she countered.

His mouth thinned. "You sure?"

She was so confused. "Sure of what?" she asked, keeping the snarl out of it only with effort.

He turned half away, hiding his face. "Of knowing more than you might want to."

What was with this guy?

She sighed and crossed her arms. "Look, ignorance is truly bliss, I've learned that the hard way, but information is also power. We need help with these damned things. I guess I'll take the risk."

He obliged, his head still down as he sorted through the bins. "My older brother was on the team that designed the original NECS."

She was stunned to silence. Her mom led that research, it was her baby. It was what took her away from her husband and daughter so much. And what had put her in harm's way when anger rose, fuelled by fear of artificial intelligence, and she died in one of the attacks on the nanite labs.

He went on, describing resonant frequencies and how

everything had a natural frequency at which they vibrate, and that anti-resonance is caused by destructive interference, "and that might explain the dissonance you're experiencing."

"Did you know her?" she asked softly.

He stopped what he was doing, but didn't look at her. "No, I was a kid, and my brother was a sub-contract of a contract to the official SpaceOp team she ran. My brother tried to reach her. He wanted to explain that the NECS shouldn't go in *people*, but his reports and calls were always ignored. How is she?"

"Dead. She never left Earth. She thought her NECS could help humans survive the conditions here as much as it helped those in space. But she was killed for it by fanatics that were against nanite technology."

He stared at her now. "Damn, I'm sorry. NECVengers?"

She could only nod. The memory felt too fresh here, despite all the years that had slipped away.

"They had a point, though."

She glared at him. "Tell me about this, 'not in people' idea? Was your brother a NECVenger?" She could feel her gut clenching with anger. Again, this guy looked like a bad guy.

He sighed. "No, he was such a pacifist he wrote letters to them urging peace."

Janlin sat with that for a moment. "My mom probably would've liked him, then."

He gave her a sad smile. "He taught me that human cells vibrate between three and seventeen hertz. I suspect the NECS are off, vibrating in such a way that it is causing infrasound, and directly affecting your nervous system, causing disorientation, anxiety, panic, nausea, dizziness . . . sound familiar?"

"All too much."

"Folding space must have made it worse, and that disruption in your body could eventually cause organ rupture or brain aneurism from prolonged exposure."

"That, too, sounds all too familiar . . . and terrifying."

He went on about certain frequencies that could possibly calm the dissonance, but she wasn't really listening. Her mind finally figured it out. "EMP?"

He looked impressed, but she knew EMP devices of any kind were forbidden on any SpaceOp platform on the basis that too many life support operations ran on tech that would be compromised, to say nothing of the NECS themselves. A device like that wasn't going to help out there.

"Tell me about your life here before, when you were a kid." She remembered the cabin, the summer holidays with cousins, good times of swimming and campfires, but she also remembered her dad being gone a lot to the orbitals, and her mom being distracted by her work even when she was home. It had been a lonely existence, despite having money. Her friends changed so often there was never time to connect.

For her, moving to orbit had been the best change of her life, with more stability and friends like Gordon. She had stayed in one bed the longest, and had a routine and a job.

Buddy didn't reply for a long time, and she began to wonder if he would. It was going to be a long wait if they couldn't tell stories.

"We were poor," he said, and she breathed a silent sigh of relief. "We worked hard to live simple, close to nature, like so few could by that point. It was incredibly hard with the wild weather patterns. One season would bring drought, the next floods, the next, disease. Most of the population had gone to dome life if they could afford it, or up to you. When WWIV brought Water Covid, people flocked back out of the domes, desperate for somewhere to go to ground. We tried to help people, then it got bad, we got overrun, and we had to protect our own." He shuddered. "We never had the option to run away off planet like you did."

It stung, probably because it was true. "I was fourteen. Would you have done any different than I did when my dad called me to join him?"

There was the scowl she'd come to know. "No." Begrudgingly. And she could see him counting, figuring out her age. "But why didn't you try to get more people off planet?"

"You've been up there," she said, guessing him in his mid-thirties, a handful of years older than her at most. "We want nothing more than to return here, and we've had our own issues. Also, I'm not to blame for my parents' actions," she pointed out, "even if I benefited from them."

She'd pissed him off again, but hell, she was pissed too.

"You could've cared at least a little about the rest of us," he said.

"There were five waves of Covid viruses in less than two years after my dad brought me up. I'd already barely survived a go with a variant. Between the basic pandemic rules of quarantine and the massive storms fuelling fires and coating the skies in ash, Earth became a no-fly zone. We lost five Shunters before that became ironclad rule, and the last rescue attempt brought Water Covid to an Orbital and eighty-three percent of those aboard died."

It still wasn't good enough for him. "And since? Did you even think about those down here after you returned last time?"

She gave him a pained look. "Do nightmares count?"

His lips thinned, and he looked down. All the fire seemed to go out of him, and the hollow, defeated look returned. "Fair enough."

She looked down at the cup. "Is Water Covid still here?" she asked, her throat tight.

He shrugged. "We're pretty sure it died off a long time ago . . . not enough hosts. If not, that rainstorm you flew out of the first time we met would've been loaded with it. You would've taken it to the Orbitals, the Jumpship Station, even the alien planet you visited."

Her mind reeled with the implications. "Perhaps I did, but wouldn't the NECS handle it?"

He shrugged again. "That was my brother's work, and he died from Covid over ten years ago." Now he just looked tired and beaten.

"I'm sorry." She chose an outcropping of rock and sat down with her tea. "If we can communicate with Spectra, maybe we can get a shipment dropped. There might be a drone or two left that could handle the run, so no one needs to risk the flight. And, seriously, we should let them know about this infrasound problem."

He lifted an eyebrow. "Nice thought, except your friend Gordon wouldn't hear of helping us . . . am I right?"

Janlin closed her eyes with a wince. He was right.

"I don't even know your name," she said.

"Ceirin MacNair," he said with a flourish, and then with a really bad Irish accent, added, "at your service."

"Kee-earn," she tried. He laughed. It did something funny to her insides. *None of that,* she told herself. *Last thing you need.*

"Yes, like that only quicker, run it together." He spelled it out for her, using a "c" with a hard "k" sound to it.

"Key-ern." She thought of Anaya trying to pronounce this one and felt a sudden deep fear that Anaya was dead, and Janlin would never be able to take her home. She gasped, the shock of the thought sucking all the air out of her.

"What is it?" Ceirin asked, a line of worry appearing between his eyes.

She waved him off, taking deep breaths to regain her composure. "Nothing. Well, Anaya. I still don't know if she's dead in that medbay, or in need of some kind of action. It was one thing holding me back from leaving, although I did have hope that new nanite supplies or an upgrade of some kind from Mars would help Linder or Steve find a solution . . . if she's still alive."

"Don't beat yourself up," Ceirin said. "You did everything you could. And I'm sure you warned her how the Jump affected you."

"We did." Janlin gave him a sad smile. "Thanks."

He got a funny look. "Have you had any upgrades?"

Janlin was puzzled. "Of course not. There are strict rules against adding any nanite anything to your system. Getting clearance for medical procedures is a pain, and those nubots are programmed to do just one thing and then exit the system. But in order to work with them, they need to network with a datapad or something, and everyone was terrified of that . . ."

"Because that could lead to AI," he finished.

"Is that how it is," she asked, "or have we been lied to all this time about that, too?"

"Yes, and yes," he said with a "what can you do" attitude. "We do always have to adhere to safety precautions so we don't start something we can't stop, but you've also been lied to. The NECS were designed with upgrade slots that should be administered around the ten-year mark."

Janlin felt her blood pressure rise. "How much you wanna bet Mars has had said upgrade?" And did Stepper know these things, being a Jordan? Likely. *He* probably had it. He did recover well from the Jump and was one of the very last to fall sick on Huantag.

"The other thing that amazes me is they don't teach you guys how to scan and monitor your own NECS."

That pulled Janlin right out of worrying about Stepper. "Scan and monitor my own NECS? Space me, you can't be serious."

"Of course, I'm serious. They're in your body, shouldn't you have access to those systems?"

Janlin just stared. Her brain had overloaded, it was just all too much.

"Look," he said, going to the storage and returning with an old datapad from the first aid kit. Soon he had a basic med scanner app running and, with her nod okay, ran the laser over her from head to toe. A few more taps and he had a holo of her diagnostics floating before them. He indicated a side drop-down menu, and selected "Nanite Settings" to reveal a completely different scan of her.

She actually gasped. There were tiny pinpricks of light marking each nanite as it travelled or nested throughout her body. Some of them were faint, some strong, and all variations between, like viewing the stars. "How do they still light up like this, when you disabled them?"

"This is residual energy; it should fade in time. But this shows you the ones that are failing," Ceirin said, pointing at the clusters of dimmer lights. "Our designs were intentionally limited to ensure there was no way the NECS could ever go AI. But I think it was a bit overkill. I think it was an easy excuse to keep people from mucking around with their own nanites. You could do a lot more and still keep them from linking up. I mean, formation of an AI would require a strong central power source—where is some magical AI entity going to find that?"

"Good grief, this is insane, and while it makes sense in some ways, it also pisses me off. SpaceOp was hiding things, withholding knowledge in the quest for power and control."

"Yeah, and then that knowledge gets lost." Ceirin shook his head. "I didn't know if I should speak up while I was on Spectra, but any way I saw to do it would only out me as an illegal."

"There were pretty strict rules about that back in the day, so you were probably right to not let on," Janlin agreed, thinking again of how Lauren was being treated.

AT ONE POINT in the conversation, somewhere after deep talks on immigration and around daydreams of old Earth pizza joints, Ceirin stopped mid-word and looked to the cave opening, lifting his nose. She, too, could hear the drop in volume, and yes, there was a different smell to it.

"A pocket," he said, climbing to his feet. He groaned when he leaned on his hurt foot. "I could use to stretch a leg, you coming?"

She scrambled up, eager to step away from the small musty confines. They emerged into open air and checked the situation. A storm building quickly in the northwest roiled towards them in a fascinating and terrifying display of force.

"We'd never make it anywhere in time," he said, gauging the approach. "But there is a nice view up here." He waved her on upslope, and they climbed to the ridgeline. "Watch," Ceirin said, tipping his chin at the coming storm.

Across the arid plain she saw the clouds churn and build, then slide over mountain tops until they were obliterated from sight. The mass then surged across the barren flats to push grey lifeless soil up into billowing clouds of driving sand. It grew as it moved steadily towards them, the roar of it reaching them over the constant howl of the wind. It looked much like the dust storms of Mars, really, just not so red.

He moved closer and shouted over the wind noise. "See that ridge there, and the folds of foothills behind?"

She nodded.

He dropped his finger down and to the right. "See that dark cleft between?"

"Okay."

"Watch how the storm moves over that area."

It raged closer, sure to envelope those little hills as easily as the rest. Yet, as it hit the rise before it, the clouds split and opened, leaving the cleft safe from the worst devastation.

Ceirin watched with satisfaction. "My great-grandfather chose that spot a hundred and fifty years ago just for the way the worst of any storm was always pushed aside."

That little valley might be safe, but they wouldn't be in a moment.

"Back to shelter," he said with a shrug. "Woulda been much easier if you hadn't . . ."

"I know!" She sulked about it for a minute, then decided she had little to lose. "Woulda been much easier if you hadn't've tased me."

"You didn't look ready to listen," he shot back. "And I was terrified of losing a chance to get back."

"Why? If it's so god-awful down here that you hate me for

living up there, why the quest to return at all costs, and with supplies?" Janlin realized the answer meant more to her than she liked to admit.

His lips thinned out, and the anger drained away. "I have family down here," he admitted.

Janlin took it as gracefully as she could. Of course, he did. *Wife and kids and everything, I bet.*

"My grandmother. And my daughter, Harriot," he said, and Janlin stood amazed at how he transformed as he thought of her. "She's so little, I hope she remembers who I am."

THE STORM DROVE them back to the cave, and sheer lack of anything else to do led to more conversation. Janlin found she couldn't deny her interest. He had great stories of their survival down here, although many were heartbreaking, and she told him about their adventures in another galaxy.

They talked dreams and what ifs, if there were no obstacles like reality had dealt them. He talked of simple things, just wanting good soil, clean water, easy weather, and sufficient crops.

"Just to have enough, so I didn't have to worry all the time," he said with a sigh.

"So, there's no daydreams of exploration?" she asked him.

He thought about it before replying, just as he always seemed to. "I did want to be a pilot like you when I was little. I thought if I could fly, they would need me in space. I thought it would be my ticket to freedom. Now I realize nothing's ever that simple, and I question whether I wanted to fly because it would get me to space, or because I just wanted to fly."

Janlin lit up. "Maybe I could teach you how to use this someday," she said, patting her pack. The idea of being able to go for a fly down here tantalized her. What a treat that would be.

"What the heck is that, anyway?" he asked, his scowl returning but without the edge it once had. "Felt like some mangled, half assembled tent or something."

Janlin laughed and carefully removed the flight suit. "This is from the planet we visited, Huantag. The people there looked like birds, flew like birds, sounded like birds . . . had a lot of the same physiology apparently, like hollow bones. They built these suits for us so we could fly with them." She spread one wing out so he could see the structure better. "I can't imagine not flying," she admitted.

He inspected the suit with interest. "So, what would you do if there were no obstacles?"

"All I want is for Gordon and Ursula to be able to have kids, grow food, feel safe enough to do all that."

Ceirin gave her the oddest look. He almost spoke, then clearly changed his mind with a tiny shake of his head.

"What?"

But he wouldn't answer, waving it off.

"No, seriously, what?" Janlin insisted.

Why did this guy both fascinate and infuriate her in equal measure?

He met her gaze and decided to take the challenge. "What do *you* want, Janlin?"

She frowned at the emphasis. "What the hell? Didn't I just say?"

"You told me about how you want to see Gordon and Ursula achieve what they want for themselves. That's nice and all, but what do you want for you?"

The question threw her. She hid her face in shadow, feeling attacked and wanting to defend herself, but she wasn't sure what from. Ceirin didn't pressure her for an answer or even seem to expect one, just rose to prepare for sleep.

She lay awake a long time in the darkness. Ceirin's soft snores undercut the shriek of wind outside.

What *did* she want?

The question was valid. Freedom, for sure. Mostly she wanted to pilot. Flying was the one thing she always trusted herself on. But what else? That was a job, not a life.

For so long she had thought she and Stepper would have a life like Gordon and Ursula's . . . together. A partnership. Even now she envied her friends for being on the same mission together, side-by-side once again. With her parents both gone, it was no wonder she wanted to help others accomplish their goals with her skills. She didn't have any plan for herself, Jump tech or no Jump tech.

The realization left her unsettled. If there were no obstacles, how did she want her life to look?

She thought of Huantag, and the possibility of so many other planets in the Universe. She wanted a chance to be free to wander and explore, to fly everywhere she could, and have adventures. But the idea of having a home base, a true home again like she once had right here on Earth, she couldn't deny the longing for that too.

So, both a home base and the freedom to come and go, if there were no obstacles like Jump sickness, bio-nanite fouling, and crop failures holding them back. If she was going to dream big, then that would be the ultimate freedom for her.

CHAPTER TWENTY-FIVE

"W HAT DO YOU mean I can't tell people about you?"

"You go talking to everyone about me, next thing you know, I've got more people here than this place can handle."

"Harsh."

He didn't like that. "Reality," he protested. "It was density, sheer numbers, that nearly wiped this oasis off the map fifteen years ago. One person pooping? No biggie. Ten? Hmmm, builds up quick, but okay, let's compost. Hundreds? Too much shit."

"Fine, I'll keep my mouth shut," she said. "Just don't tell me I can't leave. I have people I care about up there. It's become my home. You can't keep me prisoner."

He just shrugged, as if there wasn't anything much she could do about it anyway, so it didn't matter what he said. It sent Janlin into a funk, her mind stewing on her now-limited options. He wasn't much better, pacing around the small space muttering under his breath before laying down far too early, putting his face to the wall.

Janlin laid down to face her own section of wall. She waited until his breathing slowed into sleep, then let go of her emotions in quiet racking sobs. Gordon, Cassie, Steve, Linder, they all would think she ran off and was now too snarky to reply to their calls. Instead, she was dirtside and stranded, no help to Lauren. No help at all to Anaya. And now she might never see them ever again. That set her off crying harder.

A touch on her shoulder made her stiffen and gulp down her tears. Next thing she knew, he had laid behind her. He gently, cautiously, wrapped his arm around her. She stayed still, tense, while he relaxed. His arm became heavy, a strange comfort, and his breathing returned to sleep.

Micro-bit at a time, she allowed her muscles to relax. The last time she was in a man's arms was with Stepper, on Huantag. That should be a good memory, but it was marred by the trauma that followed. She had wanted so much to believe in him, in a life together once again, and he ripped it all out from under her.

Had Ceirin even been fully awake to know what he'd done? His anger at her earlier, was that about the situation and not necessarily about her?

She drifted, tears flowing quietly now, the terrors and grief still there but distracted, quieted, and his heavy arm a shield, a defence against the darkness, a warm comfort. Who was she to refuse it?

THREE DAYS LATER the storm pack ran itself out. They had talked history, politics, family, childhood, parents, and future speculation without finding much hope. Janlin had wondered aloud if more places like his could be founded here for the orbital population, and Ceirin looked doubtful.

"With time to prepare, perhaps," he said. "You have to remember we're starving down here."

"And if they arrived with shuttles to shelter in and seeds to plant, fresh water and soil?"

He considered. "Still need help with somewhere to shelter those new crops, but maybe, yeah, maybe." His gaze met hers, and lingered. "I know you won't give up on the people out there, and nor should you. I never meant that."

Now Janlin thought about that conversation as they prepared to leave. Contacting Spectra would be her first goal, which would mean getting back to the shuttle in hopes the comms still worked. Ceirin only shook his head at this idea. Apparently, the storms made communications useless a good ninety-nine percent of the time.

Janlin looked around the cave, feeling weird after being stuck there for so many days, and a little astounded that she had sheltered inside a natural cave on a mountainside on Earth.

Stepping out into open air, though, what a relief and a surprise, even if it stunk a bit. After more than fifteen years living on Spectra, to emerge out under an open sky was something, and brought her mind around to Huantag again.

Ceirin moved on ahead, obviously anxious to get home. Janlin found it difficult to keep up. She huffed her way along, struggling to lift each leg against the heavier gravity. Ceirin pulled ahead on a long, steady climb, and stopped to wait for her at the top.

Janlin wanted to gawk, but she also needed to watch her feet. She'd forgotten, walking smooth halls of space all these years, and even the pathways of tamed Huantag, how difficult it was to both watch the scenery and where you placed your foot. She pushed along, catching glances ahead when she could, and climbing hard in anticipation of a break at the top where Ceirin stood.

The wind was a boon for a change, at their backs and with a touch of humid warmth to it. She commented on it breathlessly as she reached Ceirin.

"Usually signals a big blow coming, hurricane style," he said, frowning. "Means it'll be even longer and stronger than the last one." He set off again immediately.

Longer? "Stop," she gasped. "You just stood here waiting for me to catch up, now I need a chance to rest a sec."

He looked distraught, glancing beyond her. She looked back and had a sudden respect for his urgency. A dark ridge edged across the landscape, and already the winds were picking up. "That's what I mean by hurricane style," he shouted.

"Never mind, no break required," she shouted back, pacing by him, and a humourless laugh tore from his lips as they continued.

They climbed silently, saving their breath, and cleared a ridge. Janlin gawked at the vivid green scenery she could see running up the sheltered valley across the flats. Ceirin had said a "protected canyon" and he wasn't kidding. Now they were close enough, and it was clear enough, she could see verdant waves of grasses, and small living trees banked the creek that tumbled through the rocks to flatten out over the sands.

She realized she had stopped to stare. The winds had settled again, a weird calm before the storm, and she savoured the moment. Ceirin grinned at her, unable to hide his pride. "That's the other cool thing about this place: that creek keeps running, and it's from a natural underground spring that is fairly well filtered, all considering."

Janlin waved helplessly. "How could you leave *this*," she started, "and how are you *hungry*?"

His smile faded, and he looked sadly at the vista below. "The soil is deficient, unable to nourish us the way it used to, despite what you see here." They were walking again and had to stay close to be heard. "Mammals of any kind are really hard to find, although I heard rumours someone has a herd of whitetail deer in the Kootenays they've managed to keep alive. Farming is, obviously, not an option. Storms take most crops, bugs or fire take the rest. Warmer temperatures accelerated the metabolism of insects like aphids and corn borers, making them hungrier and hornier. And what do we plant in, with the soil so dead? We found significantly less protein in all our cereal crops, calcium and iron have depleted, and zinc is rarely found in our soil tests."

"But . . . you have water, you have waste . . . make better soil and work inside, like we do," she said.

"Of course," he said. "We're not stupid. We grow indoors. We compost every single thing we can, but it's full of toxins, and it's never enough. We were trying a new enzyme that helped us to digest things thriving in this," he waved a hand randomly, "but most get a bad gut ache that never goes and then stop absorbing nutrition at all, so we stopped that experiment." He shuddered. "We're starving. The Earth . . . the very *earth* . . . no longer sustains us. And everything is so riddled with toxins and old chemicals from the before times, you eat anything and risk paralysis, heavy metals, cancers over time . . ." His voice trailed off as they negotiated the climb down onto the flats. "We've had sickness come through, too. The Traders bring it, of course."

"Traders?"

"Yeah, they have rigs built to withstand the storms, and shelters strung like beads through the landscape. But they almost always bring illness. These days Traders are both welcome and shunned. We call out our orders and set out the fee, then retreat. They leave the goods and take their pay and move on. Then we mask up and sanitize the entire lot. It's the only safe way."

They made the flats, and Ceirin picked up the pace. The wind seemed to pick it up, too—that and everything else around them lighter than a twig.

"Traders wear wild masks that hide their faces, with long downward-drooping noses that have layered filtering systems inside. The masks used to be outfitted with nano-filters that scrubbed their breath before venting. Now, of course, the filters are worn, useless, the nanites failing and in desperate need of upgrade. The Traders insist the masks continue to protect the healthy, and often beg us to be allowed to visit, share a meal." He shivered. "I always turn them away. I wouldn't want one near me."

Janlin thought about it. "Aren't they just people, under the mask?"

He gave her a strange look, like what she said was in a different language. Then he waved her on. "It's still a good hour from here."

A FEW MINUTES later she saw distant movement as little specs rose into the air and circled. "Birds!" She stared in wonder, flooded by memories of childhood. *We all took birds for granted, even then when things were already bad. Never thought to see them again.*

Ceirin grinned. "Yep, there's a few tough birds still around, like ravens. They are descendants of dinosaurs, after all. They're good at surviving. We've found food by following them. I read once that wolves and ravens worked together, the ravens circling on high to find the kill, and the wolves helping to tear the carcass open so the birds could get at it. A mutually beneficial relationship." He shrugged. "Now we're the wolf."

He looked so alive then, like the cares and worries lifted and showed her who he *could* be, without so much struggle. He strode along, waving his arms as he told his tale. But there were still things she didn't understand.

"Tell me more about Tanner."

He wrinkled his nose. "Tanner came, with Galena and Mitchell, and Mitchell's brother Rickard, plus a few others. At that point, we had food stores we couldn't use up alone, and . . . well, it would be wrong to turn them away." She saw a hollowed look in his eye now. "Galena and Mitchell had a baby, but the little thing died soon after."

He was quiet for a few paces. Janlin focused on keeping pace.

"They found the grave dug up, everyone talked about how long it was since we'd seen any big predators around, more than five years running now. Then Tanner claimed he caught a small boar on his scouting, said it must be a leftover from some old farm." He looked at her with helpless horror. "But he had cooked the infant. It was so obvious by the bones."

Janlin swallowed hard.

"Mitchell's brother Rickard was in on it. They were both a few screws loose."

He didn't speak for a time as they marched on. She could see his eyes glisten and his Adam's apple bob as he swallowed down his grief. Finally, he took up the story again.

"Galena was really great. She was a food scientist, taught me a lot." They left the old road, taking a footpath through a young, dense forest of scraggly pines about six feet tall. Old burnt stumps and fallen logs were mixed in, forming a stark contrast. "She taught me how screwed we were." The pines were stunted and warped by the constant winds, and many green trees were blown down in one section. "She's the one Tanner killed in front of you."

He had a new harsh tone, and it sunk in what the implications of his long absence might be. "I couldn't turn down a chance at space, but I really thought I'd be back here a lot quicker than I was." Then he faced her square on. "It might be bad. And there's more, lots more."

She had got that sense there was something he was keeping back. The desire to like the guy, to want to help, warred with her mistrust. But if she was actually stuck here—could that really be true? Surely not forever?—that meant relying on this human far more than she might like.

They were climbing the valley now, and he stopped to take her down to the water where a filtration system had been set up. He removed the cover, dipped a cup, and handed it to her.

"A drink not boiled," he said as she took a sip, then gulped the rest down.

"That is . . . I mean . . . oh, wow."

He laughed. "Yeah, the water you guys are drinking up there is really stale. I don't know what process it goes through after mining, but good grief, it's nothing compared to this, eh?"

She had to agree. The filtration looked complicated, with wires running into conduit that ran underground to a pole nearby, and a small power generator tucked under a rock shelf outside. Pipes and connectors and control panels with glowing digits filled the enclosure, and pure clean water sat in a storage tank at the end.

Ceirin filled a couple water pouches, these also fitted with filtration units inside. "Come on, we still aren't safe from that next blow, even here."

The landscape had darkened, and the wind turned cold again. She shook her head. "I really forgot what weather was like, you know?"

"I can imagine. The time up there was quite the experience. It's a bit weird being back again after months away."

They regained the path and climbed the valley. He had a new urgency to him now, and it wasn't just the storm. Here a few willow trees grew along the water, and grasses waved in the wind. Little birds peeped and whistled, and Ceirin said they tried eating them. "There's just nothing to them, they're so tiny. We had grouse years ago, but ate them too quickly and depleted their numbers, and they didn't recover.

"I had chickens way back. They laid less and less as time passed, so again, as we ate them and since they weren't replaced by new young ones, the stock became depleted. I keep asking the Traders about chickens, and they just stare with those empty mask eyes before slowly shaking their heads."

Janlin had other concerns. "Are you sure we won't be a risk to your people? We still don't know for sure how the Imag virus works, or how it transmitted to the Huantag if it was purely nanite-driven."

"Because it's nanite made, people here are safe. We don't have NECS. But for safety's sake, we will quarantine. It's actually standard procedure for anyone coming in from elsewhere at any time."

"Quarantine." They just spent how many days in a cave, what was this going to look like?

She could see the main house now, and more in behind. His pace quickened, and his body carried tension in every line. "Yep," he said, feigning a light-hearted tone. "Fourteen days of our filtered water before you can enter. You play crib?"

CHAPTER TWENTY-SIX

A COUPLE WEEKS later, Diona's earcell chimed, the sound indicating an unknown contact. *Strange, I haven't heard that sound in years.* She accepted the call.

"Who is this?" she demanded.

A very deep and stilted voice, with the strangest accent she'd ever heard, spoke in her ear.

"Dis is Anaya, Gitane Captain, friend to Ja'nin. I in geo-fixed orbit over you wit guns ready. You free Ja'nin now!"

The deep, strangely accented voice growled as Diona struggled to process what she was hearing, and how best to turn it to her advantage.

"Where Jan'in?" the alien demanded again, its voice grating. Diona shuddered, then clued in.

"Janlin? What? I don't know," Diona said, being sure to sound as confident as possible, scornful even. "Thought she died on Earth days ago."

"No." The pain in that denial gave Diona pause. "No make sense. Jan'in go Mars. She say."

"Welp, she's not here."

"No true. I get Jan'in now."

Cold fear cut her. She had to contain this beast and fast. She should have prepared better. Then her thoughts turned again. "Wait, let me call you on holo, okay?"

Who needed Janlin's body anymore? She had the alien,

delivered right to her doorstep. Could this be any more perfect?

"Okay." The link went dead.

I must ensure complete control of the situation, Diona thought, calm as ever, but her hands were ice cold as she swiped the comm link off. She gripped her fingers with her other hand to stop them trembling. She could show no weakness.

The alien must be contained. She would lure it into a place that Diona could lock down. She didn't even need to be there.

Trouble was, there were only two places that met her needs, and one of them contained her brother.

The other, her daughter.

Diona called up the holo-comm and linked to the alien ship. Fear of a digital hack made her pause. Her quick fingers set up an extra firewall, and a couple of alarms.

She placed the call.

She waited, standing tall. A dreadful beast materialized in front of her, all leathery skin and hulking, neckless, eight-foot ugliness. Diona clasped her hands behind her and breathed a sigh of relief it was only a holo.

"Where Jan'in?" the brute demanded. "Did you . . . is she . . . dead?"

The thing's accent wasn't so bad, and the obvious sappiness revealed here gave Diona more confidence. This creature actually cared about Janlin, obviously quite a bit. People who cared too much for others were easily ruled and fooled, in her experience.

"Greetings, and welcome to Mars," she said. "I am very sorry I don't know more about Janlin, but I would like to invite you to come down and see our home for yourself."

The alien stared at her. "How you know Jan'in dead?"

Her signal's dead. Interesting that her friends didn't know something happened. "I can show you the NECS tracking system, state-of-the-art technology that we can share with you. Again, please come and enjoy our hospitality. We are honoured to have our first guest from outside our solar system. It is a momentous time of new opportunity." Diona put her palms together and bowed, though it pained her to do so. *Whatever it takes to get her down here.*

The alien matched her gesture and actually apologized. "I am Anaya of the Gitane," she said, "tank you for invite. Where put 'ip, pease?"

CHAPTER TWENTY-SEVEN

CEIRIN VEERED OFF the main path towards a post that held a large bell, which Ceirin rang hard. The storm was upon them now, howling vengeance for some wrong she wished she could right.

The bell must be how the Traders announced their arrival. Only now did she notice the rough cabin backed in under the canyon rock face to their left. Quarantine quarters?

A fence with a sturdy, if old, steel gate blocked the way in. A shimmer in the air told Janlin the barricade was far more effective than it seemed at first glance. The canyon walls rose up both sides of the little farmstead and narrowed as it went up the valley beyond.

A head popped up in the house window. Janlin thought it appeared child-sized. Now that same window also held a woman, the little one at her side.

Tanner charged out of a barn that had clearly suffered too many brutal hailstorms. Its pocked sides looked like a sieve, but the roof had new metal sheets on half the slope. A ladder was mounted with supports against the wind, more evidence of the hard labour involved in maintaining shelter even in a protected valley like this one.

"Ceirin? You fucker! Did you really go to space?" Tanner's sharp-nosed face poked out from under his hooded coat, his suspicious gaze shaded.

Janlin noticed the woman cranked her window open.

"I did go to space," Ceirin shouted. His voice carried easily to Tanner, and to the window. "I was trying to bring help, food, maybe seeds. Not only was I delayed, on our return the shuttle crashed and burned, destroying the stores I was able to secure. I'm sorry." Tanner sneered, but the storm wasn't going to allow for pleasant conversation. "How is everyone?"

"Still alive, no thanks to you."

Janlin looked to see Ceirin's response, but he was looking at the window, not Tanner, with a smile of brilliant relief. He waved like a fanatic, his eyes filling with tears.

The girl waved back, tiny, hesitant, only to turn and toddle off again while sucking a finger.

THE STORM DROVE them to shelter without much more interchange with Tanner, but the dark stare that followed them made Janlin mighty uncomfortable. She glared back, until he lifted his lip in a snarl.

They ducked into the relative quiet. The quarantine shelter had a solid stone foundation with hewed logs stacked in the butt and pass method, and it was built under the rock face to protect it. It had two large bunks with ample bedding, a bioplaz table and chair set, and a sideboard with an old food unit plugged into an actual wall outlet. How much ingenuity had to go into surviving all this time, through all this grief and destruction? It gave her a level of respect for these folks, even if Tanner made her want a long shower.

Ceirin looked gutted and elated at the same time, and relief came off him in waves. "Your daughter?" she asked. He nodded, biting his lip. Watching the play of emotions across his face, she wondered if she should just give the guy some time to himself.

He sucked in air and blew it out, clearly near tears. "I'd give a lot to hug her right now." His anguish was plain. "I never meant to be gone this long."

Her heart went out to him. "She probably won't remember you were gone, at that age," she said gently. "Doesn't help much though, does it?"

He agreed, and opened a panel to reveal food packets. "You are probably right, but I abandoned her. That leaves a mark." The little kitchen had a hotplate, and opening a cupboard revealed the pots and pans needed. Ceirin kept stopping and staring out the window towards the farm, and Janlin noticed his hands were trembling. She stepped up to the counter.

"Can I help?"

It seemed to pull him out of his thoughts. "Sure, that'd be great."

They pulled together a meal. The packet he tore open and mixed with water said "veggie broth" on it, and another packet had a strange kind of hard cracker. One cupboard revealed jars of preserves, and she chose pickled beets. She set out dishes, found cutlery. Ceirin was quiet but subdued.

The question hammered at her skull until she couldn't stand it. Innocent enough, wanting to know, right? But somehow, she knew the answer couldn't be good.

"Her mother?" she finally said out loud.

A drop fell to the counter, and she realized he was weeping, his head hung low. "She died in childbirth," he whispered. Janlin swallowed down her own despair and tapped his shoulder, offering a hug.

He took it, his body shaking with grief, but pulled away before too long and went to wash his face. Janlin quickly finished up the prep and put the meal on the table.

"Thanks," he said as he joined her. It might've been thanks for setting the meal, or the hug. She wasn't sure and decided not to worry about it. Maybe it was both.

They settled in, both more than ready even for these meagre rations. Ceirin dunked a few crackers and spooned some broth, then eyed the spoon with a look of disdain, only to drop it and simply drink from the bowl.

"Very sophisticated manners," she commented wryly around her own mouthful.

He looked completely unapologetic. "You even watch the crew eat on Spectra? You folks aren't so sophisticated either with your tube soups and sippy straws stuck in pouches."

"What's wrong with that?" she protested while laughing, because it was too true. So, with a bit of sass, she put her own spoon down and lifted her bowl to take a long drink. It actually was much nicer than getting it only a spoonful at a time.

His grin was infectious, and she grinned back.

"By the way, we will go back to the shuttle, but to stay there then with no surety of food or water, and no close shelter spot until the fire burned out, wasn't an option. We would've died."

"I get it. Plus, you were a little pissed at me, and I kinda deserved it." He had to agree. "I hope no one else gets it in their head to try and beat us there." Janlin looked significantly out the window towards the farmyard.

Ceirin sighed. "That could be a problem, but the storms prevent him as much as they do us. Besides, Tanner won't know what he's looking for. And I resealed the hatch, hoping it would tamp the fire."

They talked over what they might salvage. Janlin couldn't help but repeat her stance from before. "If we can communicate with Spectra, we might be able to get some small help sent down somehow."

Ceirin looked doubtful. "I'm still not sure about letting them know we even exist."

Janlin chewed on her thoughts a while. There was no point arguing with the guy. *It's not like I have a choice in the matter.* With no NECS, no handheld, no comms, no knowledge of this place, she was helpless. If the Seraph wouldn't fly, she was worse . . . stranded.

CHAPTER TWENTY-EIGHT

WHEN ANAYA ENTERED the airlock chamber, Diona gaped. "My, but you are big and ugly then, eh?" she muttered under her breath, grateful beyond measure that the alien would stay on that side of the bioplaz. The beast wore an altered SpaceOp issue coverall like much of the colony still did. Diona never wore one, as it would be beneath her, but she made a point to create a wardrobe in the colours of her family's business. It reminded everyone that she was both one of them, and above them.

The hulk stood and stared through the bioplaz window. Despite the alienness of the creature, her resigned look somehow communicated her knowledge that this was most likely a trap. Why would she come, then? Was there something at play that Diona wasn't thinking of?

The alien creature had obviously not been taught how foolish it was to trust humans. Diona had simply uttered all the usual platitudes of welcome over the comm and guided the beast to land by her bunker.

Once Anaya was in the chamber hall that doubled as airlock for Stepper's cell, Diona flipped the switch and the room sealed shut, explaining over the comm link that Anaya was just going through a "safe" room, a decontamination process. She even asked inane questions about the virus as if she didn't know it was all nanite-driven. The hulk bought it, and soon Diona cycled open the door that led to Stepper.

Her brother looked up and screamed, his whole body jerking in spasm, launching him to his feet and into the furthest possible corner away.

He is so weak. Had she faced these Imag aliens, she would not have let them render her so useless.

"Oh, it's you," Stepper said, recognition dawning as he struggled to regain his cool. And then realization. "You've been tricked."

"Where Ja'nin?" the beast demanded.

Stepper threw his arms up. "How should I know? My sister says she's dead."

The hulking thing stared, then slowly sank down onto a bench. Diona watched Stepper side-eye the alien. "Thought the Jump killed you," he said offhandedly. Maybe he really was over Janlin. The alien's grief had no outward effect on him.

Anaya lifted both hands to her head. "Still bad."

Stepper grunted. "Yeah, I get that."

"Well, let's see if I can help," Diona said. "It's the least I can do, as your host." Stepper only sighed, but Anaya lurched up and came to the glass.

"Dis wrong," was all she said, but it was a deep growl, and her stare was intense. Good thing it took a lot more than that to unnerve Diona Jordan.

"Right or wrong never meant much to me, my new friend."

"Don't ca me dat," the alien sputtered. Diona caught the lack of "l" and "th" sounds, but what was more interesting was that it was Janlin's line. Every time Stepper used "Jannilove" she would spit, "Don't call me that," right back. Funny. Diona's curiosity grew, but none of it was truly important. What mattered was acquiring an alien blood sample to further her nanite research.

"Where Jan'in?"

"Like I told you, I thought she was dead. I'm beyond surprised that you expected her to be here." Even as she said the words, a little spike of fear shot down her spine. Then she shook it off. Janlin's NECS were out, gone, and the only working Jumpship still remained, so she must've died. How she ended up dying on Earth Diona had no idea, and didn't really care anyway.

And now she had the alien, just as required, without the problem of Janlin hovering over her head anymore.

The drama, and the alien shuttle parked in the red rocks

outside the airlock, well, they made it all even more fun. She was winning.

Her father would be proud.

ONCE THE GAS filled the chamber and a bot extracted the alien's blood, Diona sterilized the container and brought it herself to her tech.

"I have a new sample," she said, thrusting it into the woman's hands where she sat at the microscope. Thea's was sample two, and hers was always the control, known as sample one. Then Stepper's blood, full of wonderful new alien tech for her to play with, became sample four, three being the other child that died. And now, sample five, pure alien blood, grey and odd-looking. "It's some new tech in a biogel," she lied. "Split it in two and run the new update on one, and the usual tests on another. I'll wait."

The tech enclosed half the sample in a shielded case, and ran the usual tests. Diona watched every move. She would take all of it with her when she left. She didn't understand this secret yet and had to do whatever it took to avoid it getting out, and the tech would never be believed if she didn't have anything to show for it. So Diona waited, leaning in to watch which slides were smeared, and where the rest still sat, and that none were put aside.

The woman was jumpy. To be expected, Diona supposed, but irritating too.

Diona reached across her and enlarged the images of the scanned blood cells drifting in holo. She had seen the bio-fouling affecting the SpaceOp NECS and human cells. These alien NECS were so much more robust in comparison, with no sign of fouling at all. Did she dare use them herself?

The tech lost her jitters as she gazed at the holo scan results. "These new nanites are amazing. Were they designed for upgrades? How are they protected against networking?"

Diona ignored her. "Run our upgrade now, separate from the controls. And be ready to engage the fail-safe."

The upload finished and they both leaned in. In the other three samples, a few nanites that had stopped signalling had lit up and began an operating reboot. In the new sample, nothing changed.

"Okay, now how do we test the reboot results?"

"Oh, easy," she said, and swiped a side holo screen to start the diagnostics scan. The tech gave her a sideways glance. "There is some big potential for increased communication between the nanites as we move forward with this upgrade," she started. When Diona didn't speak, she kept going. "Even from person to person, above and beyond the earcell."

Diona gave the woman a raised eyebrow. "Yes? Your point is?"

The tech swallowed, but continued. "This upgrade contains a lot of networking software."

"And?"

"That introduces a risk of integration, of the parts becoming one unit."

"Are you accusing me of trying to create an AI? How dare you?" The tech cringed. "You know we are trying to save lives here, especially the lives of the children whose bodies don't accept NECS well. The upgrade must allow for integration in order to repair the old gear. They have to communicate somehow." Diona stared at the woman, who dared stare back. She huffed. "Make it work."

The tech ducked her head but still had the gall to continue. "It is true. Any networking software introduced into the NECS environment has the potential to create artificial intelligence. By my training codes, and that of SpaceOp, I have to point this out. Ma'am."

Diona thought her head would explode. "Which is why we are building in the fail-safe," she said through gritted teeth. "Why don't we run that. Now."

The tech scrambled. "Yes, Ma'am."

Diona almost screamed at her. *Don't ma'am me, you little shit. You know we're the same age, and you're in too deep to get out safely anymore.*

"Sample five contains programming language similar to what I found in sample four, which I was unable to link up with. Until I know the language, I can't affect them. They aren't reading our signals."

"Noted."

The tech squirmed. "Will I get access to that language at some point?" she finally braved.

Diona regarded her with some small respect for her audacity. "Perhaps," she grated out. "For the time being, you need to have some faith in your leadership."

"Yes, ma'am."

The old NECS were finished their upgrade and all running between forty and seventy percent, which was better than nothing but showed the limitations. She needed more materials, and these alien NECS might be just the answer. How kind of an alien to deliver herself here all full of them. And who knew what the creature's ship might contain. That treasure chest made her giddy with anticipation.

"Okay, it's ready."

"And it's fully contained, for certain?"

The tech nodded until her head looked about to pop off. She knew the dangers of this. Still, Diona wondered if she should step away.

Too late. The tech engaged the fail-safe.

They watched in fascination as the microscopic machines each ceased function and shut down, in a wave through the cells, spreading like a contagion. And when they reached the alien nanites, their "active" lights also went out, the signal dead, each and every Nano Electrochemical System gone dark.

"It worked!"

The tech seemed both elated and terrified. As she should be, since without functioning NECS, life in space was rather impossible for human anatomy. For her part, Diona was simply relieved the alien junk could be disabled if needed.

The tech woman was back studying the alien sample, puzzling out the details. She didn't know the half of it. And now, the tech's new program, with a few small additions of code that Diona had ready, would allow control of the enmeshed NECS. The fear of AI had always been holding them back. Now she would be able to keep everyone reliant on her. Everyone! The whole population would be completely dependent on her good graces, and grateful for her repairing the bio-fouling.

She smiled and tipped her head at the tech. Maybe one little tidbit for her would be advantageous. "Nice work. Now dismantle a nanite from sample five to see what you can learn." The woman's surprised look told Diona that the tech had already entertained the thought. "I want to see what you're capable of."

It was a flimsy cover, but it should work.

WITHIN TWO WORK shifts the tech had prepared an upgrade. Diona used the time to ensure the woman's water contained a rough version of her final upgrade. Little did the tech know she now carried new NECS ready to respond to Diona's commands.

Diona arrived at the lab, noting the woman's name on the door panel. "What have you got, Moran? Can you fix this?"

Eliza Moran waved her in. "It's only possible by adding more NECS programmed to do repair work," she admitted. "The sample already had some familiar surgery nanite systems working that I was able to augment in this upgrade."

"Excellent. Now add in this." Diona sent the last few lines from her datapad. Sure enough, the woman blanched on first sight.

"I can't," she said involuntarily. "Ma'am."

"You can, and will. They are necessary in ways you don't understand, and I don't have the skill you do to weave them into the existing programming. My version is somewhat ragged, wouldn't you agree?" Poor woman didn't know how ragged the NECS were she now carried. Hopefully they would do the trick. Diona made a few more taps on her datapad. This would be the ultimate test before the big day. It hadn't worked on Stepper, would it work here?

"Go on, add the programming, smooth it out."

The woman's eyes widened. "What are you doing?"

"Unfortunately, the upgrade I put in your water is a bit of a mess. Still, I need this done, and I wanted to do a little test, so I'm sending a little command to your new NECS." She watched the emotions exploding across the woman's face, a fine mix of anger, fear, panic, and loathing. "Can you say no?"

"No," Moran whispered.

"Now, add the new code and run the test."

"I still think it's wrong," the woman cried out. Terror contorted her face as her body did the things Diona ordered despite her protest. "This. Is. Wrong." Each word was a gasp.

"I'm just glad to know it works," Diona said. She gathered up all the samples, the test work, and doses of the upgrade, and headed back to her safe place.

THE ALIEN STILL suffered spiking pain in her head, along with dizziness, balance issues, nightmares, and vision issues, as did Stepper. Diona added the new NECS to their water supply, and ran her upgrade from her trusty datapad.

It worked.

Diona did a little bounce on her toes. If she could get repair upgrades to work on an alien, surely she could do the same for Thea.

"What you do?" the hulking brute asked, touching her forehead. "It better."

"I need your cooperation," Diona explained. "And I am, well, experimenting on you as well. You should be grateful. The pain has gone, yes?" The alien nodded. "Your NECS have been upgraded. My tech actually found a way to utilize the ports with our own set-ups. They are close enough to ours anyway, aren't they? Isn't that why your anti-viral-that-isn't worked so well on the virus-that-wasn't?"

The little white lies worked, because there was enough truth mingled in. The brute didn't deny it. Stepper sat up, his disappointment palpable. "You think fixing a headache is worth having your new junk? What gives you the right to do this to people?"

"I will do whatever I have to," she said, fighting for calm.

"How is your daughter doing, anyway?"

Diona scowled at him. "What the hell do you think I'm working on? Every day I'm faced with the operations of this colony, without backup of any kind anymore, while solving the issues of the day, which now include our NECS degrading and my daughter's blood disease that rejects nanites of all kinds . . . and you have the nerve to demand more from me?" She began shutting down the systems in their chamber, starting with lights.

"Now, Diona, don't get all in a huff," Stepper started, but she cut the comm link before he could say more. She turned her back on him and walked out.

What an asshole.

CHAPTER TWENTY-NINE

THEY TRIED A few different cards games, but cribbage was their favourite. One morning, as Janlin wiped the table and set out the deck and board, Ceirin dug in a back cupboard. He let out a crow of success and held up a thick black data pad with a glass screen that had to be a century old. A spiderweb of cracks snaked across the surface.

"What is it?" Janlin asked.

"An old cell phone that I loaded with music off an ancient laptop," he said, drawing out wires and cables that had come along with it.

She couldn't help but laugh. "Can't believe our ancestors had to deal with all that!"

"Right?" he said with his own chuckle. "But this has songs on it I couldn't get off the Cloud. Stuff that goes back decades before this thing even," he said, waving the cell phone. She realized that must be where the term "ear cell" came from. She'd always thought it was because the NECS integrated with their cells to build the internal comm unit.

He plugged the cell into the ancient wall plug and pushed buttons for a while. Janlin got bored and started poking through the other gear in the cupboard. There were wooden puzzles for kids, tiny metal toy cars, random devices, wires and bits of electronics, and an old umbrella.

"Powering on," came a voice that made her jump. "Welcome

to Gigantech Logistics.”

“Sorry, forgot that it did that,” Ceirin said. A speaker sat on the table by the deck of cards with a cord running to the cell phone. Janlin looked at the screen of the cell. She tried a scroll swipe like she’d seen him do. It wasn’t much different than swiping holo lists.

“I found a databank and it had everything to play all these songs, goes back into the nineteenth century if you can believe that.” He waved helplessly. “I’ve only just scraped the surface.”

Janlin scrolled and scrolled, song after song sailing by. “How do you even choose? Where do you start?”

He got a philosophical look and ducked his head. “You’d laugh.”

Janlin quirked an eyebrow. “So? Tell me anyway.”

He laughed. “Okay, fine. I pick one at random and trust I’m gonna hear exactly what I need in that moment.” He shrugged at her predicted laughter. “It’s never failed, and sometimes the results are astonishing.”

She considered, still smirking at him just because it was expected. “Let me try,” she said, flicking her finger to make the list spin along. She flicked one more time, purposely watching him and not the screen, and tapped.

On the opening notes, he blanched, sinking into a chair with the most bemused look on his face.

“What?”

He laughed again, a true laugh of hope, a sound she thought made life worth living. “It’s only my favourite.” His pleasure was so delicious. “Listen.”

An electric guitar strung out notes that made her heart ache. When was the last time she listened to music like this? Well before her mom died, before her dad went to space fulltime, before Earth was considered unlivable. Those last decades things really devolved fast, and while music was a thing in orbit, it sure wasn’t a main focus in life.

As we settle into sleep,
Our souls the machines do keep,
May we one day see the dawn,
Sailing through the deep.

Across the Milky Way,
We quest another day,
Our roots torn,
Our vows sworn,
Our humanity stored away.

Light years pass, the risk so high,
How will we survive the eons we fly,
On the wings of maybe comes the dawn,
Sailing through the deep.

The music quieted, poignant, drawing emotions out of her she forgot she had, then swelled in sound and drive, pounding out hard rock chords before the whole chorus was sung again, then faded in a melodic guitar bit.

"On the wings of maybe," she whispered. When the last note faded, she turned to him. "Play it again?" she pleaded.

He grinned. "Right? It's that good. One of my all-time favourites. I can't believe that's what you landed on."

He tapped and it began again, and then they let the bulky machine play on down the list. Ceirin regaled her with stories about this song and that, memories that sometimes left him laughing, and sometimes made him sad. A few she had heard before, and they belted out the words. She told him of her father's love of both flying and music. "He would've loved that first one you played," she said, feeling wistful.

"Again?" he said, hopeful.

"Yeah, play it again. It's that good."

He really grinned at that.

The notes peeled out, even better than before. "On the wings of maybe comes the dawn," the guy sang, and it made her glad she had that Huantag flight suit. Maybe, someday, it would be useful again. *On the wings of maybe . . .*

"Is there a story to this one?" she asked as it ended and he turned the unit off.

"It was a song about using cryogenic sleep chambers to try and reach new solar systems, but most people didn't even realize that, it was just another cool tune going around online."

He set the gear aside. It was quiet now, but for the muffled ever-present sounds of the storm. "Well, we can do *that* again tomorrow if you like," she said, and he agreed wholeheartedly.

THEY FELL INTO a routine, until each knew what to do without thinking or comment to land dinner on the table. That night, Ceirin warmed vegetable soup, she put out bowls, and they sat in unison with a sigh, everything ready.

Ceirin looked at her kinda funny. Music played on in the background, a thing with each dinner now. She gave a questioning look, and he shrugged it off.

They cleaned up after, again with little said, just a nice comfortable routine of Ceirin's hands in sloshing warm water, the clink of cutlery, the feel of the towel growing damp as she dried and set things away again.

He set out the cards on the cleared table.

"Ready to lose again?"

She mock scowled. "You might regret giving me a chance to catch up."

They played for a bit, the sounds of the stormy day a quiet backdrop inside the shelter. She won a couple, lost a few. He was by far a better card player than her . . . or was she just distracted?

She tossed down her cards. "I'm bored."

He pursed his lips as he gazed at his hand. "Me too, and my hand is crap."

His gaze came up and met hers, and that now-familiar zing went up her middle. It melted her inhibition away, and she felt daring.

"We're not quarantined from each other, are we?"

He lowered his cards to the table, a little smile teasing his lips. "Clearly we're not."

She let her eyelids droop, wondering if this was okay. Her body sure was interested, but the bravery had passed, she didn't know what to do next. Words caught in her throat. He probably still missed his wife. He might not be interested in her at all. What was she thinking, even bringing it up? What an idiot.

He slid his hand across to her, palm up.

For a moment she couldn't move. Fear bore down. But some desperate cry for attention and touch met that wave and broke it. It might just be worth the risk. She placed her hand in his, skin atingle, and he rose, drawing her up with him.

They moved easily into an embrace, and she sighed with

pleasure. The first hug had been so fraught with anguish and grief, and there'd been no good excuse for another. She had thought a lot about asking. He snuggled her closer, and she lay her head on his shoulder, comforted beyond measure.

He moaned out a sigh of relief. "This might be all I needed." His voice was husky. She leaned back to look at him.

"It is mighty nice."

But then he kissed her, and it was not all they did.

CHAPTER THIRTY

As SHE GAINED consciousness the next morning, her mind drifted, considering the new ferocity of the wind lashing the window with rain, and how much her knee still hurt from that moment in the Huantag shuttle, and . . .

She remembered the previous night with a sharp little intake of air. Her eyes opened to find him regarding her.

In an awkward moment, her usual go-to was to say something funny, or flippant, or best of all, sarcastic. This time she found herself lost in radiating lines of aquamarine. He slid a hand up her arm and gently pushed a strand of hair off her cheek, and she closed her eyes to enjoy the sensation. She reached out, without thought, wanting him closer, and wriggled her body to snuggle in. He wrapped her up tight in his arms, and they both sighed in unison. She could feel him smile at that as she chuckled.

"Well, I'm glad you decided to stay for breakfast," he said, kissing her head. "It's been a long time since I had such a wonderful date."

She twisted around and caught his wink. "That was a date?" she teased, and he laughed.

"Well, a bit spontaneous, but sure," he said. "Give me a chance, I can do better."

She cocked an eyebrow and kissed him, meaning to make some smart remark back, but the kiss deepened, and breakfast was postponed.

Later, relaxing languid over hot mugs, she asked him about his wife. She let him talk on a bit, telling stories about Harriot mostly, but then he flipped it on her.

"Story on Spectra was you and Stepper have a thing," he said.

"Had," she corrected. "Things got a little twisted up with him a few times over. You heard he is in his sister's custody on Mars now?"

"Yeah, you guys mutinied."

"It's true. If we hadn't, he would've Jumped to Mars, despite Captain Inaba dying, despite Anaya's comatose state, he was gonna Jump. He threatened all of us in that moment, so Steve put a stop to it."

"Steve did? Story around Spectra said it was all you."

Janlin studied him. "Are you yanking my chain, or questioning my version of the story?" She wasn't joking around.

He picked up on her seriousness and put his hands up, palms out. "Just making conversation," he said, then shrugged. "And letting you know, I guess. You have a pretty badass reputation that apparently matches the one your dad had."

"Really?" She brightened. "I'd be okay with that. But as for the coup, it happened before I returned from seeing to Anaya, really."

"I believe you," he said readily. "You were, after all, the one there." She gave him a grin for that. "Well, today is our last day. Tomorrow you get to meet everyone. Wanna help me give this place a once-over?"

THE NEXT MORNING, quarantine over, they packed up the cabin. The same storm that blew them up the valley still raged, battering at the door. Her thoughts battered at her brain, too.

If she truly was stuck here, and they continued to hit it off, that sounded like a nice thing. But could she simply abandon her friends? Anaya especially. And what of all those opportunities to visit new planets? Was she just going to give up and try to survive here?

Janlin wanted both a chance at this kind of happiness, and a chance to be free to explore the galaxy. After some thought, she decided it was best to just go with the flow. No demands, no expectations. If nothing else, it had been a wonderful sharing of quarantine time.

As she put the broom away, she turned to find him close,

expectant. He held his hand out, palm up, just as he had over their abandoned crib game so many days ago.

She willingly placed her hand in his. She felt like she had known him forever now. Such lines were so cliché . . . until they weren't. This was a depth of feeling that she found exhilarating and rather terrifying all at the same time.

He drew her close and kissed her nose. "Ready?"

She squeezed him and kissed him back. "I am."

"Are you nervous?"

"A bit, yeah," she admitted. "It'll be fine, I'm sure." Then, "Are you nervous?" He never expected to be bringing her home with him.

"Yeah," he said. "It's just, Harriot, I don't know how to be around her, with us."

"I can behave."

He lifted his eyebrows. "You can?" His voice hit a funny high pitch and cracked with his fake surprise. She laughed and poked him.

"We don't really know what this is between us yet, do we?" she said.

"Guess not, no."

"Then I promise to behave, even though I challenge that it's the others, not the baby, that you're worried about."

Ceirin looked at the holo screen depicting the ongoing text argument with Tanner. "You are likely right about that, but there's nothing to do but face it." He opened the door and gestured out into the storm. She scooped up her backpack and pulled on the big heavy slicker he had found. Unfortunately, there was only one.

Tanner was waiting at the gate.

It was clear the fence shield was still charged.

"Ceirin, you look quite the ass wearing that monkey suit."

Janlin looked to Ceirin's coveralls, standard SpaceOp issue like she was wearing . . . that she'd been wearing now for nearly sixteen years. They came in various shades and sizes, but all had long cuffed sleeves, zippered pockets, and strategic zip-ups for venting or adjusting the fit. Many liked to add adornments of various kinds to personalize them, but overall, they were rather recognizable, particularly by the SpaceOp logo on the shoulder and front pocket. Made her think of how they'd cut off arms and legs on Huantag in an effort to beat the heat.

Ceirin shrugged. "It's comfortable," he said, easy-going but immovable despite the fact he was being pummelled by rain while she and Tanner wore long, heavy slickers.

"Tell me why I should let you . . . and especially her . . . in here? You still haven't convinced me."

"My family?"

"They're likely safer without you," he leered.

The storm surged. Ceirin took out a taser gun, making Janlin step back. It flashed yellow in the gloom. Tanner's scowl turned the darkest yet. Janlin got a better look, realizing it wasn't a taser but a weird box with dials and switches on top.

"You wouldn't, not with them in here."

"I would if it meant I could throttle you with my bare hands," Ceirin said, as mild as could be while shouting over the wind. He looked ready to do it. "I can always restart the systems afterwards, yeah?" A few tree branches whipped by, striking the fence with a flash of sparks. Tanner leapt back, his arm up to shield his face. "Damn it, Tanner, open the gate before the storm does us all in!" Ceirin shouted.

Lightning cracked, seeming to split the air with its intensity, and the boom of thunder that followed left her gasping and whimpering with her hands over her ears. The wind whipped about harder than ever, and hail replaced the sleet. The pummelling became more intense by the second. It was hard to catch her breath, there was so much water in the air.

"Tanner!" Ceirin roared, brandishing the device.

"Fine," he yelled back, and he slapped the datapad he carried. The shimmer went out of the air. Tanner turned and walked away at once, not opening the gate or waiting to speak to them.

"Such an ass," Ceirin growled. They got the gate open and reclosed, fighting the wind, and Ceirin marched after Tanner. "Hey, have the Traders been through?" he called.

"I told you, they returned and left again. Been a few weeks, that's nothing with the storms, you know that."

"True," Ceirin agreed. Slowing to let Tanner pull ahead, he turned to Janlin with, "That man's wearing guilt like a coat." She, too, could see something was riding Tanner just in the darting glances and wincing posture. His shoulders were up around his ears. Ceirin must be dreading what he might find.

"There's talk of gopher east of here," Tanner said as they caught up. He stood at the door to the barn. "Be out there trying myself but you left me with all the work around here, and two useless mouths to feed."

Janlin stared at the guy, appalled. Ceirin's fists bunched, but he let them go with a deep breath. "I'm sure it's been hard. Like I said, I didn't mean to take so long."

"Or return with nothing," Tanner snarked as he lifted the bucket and went in the barn, slamming the heavy fortified door behind him.

Ceirin let air out like a punctured tire and ran his hand through his hair. "I'll pin him down later," he said. "Let me show you the big house."

Ceirin had built a reinforced bioplaz fortress to enclose most of the old farmhouse, adding a steel beam roof with welded sheet metal panels and a thick steel outer door. This outer shell created an inner chamber to dump wet things off, and it protected the old farmhouse from the thrashing outside.

They entered the old house to find a country kitchen that made her heart melt. A hint of woodsmoke tickled her nose under smells of stewing vegetables, and warmth enveloped her. It was reminiscent of the cabin kitchen her family had once had, with gleaming wood floors, hanging pots and pans, the black wood stove, and a cast iron pot set on top steaming away.

Ceirin's grandmother was waiting for them. She stood from her wheelchair, straight and proud, her own blue eyes sharp and quick.

"Grandma, this is Janlin Kavanagh. Janlin, this is Natl McNair, my father's mother."

Natl just gave her a smile and a nod. It was a different voice that piped up from behind the chair.

"Hi!"

Natl reached out a hand, and Harriot came out into view and grasped her great-grandmother's hand. Ceirin knelt down to her level. "Hello, little one," he said, his voice soft. "Remember your dada?"

She held Natl's finger tight while she regarded Ceirin, then Janlin, then Ceirin again. "Dada?"

Natl encouraged the girl. "Remember, sweetie? We watched the holos every day so she wouldn't forget you," she told Ceirin.

Ceirin's grin was so big Janlin thought it might split his whole head in two. Then Harriot let go of Natl and ran to Ceirin's outstretched arms. "Dada!"

Ceirin held her tight, eyes closed. "I missed you, little bit, missed you tons." His voice was choked with tears.

Janlin looked away, fighting tears of her own. She found Natl watching her, making no effort to hide it.

"And how is it you find yourself helping my grandson?"

Janlin shuffled her feet. "Well, I was the pilot of the first shuttle that he stowed away on."

"Oh, sure, I figured that out listening to Tanner rant on these past two weeks. But how did you end up here this time?" Her eyes sparkled with mischievousness, and Janlin decided honesty was the best policy.

"He kidnapped me and hijacked my ship."

"Now wait a minute," Ceirin started in at once, but Janlin continued.

"And then I crashed it."

Natl nodded in approval of this brutal and simple honesty. "So, you weren't always lovers?"

Ceirin choked a little, standing now with Harriot in his arms.

Janlin felt a grin growing. "Ah, no," she admitted. "Quarantine was boring."

Natl burst out laughing. Harriot joined her, her toddler's chuckles making them all laugh, until the whole room dissolved into near-hysterics. Harriot got the hiccups.

"Oh, my," Natl said, wiping her eyes and chuckling still. "I think I like you, Janlin Kavanagh." Then she turned her steely gaze on Ceirin.

CHAPTER THIRTY-ONE

"Gran," Ceirin said, "I'm so sorry, I never thought to be gone so long."

"Oh, clearly, and thankfully your plan to keep us safe worked."

Ceirin glanced at Janlin. "Gran holds the code to the NDB powercells that run everything here: food processing, crop management, waste disposal, you name it."

"Hey, I just learned about those. Something about using up nuclear waste from the nuclear energy boom of the '50s to create long-lasting batteries?"

He nodded. "They've been a lifesaver when all the lithium batteries conked out. I'm not surprised to hear SpaceOp is still using that technology. Anyway, we set it up that if Natl died while I was away on that hunting trip, then they all died."

"Even Harriot?"

Natl jumped in. "When he told the others, Tanner protested the same thing, and Ceirin told the whole crew of them they better make sure I lived, then. No pressure." She cackled.

Ceirin was unapologetic in his fatalism. "If Gran died, especially due to something Tanner had planned, then Harriot was in big trouble anyway. It was the best security we could think of. Made Gran an asset to protect instead of a liability to dispose of."

Natl lowered herself back into her chair, clearly in need of it, and Harriot ran to climb up into her lap. The scene was so cute, but Janlin could clearly see the cruel effects of malnutrition. The senior was frail, ravaged by more than old age. The tiny child was too skinny, but her belly bloated, and she had thin, patchy hair and pallid skin. It was a sight that would drive a father to stowaway on a space shuttle, steal food, and hijack a ride home. Janlin felt a new pang of guilt for crashing the Seraph. *In that way lies madness*, she heard her father saying. *When you screw up, own it and make amends.* She wished she knew how. They had to get back to the Seraph and see what was left, and if it would fly.

"When we met, what were you doing out there anyway? If it weren't for that," Janlin said, waving between them, "none of this would've happened."

He shook his head in wonder. "It is strange how I got involved, really. I told them it was none of my business, how other folks ran their survival bunkers. But Tanner's buddy Rickard, Galena's brother-in-law, returned from seeing them with a horror story of Galena having killed and eaten his brother. They said if I went with them to investigate, we could convince her to come back here with us for her safety. They really played on my heartstrings with that. No pregnant girl should be in such dire straits if it could be helped. But the girl ran. She knew how Rickard was gunning for her and well, you were there for how that turned out." Both of them shuddered. "When we found you, that's when I saw an opportunity and took it," he said. "I never meant to be gone so long, a few days at most. And," he swallowed, looking at Natl and then away, "I failed at bringing food or any help at all."

"You found her," Natl pointed out.

There it was, that ready grin that made her insides glow. "Good point, Gran."

ONCE NATL HAD served them tea and a fine sweet biscuit she said tasted better than it had any right to, Ceirin announced it was time they showed her around proper.

They got Natl settled in her wheelchair, and Harriot promptly climbed up into her lap, obviously well-accustomed to the motorized chair her great-granny used.

They took an elevator that had only one stop available on the panel, but it seemed a long ride. The door slid away to reveal a concrete cavern with sectioned off "rooms", harvesting tents, grow tubes, and a mess of gear, hoses, wires, tubes, tools, and bric-a-brac, all clumped together here and there for various purposes, and quite a mess.

Natl grimaced. "I try," she started, but Ceirin cut her off.

"And Tanner's men do little but make a further mess, am I right?" Ceirin had white lines of anger under his eyes in an otherwise red fury-infused face. Janlin almost expected him to growl, he was so livid.

"Dada?" Harriot shrank into Natl's lap. "Dada mad?"

"Oh, sweetie," Natl said, pulling her into a big, comforting hug and shooting Ceirin a cease-and-desist order over the child's head. "Dada is mad at Tanner, not you."

Harriot peered up at Ceirin, who had assembled the calmest, kindest face he could under the circumstances. "I am safe, Harriot my love, even if I'm upset."

Several shipping containers like the ones once used on rail cars and freighters were lined along one wall, some open, some locked up tight. "I'll show you inside the sealed grow rooms later," he said, gesturing further down the row. "They run micro-greens in moving hydroponic systems that require little maintenance. We found keeping them sealed off kept the mould growth down." He looked sad. "I miss planting above ground, in the dirt, and just waiting for it to rain."

"Sometimes it's hard to believe it was even real, that back when," Janlin said. "Things devolved so fast."

Natl agreed. "You think you've seen changes," she said, rolling her eyes. Harriot watched this and then copied her perfectly, and they all laughed.

"This way," Ceirin murmured in her ear, his warm hand on her back, resulting in a cascade of goosebumps down her neck and shoulder.

"Things were already turning when I was born at the turn of the century," Natl said as she wheeled ahead of them.

She drove up a ramp into one container and they followed. Their boots rang hollow on the metal floor, and they skirted around mounds of various and sundry building materials, supplies, tool bins, hardware, and shelving full of more. There wasn't a lot of room, but a clear and obvious path wound through it all that the wheelchair could navigate.

"This is our pantry," Natl said, and Janlin stared in wonder at the jars of preserves lining the shelves. There were hanging braided garlic and bunches of dried herbs, tubs of sand that revealed carrots and potatoes stored safely within. "This is the only reason we're still here, but the food is deficient, and the supplies dwindle. Worse, our crops produce less each year, no matter how we try. It's hard to keep hope."

They moved on, all a bit quiet, even Harriot. She kept staring at Ceirin as if he might disappear at any second, and she just couldn't figure him out.

Janlin just stared at it all. In another area stood a varied assortment of exercise equipment with what looked like a swim spa. They had places just like this on the Orbitals, and at Luna Base, and she was sure they were part of the Mars Colony too. But to find this here, now, underground and dirtside, well, it was astonishing!

"It's not a pool," Ceirin said, "but if you get the pumps going . . ."

". . . you can swim against the current," she finished for him. "We do have them on Spectra, there just hasn't been enough water to support running it."

"Yeah, I heard that. We have our own fears of when the lights die," he admitted.

He explained that one of the power cells failed last year and no matter what they tried it wouldn't run again.

"We're now eating more bugs and algae than anything else," he said. "There's even one mould we are experimenting with."

Janlin's gut flipped over. She thought about the biscuits that Natl had said were better than they had a right to be. Maybe she didn't want to know what was in them.

"Tell me more about your resonant frequency work?" she asked.

Natl answered first. "NECS can be programmed to emulate a cell, an enzyme, an antibody, or a virus. It's mostly about the signal they give off that communicates to the surrounding cells how to react. Simple, and immensely difficult. We must always ensure they are carefully coded to be very singular in their individual purpose, and to never use networking software of any kind that would allow the nanites to form their own sentience."

"An AI," Janlin murmured. "Linder, one of our accomplished nano-scientists, mentioned the dangers of that when we were exploring options to stop the Jump dissonance."

"Imagine for a moment if a group of nanites, enough of them, were able to network and create an AI . . . on the Station where life depends on digital *everything* . . ."

Janlin shuddered. "So, that's why we can't send in repair nanites to upgrade them, then?"

"Exactly," Ceirin said. "It's like molecular programming, like an enzyme does, see. The stem cells specialize as they go, and can adapt if the programming is in place, but networking them together in a being with the brain as a source of computing power is asking for trouble."

Natl waved a finger. "People's big mistake was to see nanites as mechanical beings, tiny machines, but you need to picture them more as electrical beings that send signals to your cells, to your very DNA, to change the story, hopefully in a way we like," she said. "But be aware, it could go the other way too. We could lose control. It's a real threat."

Janlin could only agree, even if she didn't understand the science of it. It made sense to trust those who did.

Harriot tired quickly. Natl took her on her lap again, and the two of them went above to put dinner on.

"It smells like stew, just don't ask what's in it," she called back, and they all laughed.

Once alone, Ceirin pulled her close and they walked together. "Down here is a lab tent where I'm growing simple nanites I hope will repair the soil and purify the water."

"Grown like plants, eh? Is that how they're all made?"

"Yes, especially your biological ones, the NECS."

"Wow, and I never thought to wonder. I guess I assumed they were purely mechanical, processed in a factory, that kinda thing. Natl is right, we've made a lot of mistakes and assumptions."

Ceirin agreed. "The first purely mechanical NECS were rejected by the host so often, they turned to growing them more organically," he said. "I knew I would have to get an injection of NECS somehow if *Hope* didn't return. My physiology was being affected by the lighter gravity and strange food. I was befriending Cassie and Li towards that end. Then you guys finally returned, and you gave me a way home instead."

Janlin ducked her head. "I'm sorry I screwed it up so bad."

Ceirin waved it off. "Seriously, I didn't handle it well either. I was in too much of a rush to get back. I'd heard you folks were suffering PTSD, and then I pointed a taser at you? I'm surprised I'm alive to apologize, to be honest."

She had to laugh at that. "It's funny 'cause it's true," she said, getting him to laugh too.

Janlin scanned the tiny lab. Ceirin waved her over to a sealed unit and proudly presented a view of . . . not much. "What exactly am I looking at here?" she asked, bending to look at rows of glass dishes with a smear of clear gel inside each one.

"There's hundreds of thousands of nanites in there, little mechanical molecules that can be programmed to do a simple thing, like deliver a microbe to plant roots, or prevent a certain fungus from destroying a plant. My thought now is to grow ones to send out a certain frequency to quell the dissonance and help with the Jumps. As opposed to simply repairing damage with surgery nubots. Isn't that what you were trying with Anaya?"

She raised an eyebrow at him. "Wow, you really have been keeping up, eh?"

He blushed a little. "Extenuating circumstances," he pleaded. She had to give him that.

"You might really be on to something, but you would have to reveal your existence," Janlin reminded him. She hoped he would waver on that point. He looked somewhat resigned to it already.

"I guess I've come around to understand the need for other humans, the sharing of research, and new opportunities for my daughter."

She squeezed him tight. "Come on, I want to watch you with Harriot and tease some old stories of your childhood from Natl."

He laughed and they made their way back. "Wait," he said, turning back. "There's something I want to give you."

CHAPTER THIRTY-ONE

WHEN CEIRIN FIRST held out his hand, she couldn't see anything at all, it was so small and thin. But it didn't take her long to recognize what she was seeing.

"It's a music player, among other things," Ceirin said as she lifted the tiny little silver disc from his palm with some astonishment. "I wish I'd had one along with me when I ended up stowing away with you."

"Unreal," she said. "I had something just like this once." She told him about the one she had managed to keep with her through all the Imag torture, and her Huantag adventures, only to have it hold a vital piece Gordon needed to fix the comm unit Stepper had smashed, thus saving the day.

Ceirin shook his head in wonder. "That bit wasn't in your public version of the story," he said.

"It was hard to cover everything," she admitted.

"Well, this is similar, able to hold songs and holo images." He showed her where he stored the song list. She tapped on the very first one, and it was the song she had first played by fluke . . . the same one they had sung along to a hundred times since. She thought her heart might burst it felt so full.

"On the wings of maybe," she said, smiling up at him. "Thank you. This is amazing."

As the song played on, Ceirin pulled out a chain so she could wear the disc around her neck. As soon as it was on and latched, he drew her to him again, enveloping her in his embrace, and kissed her forehead.

"We better get upstairs for dinner. Hate to miss that."

It might be nice to be stuck dirtside, she thought as they rode the elevator. The doors opened and they could smell the "stew". She wondered what it was made of.

"Do you think Huantag seeds would survive down here?" she asked.

"Maybe," he said. "Since there seems little hope for our ecosystem anymore, introducing new biology at this point is probably worth the risk."

Janlin sighed with relief. "Just make it clear the situation down here is no better, and maybe worse, than up there, and then you shouldn't be invaded by visitors."

THEY ENJOYED THE mystery stew, especially with Harriot being so adorable and Natl so interesting.

"The molecules that make the nanites that Ceirin is growing can be outfitted with a sensor to locate certain types of cells," she explained. "We hope the technology can enhance the soil's mitochondria, and maybe even do a seek and destroy on some of the toxins."

"Can we do that with the NECS? Even though Ceirin has disabled mine, they are still fouling inside of me and need help."

Natl gave her a pained look. "I'm sorry to hear that. It was one of the risks that SpaceOp decided to take."

"What does it look like when the body rejects them initially?" Her thoughts were still very much with Anaya. Ceirin rose to gather plates and clear the table.

Natl moved her chair expertly to the sink and ran some dishwater, Harriot climbing up to add soap in pumps. "Exhausted, feverish, and your limbs would ache."

Janlin told Natl about Anaya and how they'd injected her with surgery nubots to hopefully repair any brain damage. "When we left, she didn't have a fever, but we have no way of knowing if Gitane get fevers."

"How long had it been since the injection?" Natl asked.

"Three days."

"Machines tend to work faster as their size decreases, and can be programmed to replicate themselves, or construct things of themselves. Nubots are the nano-robots used for repairs, surgeries, power system diagnostics and patching, etc., and they're tiny, so they should work fast."

Janlin slumped. "Seems like they didn't help her, then."

Ceirin gave her hand a reassuring squeeze. "If the system is alien, it may simply take longer for the nubots to decide how to help," he offered. She loved him for it.

"I just wish I could be done with them completely," Janlin said, her voice catching. "Wish I'd never started, like you folks. Wish I could be free of them forever."

"Don't be so quick to let them go," Natl said, waving a hand. "Those things are certainly all that made your Jump possible, yeah? I mean, they couldn't correct it all . . . so much dissonance to go so far, but not move, all at the same time, yikes . . . but no, you need them if you're going to Jump, Janlin. I believe they are the answer to our survival here, too, but they need more capabilities built-in. We have to make them work for us, and find a way to control whatever develops, yeah?"

Ceirin shook his head. "Gran, we all know that way lies madness." To Janlin he said, "You won't survive space again, not without a new injection."

She gave a little shrug. "After what's happened with the ones in me, I'm not excited for any more, thanks."

"Personally, I wish we could move around more easily," Natl fussed. "Like a Jump, but without the ship, without all the muck-a-bruck. Can you imagine? Just 'pop'," she snapped her fingers, "and be there instead of here."

"Pop," Harriot mimicked.

Ceirin snorted. "Sounds like a fairy tale, Gran, and look at the damage it's caused those that Jumped," he said, indicating Janlin. Harriot snorted, a perfect copy of her father. Janlin held in her laughter, Harriot grinning at her.

"Anyone from eighty years ago wouldn't even believe she Jumped to a different solar system, yet she did! And lived to tell the tale. And it sounds like sci-fi, silly, not fantasy, get yer genres straight." He laughed at that.

"Unfortunately, the side-effects are terrifying and may very well keep us from trying again," Janlin said, taking Natl quite seriously. "We could do without crew dying after a Jump."

That was met with grim agreement.

"And if you want such easy travel, won't you have to take the NECS eventually?"

Natl sighed. "We may well need them here at some point, to survive Earth's evolution anyway, allowing us to process nutrients, survive storms, drink toxic water. The ones mending the soil won't be enough."

Ceirin stared out the window at the storm water slashing the glass brick they used to reinforce the window openings. "Some will become space nomads, while others tended the shores of home," he waxed poetic.

"I like that! Sounds like song lyrics."

Janlin sat with Ceirin and Harriot as Natl wheeled off into the back rooms. They were playing with a spinning top fashioned out of wood, and every time Ceirin made it go, Harriot squealed and clapped in delight.

Natl came rolling back at speed.

"Tanner's missing."

CHAPTER THIRTY-TWO

JANLIN WAS PUZZLED, both by how Natl knew and why this was news.

Natl looked straight at her. "He's after salvage."

Janlin came to her feet. "The Seraph?"

"But, how?" Ceirin said, also on his feet. Outside they were being thrashed hard by winds gusting up over 160 kilometres per hour. The constant banging of debris and roar of wind had become part of the background. Ceirin had told her they couldn't navigate to the barn in this weather without rope leads and protective gear.

Natl sighed. She seemed apologetic. "Remember the 'Hellion'?"

Ceirin gave her an incredulous look. "You can't be serious."

"He's been at it since you left, and been clearing old roadways during pockets, too. The Traders told me they came upon him and he tried to make it out he was hunting. They don't seem to like Tanner much. I overheard Rickard saying they would go all 'Mad Max' on the Traders."

Janlin knew that Mad Max was an old twentieth century movie reference, but had never seen it. The before time movies where they played at what was now her real life had never held her attention. There was some irony in that.

"So, Tanner's got some armoured car and he's going for the Seraph?" Janlin asked.

Ceirin groaned, and Natl sighed. "He told me it wouldn't run, but now both he and the Hellion are gone, along with some supplies. I'm sorry. We hadn't time to talk of it yet."

"Not your fault, Gran," Ceirin growled. Harriot's eyes widened, and he promptly comforted her.

"There's a good chance the thing will break down on him anyway," Natl offered hopefully.

"I want to get back there before he does," Janlin said to Ceirin. "He has no right to any of it . . ."

"Okay, I hear you," Ceirin said, palms out. "But we don't have a Hellion."

"The Traders. You told me they have vehicles made to shelter in. Ask them." She knew Ceirin had some weird aversion to the Traders, and spoke of them like they were lesser beings, but from all she could see they were just people surviving any way they could. She was curious about them.

Natl was horrified. "Traders are scum people," she declared. Janlin was stunned, but Ceirin was nodding in agreement. "They bring disease with their goods, and eat carrion. Besides, they would never agree to transport you. They're frightened of us having germs, can you believe it?"

Janlin could, actually. "They have good reason to be cautious, if they travel from place to place all the time. Maybe they stay safe by reducing contact."

Natl was waving her off, unwilling to listen. "They can't blame us for whatever diseases they carry around," she said. "You would be foolish to deal with them. They might even eat you!"

Now Janlin really did blink a few times trying to compute this. "Has there been any actually instances of this happening?" she asked.

"No," Ceirin said, recognizing Janlin's train of thought. "Tanner and his questionable crew of friends is the only place we've actually seen that." It was a concession, Janlin could hear it in his voice.

She struggled to get her head around the situation. "These Traders, they bring you goods you wouldn't otherwise have, right?"

"Yes," Natl admitted. "We depend on them for sugar and salt, and they sell hardware, medicines, and cloth, too."

"And have they ever done anything other than bring goods and take their pay?" Janlin asked. Natl's face twisted. "And didn't you just say they don't like Tanner? That for me is a vote of confidence. I'm only trying to understand why we wouldn't ask for help if they could give it. Maybe I have something they need that I can trade for."

There was a long silence punctuated only by the storm sounds.

"There are stories of people that disappeared after riding with the Traders," Ceirin said.

"Stories," Janlin said, "like urban myths?"

Ceirin's face hardened. "The bunker the storytellers once lived in was taken over as a Trader's sanctuary. The way Tanner tells the story, his own cousins were killed and their home taken from them by the Traders, and they were scared to take it back because of the way Traders carry disease."

Now Janlin really had to tread carefully, but she needed them to see how they sounded. "So, this is Tanner's story?"

Ceirin sighed and rubbed his face. "Not just his, the people I sheltered early on had stories too, ones of the Traders being faceless because they were previously convicted criminals, and worse stories of disease laying waste to whole colonies after the Traders moved through. And," he said, making sure he had her attention, "those dome colonies emptied by plague were then settled by Trader families. Our mistrust in them isn't completely based on Tanner's story."

"Okay, fine, I can see that," Janlin said, "but I still don't have a way back to my ship. If you two don't mind, I'd like to ask them for a ride."

Ceirin shrugged at Natl. "At least she has a mind of her own," he said, but his grandmother snorted and turned her chair away.

"If you can put me in contact with them, I don't expect you to be involved," Janlin said to him.

"No," Ceirin assured her, "we're in this together."

IT WAS SURPRISINGLY easy. Ceirin sent out a beacon that requested Trader help, and within the hour they heard back and Janlin had a ride to the crash site. All it cost her was the promise of two NDB batteries the Seraph was carrying, backups that she shouldn't need to fly.

When she'd first proposed this, Ceirin was doubtful. "The Seraph and her contents, including those batteries, might be damaged by the EMP I used on you," he started, but Janlin felt confident they wouldn't be.

"You said you did that outside. Stepper built those ships to withstand a lot, and they're heavily shielded. Don't worry, there's a good chance she'll fly, and there might be some stores still salvageable."

"Fair enough," he said. "We did survive the crash, after all." He handed her fresh filters and an old rebreather face mask from the locker. "Yours don't cover the eyes, and that needs protected too. Just in case."

She conceded to his precautions, and they prepared to leave the compound. Ceirin waved to the big house, the two shadows in the window waving back.

"It's going to be a long couple weeks again," Ceirin said with a sigh. Janlin blinked at him, then it sank in. Being with the Traders like this would mean quarantine all over again.

"Ceirin, you don't have to come with me," Janlin said. On the other side of the gate, the Traders emerged from their armoured vehicles. Most wore layers of clothing enwrapping every bit of bare skin, some wore old leather suits for motorbiking, one had old fireman's gear . . . but each and every one of them wore a plague doctor mask with a long, downward sloping nose piece and full facial coverage. They looked alien.

Janlin shivered. Wind tore at their clothes, but those masks were firmly in place and she expected they would stay there. Thank all the gods she couldn't spread the Imag nanite virus to them.

"Go back," she urged Ceirin, a hand on his chest to push him away. "I'll go have a look at the Seraph, bring her back here, do quarantine . . ."

Ceirin was watching the Trader's approach. "No," he said softly. He studied everything he could before he dropped his gaze and pulled on his mask.

Did he not trust her, maybe? Or did he want to keep an eye on her? She didn't like her suspicion, but how well did she really know this guy? Her gut churned.

Two Traders approached, one much taller than the rest, the other much shorter and moving in a way that indicated old age. The rest stood scattered around the other vehicles with thumbs in belts heavy with weapons. There was quite a variety of rigs;

some were shaped for speed with smaller compartments and doors and fierce-looking engines, while others were large lumbering old refurbished RVs, tankers, or delivery trucks.

Janlin pulled on her own mask, her heart racing now. Whatever his motivation, she was actually quite glad of Ceirin's company in this moment.

The tall Trader waved them to the open door of the closest car, one of the smaller, faster looking ones. Their faceless stare had Janlin spooked. No wonder they scared people and elicited urban-myth-style rumours.

At least, she hoped they were rumours.

Janlin gripped Ceirin's hand in gratitude for his presence. "Are you sure," she yelled through the mask and wind noise.

He squeezed. "Tanner is as much my problem as the Seraph, just as they are now both your concern. Like I said, babe, we're in this together."

She could see his eyes crinkle up in a smile through the full facemask viewscreen. Janlin gave a decided nod.

Let's do this.

CLOSER UP SHE could see the vehicle was an old ambulance coated in sheet metal armour welded to the frame. Within, they were greeted by a hoarder's delight of gear, wires, clothing, and weaponry. A bench seat seemed recently swept clear for them. The tall Trader had already stepped into the control seat up front.

The small, slow Trader sat in the passenger seat, swivelling her chair around to face them. Holos floated around them both, and often they would tend one or another's holos as much as their own. Still, she could feel the small one's curious regard.

Janlin wished she could see their eyes, at least. It was so hard to judge the human within. She put her gloved hands together in a gesture of thanks, and bowed her head. The plague mask bobbed in acknowledgement, and the chair swivelled back to face the windshield.

They tore around the valley that had taken hours to hike, then instead of the route through the slide area, went more east and circled the hilled ridges, following old pavement.

Janlin only knew this by following the holo live map tracking them that was part of the array within the close confines of the Trader vehicle. There were no windows but for the tiny one the driver peered through.

A strange mark in the holo eventually grew close enough to render out as Tanner's Hellion. It wasn't moving, probably broken down just as Natl had predicted. Just beyond it was the Seraph.

"He's going for it on foot," came Ceirin's muffled voice.

Janlin wondered what strange salvage rules of the dirtside world might exist saying he could claim her ship just because he "found" it before they could return. "I will fight him if I have to," Janlin said. Ceirin looked to be laughing, but he'd turned away, and it was hard to read body language in the protective suits they wore.

When their little marker reached the Seraph's, the rocking and vibrations stopped, and the layers of doors opened.

Janlin was surprised to see other Trader vehicles circling in from behind them as she exited the vehicle. "What's this?" she asked Ceirin, wondering if they could hear the exchange.

"I don't know," Ceirin said, drawing the words out as he scoped the situation.

Tanner whipped out a rifle and pointed it at the circling Traders, jerking it from one to another. Janlin realized they were honing in on him.

"You filthy diseased rats," Tanner screamed as he fired, the bullet bouncing off metal. Ceirin cursed and pulled Janlin in behind their ride. The circling cars were impervious to the rapid firing, and they closed in closer and closer before stopping. "Y'all tainted! Yer wrong in the head, you know. I seen what you done, I know more than you think, you can't deny it." He fired off a couple more shots, then cursed and began to reload.

Traders flooded out and pushed in so quickly, Janlin could no longer even see the man. She heard him shout, though, heard the fear in his voice as he cried for his gun's return. She saw the gun quickly get stashed away in one of the vehicles.

Their escorts emerged behind them, and gave them the same gesture Janlin had just done. Janlin shrugged at Ceirin and repeated it back.

"Thank you. Can you please wait?" she asked the Trader. After a pause the long hooked-beak mask nodded.

Ceirin was receiving text messages. "They are happy to help, and glad we led them to this 'stinking pile of offal' whom they apparently have charges against."

Janlin had to laugh. "They mean Tanner, I assume?" They had cuffed him and pushed him inside one of their tankers.

Ceirin huffed. "They are listing a horrid accounting of stolen goods, dead Traders, and eaten corpses that he is to stand trial for, and assuring me he would be offered appropriate legal counsel to defend him. I didn't even know they held trials, or had a legal system, or any of this."

Ceirin was then faced with the small one. Janlin wondered what the Trader had overheard of Ceirin's confession.

To their amazement, the Trader removed the iconic mask, revealing a woman easily Natl's age.

"I am Bella," she said. "Are you the McNair boy?" Ceirin could only nod, wide-eyed. "You tell your grandmother hello from an old school friend. Tell her she needs to rethink her stance on Traders. We are simply survivors just like you, and we need to work together as one."

CHAPTER THIRTY-THREE

CEIRIN COULD ONLY blink in complete surprise. Janlin cuffed him and bowed to Bella, pulling her own mask off.

"Thank you, and I hope Natl will listen." She extended a hand.

The wind spun up new funnels that made them squint, and to the west a distant wall of sand moved down the slopes of the Rockies, wiping any view a dozen klicks wide . . . and coming right at them. Janlin stood steady, her arm stretched out.

Bella took her hand with gentle respect.

"Thank you for the ride, and for keeping us all a little safer now that Tanner is detained," Janlin said. "Let me go find the batteries I promised you."

Bella had some questions for Ceirin about Tanner. Janlin paced towards the Seraph, anxious to stake her claim physically and tally the damage.

The outer hatch was sealed as promised, but the inner door wasn't, and it looked jammed. To be fair, the place was on fire when Ceirin hauled her out. She shoved it further open and climbed in.

The floor was tilted but intact, and a quick pull at a bent storage bin revealed the goods Ceirin had stashed aboard. He came up to the opening behind her, and she began passing out the bins for inspection. Two on the outer edge were melted shut, burned in the fire, but the rest seemed okay.

Once the locker was empty and closed up, she moved into the

cockpit. From within she heard him conversing with the Traders, now animated and interested, and full of questions for them. Janlin flipped switches and booted up holo diagnostics, and peered out while she waited for them to come online.

Ceirin was doling out supplies from the bins to waiting hands. "We will have to compare notes on how well these grow, and which ones taste best," he was saying. "Yes, truly, they are alien, can you believe it?"

Janlin could only grin. He had a new perspective, and would bring both his grandmother and daughter along with him, she was sure. Maybe the humans of Earth had some hope after all.

She flipped through holos, seeing plenty of minor repairs and only a few major issues, like a couple of dead thrusters. Janlin set the computer to calculate adjustments for the loss of those and tried her comms next.

"Janlin, we don't have much more time," Ceirin called. She could feel the ship rocking under the blasts of storm-driven winds.

"Can you get the inner door to seal?" she called, then activating the mic, said, "Spectra Station, this is Janlin Kavanagh, do you read?"

Nothing but static. She ran a few more tests and saw she could launch if she had a seal on that door. She would go limping into port, but it would suffice to get her home.

Except this could be home now, she realized with a jolt. Or was that just the floor, still on a tilt and rocking with the storm?

Things grew quieter. She tried the orbital a couple more times, put it on repeat, then started a scan for any kind of signal at all.

". . . Spectra . . . Janlin? Can you hear . . ." followed by garbled words and static. Then, "My name is Lauren. Please, if you can . . ." which faded out to nothing. Ceirin climbed into the cockpit area.

"Got the door closed," he said, but she waved him quiet. With a couple swipes, she put the transmission up on speaker.

Static. Warbled words fading in and out. "My name is Lauren, I need to speak to Janlin . . ."

Ceirin's blue gaze was full of questions.

"She's from the Mars Colony," Janlin said. "It's not live, it's on a loop." She shook her head. "Why hasn't anyone answered her from Spectra?"

"Either they aren't listening," Ceirin said, "or they don't care."

". . . Spectra Station or Janlin? Can you hear me?"

Janlin worked to clean up the connection before the storm wiped it out completely.

"Please if you can, we need to reach Janlin. My name is Lauren . . ."

"Dammit," Janlin muttered. It started again, a few familiar parts, nothing really new, then words came through that changed everything.

". . . Anaya's here with me, we need help . . ."

CHAPTER THIRTY-FOUR

"SHE'S ALIVE." IT took a moment to step back from the fear that Anaya had died in that medbay machine. "She's alive and, what the hell, on Mars? With Lauren?" Janlin was completely overcome. What had happened in the few weeks she'd been gone? "They need help!"

The broken-up broadcast continued to loop, fading in and out, only bits and pieces coming through, but the main point was clear.

She turned from the holo to see Ceirin standing there in the doorway and two things hit her immediately: one, that she needed to go help Anaya, and two, that he couldn't come. She felt cracked open inside, shattered at the loss she must face. "I can't leave her, I have to go . . ."

He took two steps and silenced her with a kiss. "I wouldn't expect anything less."

"Can you help me get this thing flight ready?"

They turned to the console as one and began setting up scans and testing runs on the various systems.

Janlin's brain was running overtime, and she wanted Ceirin to understand the situation, so she began trying to explain it. "I'm terrified Stepper is loose. He would be deadly to their population," she summed up.

Ceirin frowned. "But if it's all digital, and Diona figured out how to turn it off, then Stepper wasn't the danger you're making him out to be." Then he said, with scorn, "Whose bright idea was it anyway to let Diona have her brother if he was so dangerous?"

Janlin winced. "Mine."

Ceirin looked like he had swallowed a stone. "God, I'm sorry, I'll just shut up now, I don't even know what I'm talking about. Although, I sense there's more to this . . . Why do you need to run to this guy so bad?"

"It's my responsibility. It *was* my idea to trade him for freedom when Diona was going to arrest us all. It was *also* my idea to bring Anaya home with us." It was also her idea to fancy crash the Seraph to knock Ceirin out. Lucky for her that actually worked out okay in the end, but this string of bad ideas weighed on her conscience. "All of that aside, though, Anaya is my guest, my *friend*, and I have to help her now. Good grief, she probably went to Mars looking for me. I have to go. I couldn't live with myself otherwise."

"It's a bit risky, taking new NECS, and a Jump is truly a bad idea especially thanks to . . ."

She couldn't tell if he was only speaking his worst fears, or trying to talk her out of leaving, but her blood pressure soared and she shouted, "I will risk anything to help Anaya!"

Janlin realized Ceirin was calling her, holding her, right in her face.

"Listen, I'm not trying to stop you."

"What?" Janlin took a deep breath, shook her head a bit. She'd been all ready for a fight. "Really?"

"Really," Ceirin said, looking incredibly relieved that she was listening. Janlin thought on this, and recognized she was probably reacting to someone other than Ceirin. *Gordon.*

"I'm sorry. What were you trying to say?"

He shook his head. "Just be careful. A new dose of NECS doesn't guarantee safe Jumps, okay?"

She ran a shaky hand through her hair. "I have to Jump; how can I be of any help if I'm weeks away?" she said. Ceirin had that look that said only she could answer such a difficult question. He pulled her into a hug.

"You better go. This pocket won't last." But he didn't release her. "Or you could stay," he said to her surprise, sweet wistfulness to his voice. "Let them figure themselves out or not. You don't have to risk yourself, Janlin."

She cupped his face and kissed him deeply. He was tense, but then he melted, and they both came up breathless some moments later. She laughed, her heart sizzling with his love and the thrill of new adventure.

"Remember you asked me what *I* wanted?"

His eyes narrowed. "You were not my favourite person back then," he chuckled.

"True, but it was a valid question, so here's your answer. I love to fly, and explore, and take risks like folding space to find new friends like Anaya." She met his gaze square on. "Truth is, I love the thrill. I'm sorry I can't just stay here with you and let it all go. It would drive me mad."

He considered, giving her a wistful smile. "I can see the truth in that."

"I wish I didn't have to add more nanites to my system," she said.

"Maybe you won't need a new shot," he said. "I'm sure there's someone up there that could help with a reboot? That Steve guy you seem so fond of?"

She had to laugh at his hint of jealousy. "Steve who is newly and madly in love with Mark?" She winked as he made a little "oh" sound.

"I really gotta stop putting my foot in my mouth today," he said.

Janlin laughed. "Steve, Linder, Huey, and Duey are already working on the bio-fouling and possible reprogramming as well."

Ceirin got a pensive look. "I'm still worried, to be honest. I don't want a deluge of people here I can't feed."

"No, I can't agree with that. Knowledge is power, and holding back truth leads to toxic secrets and horrible misunderstandings. I might not reveal exactly where you are, but everyone up there needs to talk about the fact you exist."

"Why offer false hope?" Ceirin countered.

"Is it false, though?"

He considered. "Well, we're starving, you're starving, and we're learning Mars isn't the safe haven we had hoped for. Jumps appear potentially deadly." He squeezed her arm. "Where are you finding your hope, exactly?"

Janlin struggled with the reality of not having much, in that light. "If I think too much that way, I won't be able to move at all.

I'd rather have something to work towards and go after it. Like your resonance idea, which could make Jumps safe so we can find refuge, food, and new friends. The fact I've Jumped, survived aliens, and returned proves it's possible, we just need better gear."

Ceirin scooped her up in his arms and twirled her around, setting joy surging through her despite everything. "Janlin Kavanagh, you are a marvel," he said, setting her back down all breathless. "You not only find hope in what seems hopeless, you have solid reasoning behind it. How could I ever doubt you?"

Janlin glowed. "Whatever the case, and however it all works out, I want to be able to talk to Gordon and Ursula and want to confide in them. Please let me offer them this small hope. There could be nothing more perfect than if we could all live here one day, together."

Then it really hit them both how far away she would be going now. She gripped him with some small despair. "I'm not as cheery as I seem on the inside, you know." She walked him to the door, and he opened it to the howling winds blowing sand straight sideways. The Traders' vehicles were all gone now but for the one they rode out in, waiting there for the return ride.

"What can you do, yeah?"

They leaned on each other. "Love what's left," Janlin said.

"And try to protect your own small piece of it, if given the chance, right?" Ceirin asked.

"Would if I could."

"Come back to me," he said then, gripping both her hands in his. "Do what you have to out there, but come back, yeah?"

"I will," she promised.

Janlin looked out over the remnants of the pine and spruce forests lifting into the jagged rocky peaks of mountains. Acidic soil, perfect for trees and wild rose bushes, not so great for vegetables. There wasn't a ton of diversity here even before the climate crash. The landscape just couldn't support it. Now, everything was compounded. All the issues grew exponentially and piled on top of each other. Storms had become the norm, and the water was contaminated, the soil lifeless.

But . . . all the work Ursula was doing with crops in orbit and on Luna Base could help here, too. If they worked together, pooling their resources and knowledge, and utilized the Huantag seeds they had brought, there really was hope, in her mind.

"Truth is, I'd rather go with you," he admitted.

"Really?" Janlin felt a surge of elation.

"Oh, yeah," he assured her. "As much as I grew to hate SpaceOp, I longed to explore, and loved—still love—a good sci-fi story where they magically 'jump' to other worlds. And here you've actually done that. Plus," and here he began to turn an interesting shade of pink, "I'd like to be with you. Always. Through anything."

Janlin's heart grew larger by degrees while her own face heated. Her mouth ran off before the brain could catch up. *"Could you come with me? Could we set Natl up with that fail-safe again?"*

Ceirin gave her a desperate look. "I would have to take NECS."

"No," she immediately said, sure of herself in that one thing at least. "I'll find a way back," she promised. "I still need to teach you some crib strategies." Her teasing broke the unbearable tension she had created with such a request, and brought them to the moment. Of course, he couldn't come with her. She knew that.

Everything was ready. The opening in the weather wouldn't last.

"I'd better go." She tightened her grip. He couldn't, wouldn't, abandon Natl and Harriot again anyway, she understood that, and expected nothing else, but oh how she wished it were different. She pulled away. He let go.

"On the wings of maybe . . ." she said. She had to bite her lip hard to keep her composure.

"On the wings of maybe," he replied, his voice gruff. "We'll have our chance, Kavanagh, some day."

She turned away before she changed her mind. They both had their responsibilities, and Anaya was hers.

So was Stepper.

She shoved into the pilot's chair a bit too hard, glad for the distraction of strapping in. Glad to be powering up for flight. Glad to know Anaya and Lauren were alive. Glad she had had what she did with Ceirin. But her heart was breaking into a gazillion pieces, and she wished somehow it could all be just a little easier.

The wind was as fierce as ever. She ran her check, read the storm front to gain as much lift from it as possible, and readied to launch into the sky.

Her skin felt like it glowed from Ceirin's touch, and that warred with the ache of leaving. She would return, without a doubt, and with plenty more supplies. This gave her some small hope for the future, especially if Jumps proved too dangerous. Some small hope for her heart, too. She soared over the foothills, tears running as the thrusters engaged.

On the wings of maybe . . .

CHAPTER THIRTY-FIVE

Diona didn't mean to sleep. She had so much to take care of, so much to make sure stayed hidden. But the body had limits, and she had pushed it beyond what it could handle.

She thrashed her way through the reoccurring nightmare. Her stuffed bear dangled from her hand while the sirens screamed, sirens, always the sirens, and the flashing lights strobed across her mother's convulsing body . . .

Diona's dream self held the ragged stuffed bear in a death grip, a morbid keepsake, as she watched the scene like some separate entity.

That day they had played together, a tea party with her dolls and bears, her mother relaxing on pillows. "You must be strong," she had told Diona. She was five, Stepper two. Only five. Yet she could sense something was wrong, and had clenched that stuffie all day.

"The nanobots will help your body, so you be strong in your thoughts, your plans, and the rest will come."

Diona thrashed awake. The lights of day shift were soft yet, muting colour. She lay staring at the bland ceiling, watching the unnatural light grow in a weak facsimile of sunrise.

Later she had learned how the early NECS had caused strokes in several test subjects, but that hadn't been the main problem. She had also learned her mother's family had a genetic disposition towards blood disease and rejecting implants. Her mother died despite all the amazing tech of the day, a stroke caused by that blood disease, and now Thea might too, thanks to stupid genetics.

Her final upgrade was the only hope for Thea. For humanity. It might stretch the original rules a bit, but if she wasn't the one setting the rules, who was?

She rose and made haste to be ready, determined to take doses of the final upgrade to administer to Stepper, and later, if he was fine, Thea. But her tech lady, what was her name? Whatever, she was missing, none of the other lab rats knew a thing, and the woman's pod seemed abandoned. "That's simply not right."

She snooped through the office. She had instructed the woman to lock up these special samples with a particular code Diona had given her. She just had to find the lock box's location. The third cooler revealed the box she sought, and her code worked. Relocking it, she tucked it under her arm and left the lab, sure no one would question her but still worried someone might.

The NECS she carried could change the human race forever.

Diona was always careful when heading to her hidden bunker, yet today she found herself especially paranoid about being followed. She kept hearing skitters and echoes behind her that left her blood rushing too loud to properly listen.

"Be strong!" she reminded herself. "You must never let them see you lose control." She scanned behind her once again and, seeing no one, slipped through the door to the bunker. "Stop being a nervous Nellie," she hissed.

She entered the back room of the Faraday cage, only to turn and find her tech lady and some other woman pointing a stun gun at her from the open doorway.

Diona dodged inside the hall that led to Stepper's shielded cell and the airlock to the Mars surface. *I banned stun guns,* she thought, *for everyone's safety, how dare they threaten me with one?* There was no lock on this inner door, only a small window above the handle. The colonists advanced, probably thinking they had her pinned, but Diona activated the airlock door, slipped inside, and shut them out.

They would think her trapped in here, a link to nothing but the empty Marian landscape, but of course they were wrong. This airlock had the underground tunnel access to the forest dome. She was betrayed, and cut off, but she would survive.

The worst was, once they got this door opened, they would find the tunnel. She could shore it up on the other end, but she couldn't keep her beautiful forest dome hidden any longer. She activated the hidden panel, stepped through, and closed it, saying a small prayer that they somehow wouldn't notice it.

She entered the forest dome's airlock on the other end of the tunnel and activated her highest security protocols. If the colonists were going to lay siege on her here, that would at least slow them down a little.

Diona grew angry at this thought. Maybe she *should* create an upgrade that would allow her full control programs to run. She was the only one that could get them out of this mess, she needed people to just cooperate with her.

She passed Thea's room, a glance showing the tiny form curled on her hospital bed, facing away. There was nothing to her, tiny bones and a tiny heart and a tiny problem in her blood.

Diona pushed on. She wanted to get Thea her dose, but she needed to get to the console that would access the carefully separate and secured video feeds from the bunker first.

She called up the holo, only to see the last possible thing she expected.

The door to the cell's airlock was open, the two women at the controls. The alien moved towards the door at their urging, but turned and shoved an angry Stepper back away from freedom. He fell on his ass, the door opened, and the alien walked out. The door sealed shut before Stepper could regain his feet.

Diona watched, livid yet mystified. While delicious to watch Stepper be completely abandoned, there were some important questions to consider. One, why free the alien? Two, how did they know she was there? And three . . .

Wait. That tech, she knew more about Diona's plans than anyone, for all her caution. Did this woman think she could do something special with an alien's nanites? She must have somehow figured out the blood wasn't human.

She watched as they opened the door to the tunnel airlock. Diona swore a little as they went right inside. Next, her secret would be revealed. Would the hidden panel deceive them?

The day was full of surprises. All three shrugged it off as a simple airlock to the Mars landscape, and left.

"So stupid," she said, but the relief made her weak. What else could she do but control these people for their own good? Now she had an alien loose in the population. Those two women would regret their decisions, she decided. "Once this upgrade is complete, I will make sure no one can ever turn against me again."

Diona decided to ignore the alien and her accomplices. She had what she needed, she and Thea were safe and the forest dome still, amazingly enough, secret, and she had more important things to worry about. Without delay.

Diona prepared the lab, opened the sample case, and got to work. At one point she set up a video chat with one of the other lab rats to get the help she needed to finish. He also grew wary when he saw how complex these nanites were, but she reminded him who he was talking to and the subject was dropped. He could not know she intended on actually using it on anyone, let alone everyone.

It was her only hope.

Finally, it was done.

Time to test it on Stepper. A glance at Thea showed the girl had not moved from her napping position. The wires and machines, the lights and beeps, the tethers that kept Thea weak and tied to a bed, soon it would all be over, and instead she would have a healthy, strong girl to raise up.

Diona was cautious opening the airlock. Vid feeds could be easily hacked. But the hall remained clear as the security camera showed it to be. She moved in and brought up the lights.

Stepper surged to his feet immediately. "They took her," he shouted, "why didn't you do something?"

Diona tipped her head and regarded him in all this instability. "I have what I need," she said with a shrug, lifting his dose out of the carton to pour it into his water.

Stepper followed her movements. "What is that?"

"Just a little upgrade," she said, preparing the airlock pass-through. She placed her hand on the gas.

"I'll take it, you don't have to gas me," he said. It was the calmest she had ever seen him, but she recognized the deep abject despair and knew what it was capable of.

"It's the only time you sleep well," she said, her mothering voice having just the grating effect on him she desired. His eyes narrowed, that muscle in his cheek started to jump, and she could almost see his lip lifting in a snarl.

"I hate you."

"I hate you too, brother," she said easily. If this worked, and he was fine, she could use it on Thea. Everything was going to be okay. How fortunate to have him as a test subject.

"See, it will be fine," she said, more to herself than to her brother. "People should just leave the decision-making to me."

"Except when your actions could do them direct harm," Stepper said. She scowled at him. "Seriously, Diona, you have to think about the well-being of your peons or this could come crashing down around your ears."

She snorted in derision. "How could it? When you own everything, you control everything. And if they won't listen, I will also control them. I will keep us alive as a species!"

Stepper looked scared now. "What's in that?" he asked. The gas was already seeping through his vents, he wasn't going to be conscious for much longer. "You can't go trying to control people, Diona . . ."

Diona lashed out. "Look, Thea is dying. We are all dying more quickly by the day, as these NECS degrade inside us, but her, she won't survive the next week unless her body can accept them. I *have* to try this. I'm willing to risk anything for my daughter!"

Stepper had no smart comeback. How disappointing. No witty riposte, and she was left the victor yet again. But the thought hounded her. Was he right to be afraid? No, with foresight and care, she could fix it so everyone was happy.

She was more certain by the moment that her best path would be to make sure everyone survived, and behaved.

The gas spread and Stepper sank to the floor, coughing. "Damn you, Diona," he said as he fought to stay upright.

"Thank you, brother," she said as she leaned against the glass. She activated a medi bot, and Stepper was sat up and fed the water.

Next morning, Thea's alarms sounded. Diona ran in to find the doc setting up the oxygen again. Thea looked sideways at her, mouth gaping as she grasped for each breath, the blood blisters rimming her lips glaringly obvious. "Keep her alive," she ordered the doc.

Diona made her way back down the tunnel and set the bot to draw a blood sample from Stepper, completely unaware if he even tried to talk to her. Back in her office, she ran the stats, then sent those to her new tech.

"What am I looking at?" she asked his holo image.

He bent over the floating data. "The upgrade is not working because a previous upgrade is hogging the bus . . ."

Her look silenced his babble. "Plain speak."

"Ah, the bus, it's a port for upgrades to attach to. These ones are full with new nanites already locked into the port, hogging it. The one in the port should have a receiving port as well, but I don't see one on the top nanite so yours can't mount."

The alien NECS were in the way. Diona ordered him to create a seek and destroy, giving him the override codes for the extra power and processing he would need. She needed this upgrade to work on Stepper, so she could use it on Thea.

"Fix it, and fast," Diona said, "I want it ready now."

"These changes are forbidden in this format by your own rules, you know."

"I know. This is important, and for a limited and controlled testing environment."

Did he really think he could stare down Diona Jordan, CEO of SpaceOp, his boss and saviour? Did he really?

He looked down, but still had the audacity to mutter, "Dangerous move."

THE SEEK AND destroy worked, and bolstered her confidence. It only took moments to needle Stepper into a full tantrum once he realized she could control his every move.

"Stay cool, bro," she mocked, and of course he had to comply. Hate burned in his eyes. "If you continue to support my research in such a positive way, maybe I could let you out of here."

"You would never risk it," he grated. He was right, but how could she resist taunting him?

With new confidence, she decided on the hike back to her daughter to administer Thea's upgrade directly to expedite the process. The moment she saw her poor baby listless in that hospital bed, all doubt disappeared and she prepared the dose in haste. She would inject it to get it into the bloodstream immediately.

"I don't like needles," Thea whined, squirming under Diona's hold.

"You're fine, good grief, you get enough of them," Diona said. "Sit still!" Her jaw ached, and she loosened her clenched teeth to work it back and forth. She should've had the doctor do this, sparing Diona the trauma of it. It was in that moment Thea began to sob.

"Where's Papa Gamble?"

"The *doctor* is gone," Diona said, correcting her. It's not like there was any family connection. "Be a good girl and follow the rules, or he will have to go away."

Diona slid the needle home, her other hand keeping Thea still. She felt the flinch.

Thea wept quietly as Diona tidied up. "I had new tiny machines grown to fix your blood," she said while she set up the scans for the diagnostic holos. She would be able to see everything happening within the microcosm of Thea's blood cells.

She checked the same for Stepper, and saw how the new NECS had repaired and restarted the old ones. All the dissonance should be relieved. A feed showed he slept peacefully, as she predicted.

Diona lifted Thea's chin with a finger. "You are going to be fine," she assured the child. "Uncle Stepper tested these ones out, and they're going to fix you all up. No more problems, okay?"

Thea just stared at her with eyes pooled with tears. She probably didn't even remember Stepper. Diona sighed and went back to the scans.

"It's going to be fine."

CHAPTER THIRTY-SIX

JANLIN HAD A plan, but none of it moved forward without something to get her back into space. "Come on," she whispered to the Seraph. On a lick and a prayer, her dad Rudi used to say. *On the wings of maybe* was her new favourite.

The engines fired. Space-faring vehicles were hard to take out. If she bypassed some fried systems and rerouted them to her banks until she had a working launch sequence, she could be in the sky within moments. She stuffed her head in her helmet and sealed up her spacesuit.

Two storms now travelled across the landscape and threatened her takeoff. The Seraph didn't need a runway like a shunter did, thank goodness. The engines roared and jets rotated to lift the craft into the air. She punched the launch, using the prevailing winds pushing the storm fronts, and slammed the thrusters to full, Ceirin's soundtrack coursing out of the Seraph's speakers.

Time to face the music.

The g-forces pounded her into the seat, and it became harder to breathe with each passing second. It also triggered all the memories of her last lift-off flight away from Earth, and everything that followed from it. In the final seconds before the engines cut and free fall brought relief to her beleaguered body, she prayed for an end to it all that brought hope and peace to humanity. It had to be possible. She had new reason to fight for it.

She pulled off her helmet and opened her collar. The disc and its chain floated out, no longer weighed down by gravity, a tiny bar of light on the circumference pulsing with music. Without warning the light switched from green to blue, and the music cut out.

"Hey!" She reached for the disc only to have it project a tiny image of Ceirin.

"Janlin? You made it, yeah? How do we look from up there?" He grinned, and she grinned back, her whole body flushed with this pleasant surprise.

"Well, let's have a look," she said, turning the disc so his holo's vision took in the view out the window. Below swirled the usual storm patterns, and she could see the hole that she had flown out of. Flashes of sunlight on water showed the massive Bow River snaking through burnt out forests of the foothills. From here she couldn't make out the ravine where the compound hid, but she knew generally where it was in the folds of earth rippling up the eastern slopes of the mountain range.

She turned the holo back to her. "Your music player has some surprising features."

There was that grin again. "Love the view both ways," he said, winking. "Yeah, I wasn't sure if it would work and I didn't want to get your hopes up. It's the new tech, magnifying the signal with resonant frequencies."

Janlin blinked. "So, you're using music, or sound vibration, to improve comms?"

"Exactly!"

"Can I use this to contact others?"

"That's what we're hoping to find out. Ring me back after you try Spectra, yeah?"

"All right, I will!" Thrilled that she would have such an easy way to contact him made her glow.

He gave her a few tips on the new interface, and she tapped away at the holo console, disconnected from Ceirin, called up the Spectra comm system, and searched specifically for Gordon's earcell connection. Not having her earcell working was almost painful. Everything took longer than it should, and she still kept tapping at the thing expecting it to work. It was maddening.

She crossed her proverbial fingers and sent the call with Ceirin's new device. Gordon's voice answered.

"Sweet glory, it worked!" she cried. "My earcell's a mess, I just got off Earth, the Seraph's damaged, and the comms are out. I need help, the people I met on Earth need help, Anaya needs help, and the people on Mars need help too!"

"Well, good on them," Gordon snarled. Janlin's excitement drained away. "Haven't we already discussed this before you ran away?"

"I didn't run away," she snarled back. "I was abducted by the guy who hitched a ride up with me last time I went."

"You? Dirtside? What a load of hogwash," he said. "And crashed? Why don't you feed me a bigger line of malarky? Kavanagh doesn't crash. I should just—"

"Are you calling me a liar?" Janlin fought to keep her voice even, while wondering how this went so wrong so fast. "Dude, listen, I *have* been dirtside again, there's so much to tell you, there's hope down there—"

Gordon cut her off. "If there's hope, why are you here asking for so much help then, eh? Ursula and I finally have hope here, now, and I won't let you jeopardize that with your humanitarian efforts."

"You don't even know what's going on," she protested. "And how the hell could you let Anaya go to Mars alone?"

"Her choice," he said, no regret in his tone.

"So, you've heard Lauren's broadcasts?"

His silence spoke volumes.

"And you're not prepared to help me go help Anaya?"

Gordon let out a huge sigh, as if she were some problem he wished would stop bugging him. "I don't care about that part, you do what you want. But there's others here who agree with us about the supplies and meds, and they're not happy about the idea of letting *Hope* go either. Can't say what they might do."

Janlin was speechless. She refocused and took a deep breath. "I will go to Mars and help Anaya, and I will hunt down Stepper and his sister, and instead of running away from my NECS and their potential, I am going to chase down whatever I need to make them work *for* me," she declared. "I will take whatever risk I have to, first to rescue *my friend*, then to get us *all* to a place we can safely live *without* becoming so fearful we are unwilling to help others in turn."

"It's a ridiculous plan, right? You shouldn't be risking the

Jump. It was Anaya's choice to go, and she didn't Jump."

"Yeah, she went looking for *me*, right?"

He didn't deny it.

"And sure as hell no one else was worried about me, am I right? And now the one being in the universe that saved us all needs our help, and no one wants to help her in return. Or have you forgotten that part?"

"Janlin, you're being an ass."

"No, Gordon, you are. You are letting your fear of not enough hold you back from doing what's right."

Gordon cut her off at that point, and she stared at nothing for a long moment, stunned beyond belief.

"I'm just trying to do the right thing," she shouted at him, despite knowing he couldn't hear her. *Wouldn't* hear her. "How can helping others make him so mad at me?"

Janlin swallowed deep disappointment, the grief cutting her inside. She buzzed Ceirin.

"It worked fine," she said, still reeling from the argument and wondering what welcome, if any, she would face on Spectra.

"What happened? You're upset," he said.

"Just surprised at the reaction I got. Gordon and Ursula are no longer interested in helping anyone else if they're not on Spectra and preparing Luna for crops. He wouldn't even let me explain where I've been, didn't even believe it. I didn't even have a chance to tell him about you before he cut me off."

Ceirin slumped. "So, no help from that quarter. What will you do?"

"I'm going aboard," she said with determination. "I need *Hope*, and Gordon can't keep her from me."

"Just remember, you'll never survive a Jump without a new injection."

Janlin noted that Ceirin didn't question if she could do it, only pointed out what she needed for her safety.

"You'd survive life in orbit for a little while, but not a Jump."

She wanted to melt into his deep velvet voice, and cursed the fate that now pushed them apart. "I'll figure something out. I must have one friend or two left on board."

"Keep in touch, babe."

"I will."

With that bolstering her onwards, Janlin brought the Seraph

into line with Spectra's orbit and began setting up to enter the bay. She sent a "permission to dock" message, the standard text recording not often used because people just used their earcells and talked.

She maintained position for several moments, wondering if the bay doors would open. Would Gordon be so set against her that he wouldn't let her in? Maybe she should try Cassie.

The external docking stations would work, if she could connect with someone who could guide her in and unlock the hatch. Brighton, maybe?

At that moment, the bay doors began to iris open, and she breathed a sigh of relief. If she could just get Gordon to listen for a minute, he would understand the group effort they were going for here.

She landed poorly, the left thrusters still spouting more sparks than projection. Every move she made inside the shuttle made it sway and teeter. The bay had closed up and cycled in atmosphere, so she scrambled free . . . just before it tipped over with a resounding crash.

Cursing steadily, Janlin hoisted up her pack and headed for *Hope*, now alone on the bay floor. The spot where Anaya's ship had sat now seemed a gaping hole. The relief of Anaya being alive was countered by the fact her friend was in trouble again.

Before she could get far across the bay, an interior door opened and Gordon emerged.

He was followed by a fairly good-sized group of people, maybe three dozen or so. Most faces she didn't know, but there were a few from the Huantag settlement that she remembered, like Candice Young. Candice had never forgiven Janlin for her escape attempt when the Imag first attacked, because her and Weston were hurt in the process. And later, on Huantag, she and Weston had seemed to find Stepper's false claims quite reasonable.

"I canna bloody believe you would steal food from your own, and then come back for more . . ." Gordon started.

"I didn't steal anything," Janlin said over him. "This guy named Ceirin stole it, kidnapped me, except we crashed . . ."

"And that's where your story really falls apart. Kavanagh doesn't crash," Gordon repeated, full of true British righteousness.

Janlin felt anger begin to boil through her. "I was fighting for my life," she cried. "And I can't believe you keep calling me a liar."

Gordon's face flushed red. "Why didn't you call, then?"

She turned her head and pushed her hair aside to show the ghastly scars still healing. A few sounds of shock echoed through the crowd. "My earcell stopped working after the crash that you say didn't happen. Then my NECS were disabled . . ."

This brought a roar of disbelief. "How stupid do you think we are?" someone said. "Earcells are more resilient than that, and you can't just turn NECS off."

Janlin threw her hands up in despair. "Look, I don't care what y'all believe at this point, I just wish you'd remember I don't have a habit of going around lying."

Some foot shuffling ensued, and she wondered if she could sway them. "There's more going on than you realize," she began, willing Gordon to see that he would get privileged insider information if he would get rid of this crowd of goons first. Janlin wondered where Ursula was. The scientist was a proclaimed pacifist, and probably unwilling to take part no matter her views.

But Gordon, with that look that Janlin realized was ongoing pain from the NECS still resounding after Jump, did not want to hear it.

"There's always something with you," he started, an old track that didn't help. Janlin decided it wasn't worth trying anymore. It hurt too much.

"You listen," she cried, and for a wonder, he did. "I'm taking *Hope* to Mars to help Anaya and Tyrell's sister and nephew. Hopefully they're still alive by the time . . ."

But Gordon shouted back, "Not a chance," and the crowd's protest grew louder and drowned her out. They pushed forward and around her. Suddenly she felt threatened, as if these people no longer cared about her well-being at all.

"Gordon, please let me explain about—" she started, but he cut her off immediately, shoving a finger up under her nose.

"No more of your explaining," he said. "We have a plan here, and we're not about to let you muck it up."

"I'm not going to—"

"Right. That's what you always say, Janlin. You said you wouldn't ever go dirtside again either, but that still happened, didn't it?"

"I was kidnapped," she cried, but no one was listening as three big guys moved in on her at a nod from Gordon. Two grabbed her arms and pinned her, the third stood ominously at her back, out of her line of sight. "Gordon, good Lord, please, I was hijacked by this guy from Earth . . ."

"How is that even possible?" Candice shouted. "You're so full of shit, Janlin Kavanagh."

"He stowed away, rode up with me, before we Jumped," Janlin tried to explain. Gordon had turned away, and was heads together with some others, not listening to her at all. "Gordo, please!"

He shot her a look full of disdain. "Give it up, Kavanagh. We won't stand for your crazy bullshit. Take her away."

She blew a fuse. All her grief and rage at her father's death, the torture they had endured, the lives that were lost to the Imag and the virus, Stepper's raging, the way Ceirin's daughter looked, all of it was let loose to flood her now with incredible fury at the idea of being locked up. On some level, somewhere, where she was her calm rational self, she knew she was acting in the worst way possible, and that PSTD could do that to a person. But on a real visceral physical level, none of that calm rational self existed. She fought the men dragging her out, shouting obscenities at Gordon and the rest, spitting and screaming and trying to bite her abductors until they threw her into Spectra's small brig.

As they shut the door, one told her, "Give up. No one knows where you are, so just give up trying to steal our supplies. We won't let it happen."

"You can't—"

But they didn't wait, didn't give her a chance, simply shut the door. She felt so helpless.

She banged around the room, angry as hell, shouting and kicking and crying. Finally, after several laps, she drew deeper breaths and stopped striking out at everything.

Then the lights went out.

"No!" she cried, a desperate shout for mercy. "No," she whimpered, curling in on herself.

Ceirin's disc slipped along her skin, and she grabbed it tight in her hand. "Thank you," she whispered. She knew the prison cells were signal-blocked, intentionally of course, but at the least she had a tiny bar of light, and . . .

Soft music emanated, some small comfort, and she allowed her mind to slip away.

CHAPTER THIRTY-SEVEN

TIME STRETCHED OUT weird in the endless dark. Had it been a morning? A day? Surely, they wouldn't let her starve? Uncertainty gnawed at her brain. Anger warred with terror, and when the terror won, she found herself gasping, unable to breathe through the panic, until the room spun.

She came to on the floor.

Determined to do better, she began a systematic inspection of the cell by feel. Still nothing changed in the utter blackness, her only reprieve the tiny bar of light on the edge of the music player. She could be floating in space for all it mattered, and for a little while she did lay on the cot feeling a bit floaty, listening to a serious of songs labelled "Postrock" from the 2020s.

Angry again, she ranted around the tiny room, rehashing every point, having the conversation she wished Gordon would've allowed. She explained everything, hoping maybe he *was* listening, or *someone* was listening, and would come bring back the light. What felt like hours later, worn out and defeated, she crept onto the cot again and wept great gasping sobs of surrender.

There was no water, and the crying jag left her parched. Determined to conserve what she could, she forced herself to breathe deeply and stanch the tears.

Still the darkness persisted, so she went still. She sat, cross-legged, and tried to become one with the darkness. Carefully, one detail at a time, she counted her blessings. She could breathe, she was safely back on Spectra, this wouldn't last forever, she had to simply make it through. Time stretched, she had no clue anymore, and hunger was a familiar background ache. But her thirst grew desperate.

Surely, they wouldn't let her die of dehydration?

When the door cracked open, she backed to the wall, uncertain what she faced.

"Janlin?"

"Cassie?"

"Come on, let's get you out of there."

Janlin wept with relief.

"It's all right, sweetie, it's all right," Cassie said, taking Janlin under her wing. There were others with her, oh, Huey and Duey, those sweet young men, and Cassie's partner Li.

"They said no one knew I was here," Janlin said, sniffling and blinking in the brightness. "How did you find out?"

"Some guy named Kern or something called up Jessie Brighton, you know him?" Duey said.

"Brighton, yes, and Ceirin too," Janlin said with a little laugh.

"Yeah, he said he's from Earth?" Cassie said. Janlin grinned through her tears and nodded. "You know him? Oh wow, look at you blush, well okay then, congrats. Yeah, he said he couldn't reach you and it had been a full day, he was worried. Steve immediately put it together that the signals were blocked in the cells . . ."

Duey picked up the tale. "This Earth guy of yours ends up chatting with Brighton first, him being the comms guy he is. Brighton had seen you come limping in and never thought more of it, thought he'd hear more in the news feed later. When Ceirin explained his concern, sure enough, Brighton couldn't get a read on you anywhere. No news of your arrival, no trace of you anywhere, and Gordon acting all strange. So Brighton came to us, we asked Linder, she got Steve and Cassie and Li on it. And here we are," he said with his classic big smile.

"Where is Steve?" Janlin asked. "I kinda need to talk to him about a couple things."

Cassie snorted. "I bet. He's keeping Gordon and crew busy to be sure we wouldn't be interrupted. There might be charges pressed."

"Oh no," Janlin groaned.

"What they did to you cannot be tolerated! Just because you disagree with someone, you don't throw them in a darkened cell without any due process, charge, or justice," Cassie said.

"Sure, I get that," Janlin said. "But will I ever be able to heal the friendship?"

Cassie gave her a stark look. "Why would you want to?"

Janlin scrubbed her face. Where would she be without Gordon, through all these years? That had to count for something. "Look, if it's up to me, there will be no charges, okay? They were only trying to protect themselves and their future. Besides, none of us have time for locking anyone up. We need all hands on deck, not busy creating the due process that would make it right to charge Gordon."

"He threw you in a cell, and you don't want to make him pay for it?"

Janlin sighed and shook her head. "What happened with Anaya?"

"She went to Mars. To rescue you."

"How did that even happen? She was in a coma!"

Cassie gave a little choked laugh. "I found her swiping through holos of medical data, completely naked and steaming, that whole bag and slab set up dripping stuff all over the floor, and I swear I nearly pooped myself. Apparently her NECS blocked ours for a while before deciding to allow the procedure."

"The livestream?"

"Went dark, which is how I ended up there."

"And the weird wrap and stow move?"

Cassie's grin was contagious. "It truly was a stasis chamber, I guess. Kept her alive while the nanites sorted themselves out."

Janlin shook her head. "I can't believe she went to Mars after me!"

"Well, that's where we assumed you were when you disappeared. That wasn't where you were, though, was it?"

It was Janlin's turn to give a small choked laugh. "No, dirtside, if you can believe it. We crashed, barely survived a landslide, weeks of storms, and quarantine. Have you heard from Anaya recently?"

"No. We did okay with intermittent contact through her month-long journey, and she let us know she had reached Mars and was going down to meet Diona. Now it's been thirty-two hours and I've heard nothing, and here you're not on Mars at all . . . I'm scared for her. And we haven't been able to reach Lauren either. Then, to my horror, her recorded message was picked up."

A pox on Diona, Janlin thought. She gripped Cassie's hand. "There's only one way. I'll need *Hope* set up to run from the captain's seat, and Steve's willingness to make me that captain."

Cassie pursed her lips. "It's a crazy risk."

Janlin nodded. "Will you support me? Do you think Steve will?"

"Yes," Cassie assured her. "There's been some change of hearts among some of us. It's actually led to some strained friendships."

Janlin was both relieved, and saddened. Chances were, her own friendships were strained to the breaking point now. But there was one more hurdle she needed to clear.

"Cassie?"

"Yeah?"

"I'll need a new dose of NECS."

Cassie's mouth fell open in shock. "Is that a good idea?"

"There's no other option right now. I'll explain later."

"I tried to tell her not to go, Janlin," Cassie said, looking at her feet. "Anaya wouldn't listen. She said she had to help you, no matter the risk."

Janlin couldn't help but grin at that. "I just said the same about her to Ceirin. But that's precisely why I need to get to Mars. Immediately."

Huey and Duey both stared at her. "You're gonna Jump?" Duey asked, fear thick in his voice.

She gave them a desperate look. "How else?"

They both shook their heads in unison.

Cassie and Li didn't have the first-hand experience of the dissonance after a Jump, so they weren't as appalled. "Who is this Ceirin person?" Cassie prodded.

Janlin wondered how to nutshell it for the moment. "He lives on Earth in an old prepper bunker, with his daughter and grandmother along with a few other residents, and they are struggling for adequate nutrition, like us."

"Why did you go there? And who is this Ceirin guy?"

"Ceirin, um, abducted me."

Cassie raised both eyebrows and leaned back in shock. "This is the guy you're blushing about, though?" she asked, her confusion obvious.

"Yeah, same one," Janlin grinned. "I want Steve to hear the whole story, though. But you should know, Ceirin was onboard since before we went after *Renegade*. That's a huge breech of security, and one that no one noticed. We've become rather complacent, don't you think, considering we now know aliens exist?"

Li choked a little, and Cassie let out a long breath. "Holy cow. Nothing's ever easy with you, is it?"

STEVE AND MARK waited for them in Steve's quarters. Janlin had called Ceirin along the way, and put him up on the holo to introduce him, Natl, and Harriot to everyone. Ceirin was so grateful, and he kept thanking the others for setting Janlin free. Cassie wiggled her eyebrows at her and the grin she couldn't seem to wipe off her face.

After they ended the call, Steve held up a syringe. "We found a standard dose of NECS for you," Steve said. "Never thought I'd hear you say you want *more* NECS in your system."

Janlin gave a bitter laugh. "Right? But mine were disabled."

Everyone expressed surprise. "That can be done?"

Janlin nodded. "Sure, but the EMP blast required would be devastating in most space environments, yeah? Therefore, it wasn't common knowledge up here."

"EMP . . ." Steve said, shaking his head. "Of course. I remember them on Earth, but they were banned in space."

"It did help my head, and I was plenty glad for that."

Linder piped up. "I'm curious to study what a new dose will do to the disabled and decaying NECS."

"Do we have to use words like decaying?" Janlin moaned.

Huey piped up. "If programmed to do so, they may help repair and even restart the original NECS," he said.

Duey agreed. "You could end up with a working double dose, Janlin."

"Adding a routine that allowed the new dose to do repair work would require networking abilities," Linder warned. "That's be a good way to start an AI."

"As long as they are kept simple, it should be okay," Steve

suggested. "Also, an Artificial Intelligence would need terabytes of memory to form; where would it access that? And I think this is the kind of thing we may need to do to repair the bio-fouling." He looked to Janlin. "Are you sure you want to be our test subject on this, though?"

Janlin threw her hands up. "I don't even follow half of what you guys say, so I'm kinda at your mercy. But I'm not going to survive a Jump without them, and if they can help the fouling, then sure, I'll be a Guinea pig. Hopefully it means surviving this so I can actually help Anaya and Lauren."

They hatched a plan to use an old escape pod to send more supplies dirtside. Many of the pods had been dismantled for parts, but a few still sat in their launch tracks. It was a short-term solution that still made everyone feel good.

Li left to track down Danal for help with rerouting key systems to the captain's chair on *Hope*, and to get him to plot her Mars Jump. Janlin caught a shower, ate some Huantag tubers with Orbital algae sauce, and fielded a slew of questions from Brighton about Ceirin's tiny little device. She finally handed it over with Ceirin on the line and let them go at it.

She returned to the hangar bay to find her friends each working on different things to get *Hope* ready for her. Cassie waved her over to a console Li worked at.

"We are rigging up a dose of adrenaline for you, post Jump. It should help clear the head much faster."

"Excellent," Janlin said. "Thank you. I hope it works."

They went aboard to rig it up, and found Danal working on the helm calculations, his bulk straining the seams of his standard-issue SpaceOp coverall. He stood when he saw Janlin coming, and looked like he might call her captain or something.

"Hey, Danal," Janlin said, determined to keep it light. He nodded and gestured awkwardly at the console.

"You need to refine the calculations for where you are when you Jump, so I created a program to do it." He showed her the commands to set and the process to run. "Then you strap in there," he said, waving at the captain's chair, "and hit run on the program waiting there when you're ready to Jump."

Janlin felt a little overwhelmed by it all. "Thank you, this is amazing work you've done," she told him.

He grinned, nodding some more. "It was an interesting

challenge, I enjoyed it." He shuffled his feet. "I'd be willing to go with you," he said. "You might need help with the return trip."

Shouting rose out in the bay, and she exchanged a worried glance with Cassie. Janlin looked up at Danal's impressive height and muscle mass. "I won't put you through that, but would you mind joining us right now?" she asked as the sounds of strife grew.

Sure enough, it was Gordon and his posse of dissenters facing off with Steve, Linder, Huey, and Duey. Cassie and Li were ahead of her, Danal at her back, and Cassie called out over the repeated protests.

"We support this mission, Gordon, and locking Janlin up was completely illegal and uncalled for."

"See," Steve said to him, "like I just told you. Janlin wouldn't press charges, but she still could."

Janlin pushed through and came up to Gordon. Again, Ursula wasn't with him, but Candice was, and several others she recognized from before. She met each of their gazes and several dropped away in guilt.

"Steve?" she said.

"Yes?"

"Would you please make it formal?"

"Would be my pleasure," Steve said with a smile. He stood a little straighter and looked right at Gordon as he said, "I am relieved to announce I am standing down as *Hope's* captain, and instating Janlin Kavanagh as her new captain. Cheers to the Captain!"

"Cheers!" called half the room. The other half shifted and frowned. Gordon was like stone. Janlin faced him square on, catching his glance up at Danal's taller stature at her back. "In honour of our friendship, I refuse to press charges against you for illegally incarcerating me without due process. However, as Captain of the mighty *Jumpship Hope*, I hereby order you to cease and desist in your intimidation and bullying in regards to this matter."

GORDON DID LEAVE, taking his angry posse with him, but he was none too pleased about it. Janlin tried not to let it get to her. They finished up the preparation, and she looked ahead to all the things she needed to accomplish once in Mars orbit. She couldn't let her grief surface, or it would engulf her and she'd be useless.

They redocked the Seraph inside *Hope's* hangar despite her state, ran a test on all the systems, and finally, Cassie gave Janlin her booster shot. "Linder said she did what she could with adding some repair programming."

"I'm gonna be all robot before you know it," Janlin said, rubbing the now sore spot. It might be her imagination, but she thought she could feel the cold path of the nanites as they spread through her system. She wished they had time to make sure putting these old, unused NECS in her wouldn't conflict with the existing and cause an upset. Hopefully because the other ones were inert, things would be okay. That was Linder's take. But what happened if they repaired the old ones?

Janlin shrugged into her gear. Everyone else cleared out of the hangar bay with calls of support, but Steve pinned her down before she boarded. "Are you sure about this? *Hope* is a big rig, not designed to be flown by one person, and Jumps . . . well, you know."

"I do," Janlin said. "And thank you. Thank you to all the folks helping me set this up, too. But that's why I have to fly solo. There's no way I'd let anyone to Jump with me, even if they volunteered. And, Steve?"

"Yeah?"

"If I don't survive the Jump, please find a way to get a message to Lauren and Anaya so they at least know *Hope* is there for them to use?"

"I've got a better idea," he said. "Survive."

CHAPTER THIRTY-EIGHT

DIONA WATCHED THROUGH her live cams as her tech lady, Moran, and the orbital woman took the alien through the streets of the colony. It was before dayshift still, no one about but these idiots. She still had time to set things in motion.

Diona noticed a new blip in the list of humans with NECS. *How was that a thing?* She thought about the small handful of NECS doses she still held. Could it be someone on Spectra had taken a second dose from their old stock? She watched the scans for a bit, unable to find any that seemed doubled.

Setting that aside for a moment, Diona sent several messages to her supporters in the guise of her favourite social media persona, saying the rumours going around about an alien in the colony might be true, and called for a rising up to ensure their safety. She had several personas to choose from.

She created a post saying "aliens need shown the door" and made it seem like another's post on the colony's message board. It was immediately shared, and comments started to pour in on both posts. Then she made another that said, "fake alien is really illegal immigrant" and another mocking anyone that would help such a person, and another mocking anyone that would believe in aliens. All of them were instantly shared. Soon a mob would form to scour the streets of the colony, and when they found the insurgents, they would literally get shown the door right out onto the Martian dirt, no matter what the peons believed, and she could cast reasonable doubt about her involvement.

Diona wanted to fortify the tunnel airlock entrance to the forest dome against any comers forever, but that would be to admit defeat. Realistically, she needed access to Stepper and the colony, and wouldn't let them go even if she didn't. She watched her various cams: Thea playing, Stepper pacing, the alien and her two unlikely friends, the mob building behind them. She logged into a few other personas and liked, shared, and commented to steer the mood the way she wanted. She smiled. Her supporters would take care of that problem for her.

Better yet, if her work was successful, she wouldn't even need the subterfuge anymore.

Diona tried to put all other distractions aside. Thea was playing quietly, the upgrades working away under the surface. If all went well, the child would be the healthiest resident on the planet. Time to prepare the upgrade for the colony so that the moment it was ready, it could be released into the waterways, the people unwittingly taking them into their systems with each sip.

She would make it so no one could lie to her, no one could oppose her, no one would throw up roadblocks when they didn't understand what Diona was trying to do. Governing would become so much easier, and their survival would be assured.

Diona went through the scans again, tweaking some code, careful not to touch other parts. It was nice to work longer here. Maybe she should put out more support posts about her leadership despite her absences.

Meanwhile she had to play the hand dealt her. If planned right, it could be made to look like she saved the whole colony by supporting these righteous souls only doing what they must to protect their own.

She focused back on Thea. The girl seemed more alert now, sitting up in her bed playing some holo game. Her movements were sure and quick, her colour good. Diona didn't want to face her with another syringe, and decided to wait to get the next sample.

CHAPTER THIRTY-NINE

JANLIN WAS ABOUT to close the hatch when Brighton called on her new device.

"Hey, we're connected," she said. "Are you magic?"

Brighton laughed. "No, no, of course not. My astounding ability with communications technology just looks like magic to the rest of you."

Janlin laughed, appreciating his humour. Then Brighton revealed more, and she heard the name that lit her up.

"To be fair, Ceirin set up the initial link, I just ran with it. Listen, I've got Lauren on the line, it's not the greatest connection, but she needs to talk to you. Anaya is with her."

"Put them on," Janlin said. She increased the volume, and brought the disc to her ear. "Lauren? Are you okay?"

"For the moment," came her distant voice. "Where have you been?"

Janlin groaned. "I've been dirtside, and my earcell was damaged."

"Dirtside, sweet geezus. How the heck . . . ?"

"Not by choice, trust me." Although she thought of Ceirin and was glad it all happened.

"I've made a new friend, I think you know her?"

"Anaya?" Janlin breathed.

"Jan'in, why you no on Mars?"

Janlin bust out laughing. "Anaya, why you no in a medbay

where I left you?" Her heart swelled with the sound of Anaya's *chuff* laughter. "You also have other things to explain, too," Janlin continued, getting serious. "The Imag virus and your cure are nanite-driven, not biological. When were you going to tell us?" She couldn't keep the tone of accusation from her voice.

"I t'ought you know," Anaya said. "T'ought you know a'ways, yes? Ahhhh, de word?"

"Obvious," Lauren said with amusement. "She thought it was obvious, not anything of note to reveal."

Then Anaya called her out. "My 'ip no right, wires an' human junk. Expane dat, pease."

Janlin wished for a holo, to gauge the true emotion behind the words. Anaya always sounded gruff. Was she truly angry? Janlin cringed, her body tense and her gut churning. She wondered if her strong physical reaction was a side effect of PTSD, too, always overthinking things like this.

"I thought you were dying, my friend," Janlin said. "I was only seeking information that could help."

A quiet chuff was her only answer.

Janlin thought she heard shouting. "What is that?"

"Dammit, no," Lauren moaned. "We need to get out of here."

"And go where?" another voice asked.

"My 'ip," Anaya said.

"No," Janlin said, "that's exactly what Diona will expect."

"We've tried the way back to Eliza's, but it was blocked by an overturned sani-unit, and the next had a crowd of men that surged up and started marching on us, shouting, 'There's the fake alien,' and 'Gonna beat the shit outta you, freak!'"

"My gawd, that's terrible," Janlin said. She sat in the captain's chair and fought to breathe past the abject fear that rose like bile.

"They're pushing us towards the airlock," Lauren said, her voice hard. "It's happening all over again."

"Where's Tyson?" Janlin asked.

"With friends," Lauren said, "the ones we've been hiding with. I don't want to reveal where it is... and we're cut off from that area, in any case."

"I'm glad he's safe. I'm coming for you right now. Tyrell wouldn't have it any other way. If you go out that airlock, can you circle around to Anaya's shuttle?"

"We can't go *outside*," Lauren gasped. Eliza made sounds of agreement.

"Get the right gear, it'll be fine," Janlin said, wondering what the problem was. She heard shouts, and they were loud and growing closer.

"In here?" Lauren said. Janlin wondered where "here" was. "Eliza, will your pass work?"

Janlin began her preparations.

"It's been disabled," came what must be Eliza's voice. "I no longer have colonist status." Janlin could hear the horror in her voice. "I no longer exist."

"Hold tight, I'll be there shortly," Janlin said.

"Diona will pay for this," she heard one of them say.

"Lauren, can you get to the airlock? I'm on my way." If the adrenaline worked to revive her quickly.

If she survived.

There was no answer, and she couldn't get the connection back.

Janlin ran the pre-set commands to guide *Hope* out of Spectra's hangar bay and out into space. Her heartrate was too high, and she couldn't seem to get a deep breath.

"Easy, babe, you got this."

Janlin smiled at the tiny, comforting bar of light. "Thanks for believing in me," she said with all earnestness.

"I am here to help," Ceirin replied. "Proved an idea, too, after a little playing around with the NECS."

"Oh?"

"They *do* respond to vibrations, and dissonant sounds will make them churn up and run crazy, whereas soothing music settles everything down. Before you Jump, maybe set up some music to play?"

"Love that idea," she said. "It can't hurt to try it."

"Call me the moment you're there, yeah?"

"I will."

They broke the connection, and Janlin set the last few commands. Then, she ran their favourite song.

"On the wings of maybe . . ." She hummed along, the melodies played, and Janlin said a little prayer.

"Onward to Mars." She sent the command.

JUMP

CHAPTER FORTY

DIONA WATCHED HER people herd the three insurgents towards an airlock. *That should take care of that,* she thought with satisfaction. Lovely when she needn't get directly involved.

It was no surprise the young woman helping Moran was a new immigrant. It proved Diona was right to limit newcomers, and to bring the colony on board with protecting their borders. No newcomer would have the same loyalties. And it was thanks to her measures that they didn't have the spore that shut Luna Base down.

A new chime sounded, and she flipped up the holo. A proximity alert, ship in orbit.

Ship in orbit? What happened to her outpost alarms? Were they sleeping to allow a cruiser past them like that? What of her crew around the moon, or . . .

Jumpship.

Diona checked the live feed of Spectra's hangar bay. *Hope* no longer sat there. She flipped back to the holo of the NECS tracking system. There was that new blip, no name attached to it, but the only human apparently aboard the Jumpship now overhead.

"Janlin Kavanagh." Who else could it be?

The gutsy pilot knew Diona wouldn't order SpaceOp cruisers to fire on her, not at a working Jumpship. The new NECS must be to try and make the Jump safer. But she should still be out of commission for a while after Jumping.

Diona sent coordinates to the Mars Orbital Command. *Go immediately and arrest everyone you find. Let me know when you have boarded and secured the vessel. And hurry, or your job will become far more difficult.* They wouldn't understand her double meaning, but it didn't matter. She appreciated her own humour.

She tapped into Stepper's livestream. "Looks like your Jannilove is still breathing, and she's come to visit," she said, her voice over the speakers making him jump.

Stepper gave a humourless laugh. "Guess you got everything you wanted," he said. "Come on, sis, no holo?"

She switch over to hologram, and now had a better view of him as well.

"Why so worried?" He said it straight, but she heard the taunt.

"What do you know of the two that took the alien?"

He gave her a strange look. "What does that matter?" he asked, before adding, "I don't know either of them."

"Why did they release her, then?" Diona was asking herself more than anything.

"My guess is they know Janlin somehow."

Of course, that's why Janlin was in orbit right now. Thankfully her goons would have her pinned down and locked up before Janlin could regain consciousness.

"Well, she's not going to be any help to them," she said. "How are you feeling?"

"Fine," he said, staring off. "The headaches are gone, thank all the gods, and I've stopped feeling like my heart was going to stop. Not so dizzy, either." He refocused on her holo. "Got to give you that much, sis, you really fixed the horrid aftereffects of Jump. Do you think it will solve the bio-fouling too?"

She straightened up with the praise. "That is the intention. We won't survive anything out here if we don't have NECS supporting our systems."

Thea came out of her room and walked over into the holo view. Stepper studied his niece. Diona gained a bit more confidence. Two examples of her efforts working.

"Thea is well," she said, holding her hand out to Thea. Thea just tipped her head at it, eerily much like the way she herself liked to tip her head at people. They often found her regard disconcerting, which was why she did it, and now her own daughter was doing it back.

Diona let her hand drop.

Stepper sneered.

"Are you going to let Janlin take the alien and my Jumpship?" he demanded. It made sense that's what they were here to attempt. "You should let me out, I'll take care of it. You clearly have control over me, so what's the harm?"

"I've taken care of it all already, brother," she said, feeling calmer by the minute. "Janlin will be in my custody soon, and the alien dead." She tipped her head, shooting a wink at Thea. "Should we put your Jannilove in with you?"

Stepper made a rude gesture and put his back to her. "Do what you want, sis. I'll bet this will all backfire on you soon. Are you really going to put that upgrade in the population?"

"I am," she told him, annoyed again. "And no one realizes the hero that I am for doing it."

DIONA WATCHED THE colony livestreams, wondering how long it would be before the groups in the streets became one and forced the dissidents out the airlock. She needed to be sure things went as they were supposed to. Visual confirmation was important.

Looked like it wouldn't be long now.

Diona realized Thea still stood beside her. "What, child?"

Thea stared, wide-eyed. It was disconcerting.

"We need to draw another sample, Thea, come back to your room and roll up your sleeve."

The girl followed her. Diona turned to the cupboard with the needed supplies and braced herself for the weeping, weak protests, and whining complaints that would inevitably follow. To her surprise, Thea simply stood gazing around. Her sleeve wasn't rolled, however. Diona sighed, set the syringe down, and deftly tucked it up out of the way. She tied off the tiny arm, tapped the vein, and drew the needed blood.

Thea didn't even flinch. She watched for a moment, then went back to scanning the room, as if she memorized it. Diona decided it was a good sign. Her girl was tougher now, healthy, able to withstand small discomforts.

"Good job," she offered, surprising herself. Thea smiled back at her.

Diona's hands shook as she loaded up a smear on a plate. The scope took its time warming up, and finally the results came in.

The upgrade was parsing through the cells, and some NECS had lodged where needed. Repair work was underway, and the signs of the blood disease were diminished. Her baby carried the finest new programming that she had designed to help save the colony, and the last of humanity. If this worked, she would even share it with the Orbitals. Why not, she could afford to be generous.

Out of caution, Diona closed off Thea's room, set the seals, and initiated security. "You're going to be fine," she told her daughter through the window. "The nanites will heal you up good and strong, and this room will keep you safe."

"I know," Thea said, "I am already better than before."

CHAPTER FORTY-ONE

THE MUSIC DID help, and so did the shot of adrenaline. Or was it just the shorter distance? Janlin began the shutdown sequence before her vision really cleared. Queasy would be a polite way to describe how her gut felt, but the usual spiking pain and blackened sight was thankfully absent. By the clock, she'd also come to within seconds, instead of several minutes or worse.

She really didn't know how much time she had, so she unbuckled even as she swiped through the last few commands. A new alert popped up, and she tapped it.

Approaching shuttle craft.

Great. A welcome from Diona, no doubt. Janlin took off at a run for the hangar bay and the waiting Seraph.

She was certain they wouldn't be able to do much of anything with the *Hope* while she was gone. Nanite protocols were wicked difficult, and most people wouldn't even know where to start. Without all the help from Linder, Steve, and Danal, among others, she wouldn't even be flying this thing. It was damned *complicated.* She was also reasonably certain Diona would not fire on or damage a working Jumpship.

But she had to get gone without their notice.

She bounced off a few corners and stumbled somewhat inelegantly across the bay to the Seraph. Once sealed within, the re-routed controls worked and she was soon free of the Jumpship. She gave a sputtering boost in the right direction, then cut power to the Seraph and drifted free. The SpaceOp shuttle approached as she sank into the quiet night of space. She turned away to pull on her EVA suit, setting the helmet within easy reach.

As soon as Diona's goons were on the other side of *Hope* and fully immersed in docking, she kicked on the power and set the computer running calculations for landing with two missing thrusters. Soon she was soaring over the Martian landscape.

The colony was hard to spot in the red monochrome landscape, only its vent tubes and light-gather pods visible. The regolith was layered over the domes, which were set several feet deep, to provide shielding from solar radiation and storms. Janlin saw Anaya's shuttle at one of the airlock entrances.

She tapped the tiny disc dangling from the chain around her neck.

"Ceirin, I made it, but I'm a bit pressed for time at the moment. I'll call back soon!"

"Wait," came the reply. "Look under your seat."

She had a moment of wanting to say, seriously in a hurry here, but she reached under her seat and found a small box attached there. She brought it up and realized exactly what it was.

"Should be all charged up from sitting there," Ceirin said, his voice smug. "Just know that if you set it off, it takes a while to recharge, yeah?"

"You are a marvel," she breathed.

"Be safe, luv."

Then she buzzed Lauren. "I'll be at the airlock in minutes, please tell me you're okay?"

There was no reply.

Meanwhile the Seraph had a funny smell coming from under the holo console, and another thruster was not responding. Janlin fought with the controls, careening her way over the massive colony towards the west side airlock Lauren had spoken of.

Anaya's shuttle better be in working order, or they might not have a way off planet.

Lauren's voice came over the comm.

"Janlin, thank god you're here. We are being pursued by an angry group of people who seem determined to put us out an airlock."

"The one we are to meet at?"

"No, we couldn't get there. We're nearly at the SSW gate, can you land there? We don't have a lot of choice about where to go at the moment. Can you connect with the airlock gate?"

"Not sure, but get some gear on if not," Janlin advised. Every airlock on the orbitals has emergency suits stored in them. Surely this one did as well?

Janlin could hear a low growl like that of an advancing wildcat, with occasional shouts punctuating it.

"Are you seriously willing to murder us?" Lauren called out, her honest curiosity laced with desperation.

"We will protect our own," cried a man's voice. A woman picked up the chant, and more voices joined it. "Protect our own, protect our own." It was all too clear over the comm, enough to give Janlin chills.

She heard another voice, closer, raised in protest. "She's a mom. A *single* mom!"

"Less mouths to feed," another voice called back, more distant but still uncomfortably close.

Janlin swore, fighting the wobbling Seraph to accept her directions. She wasn't going to be able to land as close as she'd like. Close and alive was preferable, but how would she help them if she wasn't close enough?

Lauren moaned. "We're backed into a corner now, there's no way out." Her voice became desperate. "Stop," she cried. "Stop!" Then her voice came back closer to the handheld. "We don't have long. Their faces are twisted in rage, Janlin. They don't care. They are willing to kill us." The defeat in her voice was crushing.

"I'm almost there." Janlin focused on her landing, the voices a terrible background distraction. She got the Seraph down in a spray of red rocks. She ran the shutdown procedure, and stuck the EMP device in her pack.

She stuffed her head back in her helmet and was out the hatch, making her way across the Martian landscape. Lights peeked through the regolith where windows had been allowed, and the airlock tunnel stuck out, easy to recognize. She could see movement within, one figure much taller than the other two. She reached the outer lock and peered in at the advancing wall of hatred.

Janlin stepped back in the face of such ugly anger, so

righteous and eager for violence. They believed Lauren and Anaya were a threat. An unfounded fear, but real enough to condone murder in their minds.

"Eliza isn't infected by anything, nor am I," Lauren said. "Anaya is our first alien guest in the history of humankind. Is this the welcome you want to give?"

"Lies," cried a woman in the crowd. "There are no aliens, that's just an elaborate costume to throw us off. We know about the secret plan to take down our colony. We know that's just bullshit to scare us so you can move right in."

"If you keep coming, I'll let her in."

Janlin looked over to see Lauren pointing at her.

"You won't have a chance," the front man shouted. "We'll throw you out to face the Martian pathogens."

Janlin sputtered into the mic. "What? What Martian pathogens? What the hell is he on about?"

Lauren made a sound of dismay. "It's real," she said to Janlin, her voice tinny over the airlock comm. "Every colonist knows it. It's in the NDA waivers we had to sign to work for SpaceOp. We won't last out there, even with suits."

Janlin looked down at the dust coating her suit. Such a blatant lie, as it just had to be, would keep people within the confines the Jordans wanted them in. The whole thing stunk like manipulation.

"I think you've all been misled," Janlin said, but no one was listening.

Lauren, Anaya, and Eliza were backed into the airlock chamber now, nowhere to go, but they made a valiant effort to keep the mob from being able to close the hatch. Safety settings made it impossible for them to let her in. "Put me on speaker," Janlin called to Lauren. "Let me talk to them."

Eliza made some adjustments to a panel, then gave her a nod.

"Look, my name is Janlin Kavanagh. My mother designed the NECS, and my dad," she choked a little, "he was the finest pilot SpaceOp ever had." Janlin touched her helmet to the outer glass. "There's a lot more going on at the Orbitals than you guys are told, and to be honest, Diona's lied about a lot of it. Is there any chance she was lying about the Martian environment to keep something hidden?"

"You're the liar," the man shouted, and many seconded it.

"How would you know any of this? You must be one of those 'forest dome' nuts, thinking the ban on going out there is to hide it instead of being a protection for us all. Instead, you'll be dead in hours."

"Yeah," the crowd cried.

Wow, how did she reach these people. "Maybe I will be, and maybe I'm crazy, but is that enough to kill these people over?"

"You bring those pathogens inside," the man said, gesturing at her EVA gear, "that's how we end up with some spore killing our crops, just like the Orbitals did."

"Fine, leave me out here, but let Lauren return home to her child."

"Oh, no," said the woman, poking a metal rod at Lauren. "I know this one, she likes to cause trouble, and now she's proven she's trouble, here with you. No, no, trouble can go out with the trash."

"That's murder . . ."

The angry couple began shouting, denying her words, shoving forward as they spit defensiveness, and some chanting "clean house" as they surged forward. Janlin was stunned at their unwillingness to listen to any reason.

Someone fired a stun gun at Anaya, knocking her back, and someone else slapped the controls to cycle the inner airlock door shut. Lauren and Eliza surged forward, but they were shoved hard, both falling back into Anaya, before the inner door sealed shut.

"Janlin?" Lauren cried.

"It's okay," she said. Was it okay? A glance showed her the Seraph to be just far enough away they wouldn't make it there without suits on. The thought also crossed her mind that Anaya might not be able to use a human rebreather.

Lauren moaned. "Tyson," she grieved. The airlock began to cycle open to the Martian environment, and the mob cheered.

CHAPTER FORTY-TWO

DIONA SLAVED OVER the upgrade. It truly was a work of art. Too bad her tech woman was a traitor. She could've enjoyed nice rewards for her work instead of bringing problems down on Diona's head. What a waste.

Diona merged her changes with the final programming for the new NECS. One day, she would be seen as the one who saved humankind from self-destructing. Someday people would understand how important she was.

She flipped a few holos out of her way, the processing done and finalized and ready to package, only to notice the live cam footage.

The mob had forced the three troublemakers into an airlock out the west side, which was now cycling open to the red dust, just as she had planned . . . only someone waited for them. How was this possible?

Janlin again.

Diona called up her orbital team.

"We have the ship surrounded, ma'am, no one could've left. We haven't been able to get access, but we've been here the whole time."

Diona could see the small shuttle Janlin must've flown down. It looked like a heap of junk. "Well, you bloody idiots, you missed everything important," she screamed into the mic. "You're all fired."

She broke the connection with shaking fingers. She flipped holos, looking for good news. Thea. She sat on her bed, healthy, smart, alive.

Her only chance was to get this upgrade out before Janlin found her way in. Diona's father had helped her long ago with the plan for this, and now she modified it to fit the current events as they stood. Her parents' insight made it so she even had an access feed to the colony's water supply.

"Like they knew I would need it," she said. She checked Stepper's feed. He paced, his fingers moving as if they tapped out commands on a keyboard. "Still crazy," Diona muttered, pushing his holo aside. At least he was safely tucked away.

A new chime echoed, and the upgrade was ready. Basing it on what the tech had done to save Thea, Diona had created a run of NECS that would knock out contenders, piggyback onto the old nanites, and repair the fouling. It would also give her control of every single individual. They would be linked to her command centre, and she could influence how they felt, what chemicals were released in their brains, what actions they could and could not take.

Sweet heaven.

She would keep them all safe, Thea would survive, and she would remain their beloved leader. They would be the future of humanity, and she would eventually lead them to expand into the universe.

Janlin Kavanagh could not ruin this. It was done. The upgrade was ready, her daughter was healing by the minute, and soon she would have no more worries. People had to drink water, after all.

As the airlock opened with a whoosh, Janlin grabbed Anaya and pulled her out. She was groggy but regaining mobility. Janlin stuffed the rebreather in the giant's hands.

"Try this on, I don't know if it will work, and run for the Seraph! Go now, I don't know how the lack of pressure will affect you!" Janlin pointed the way.

The other two stood plastered to the inner door, terror in their eyes as they gasped for breath. "You only have a few more seconds before you begin to decompress," Janlin cried. "Get some suits on!" Neither moved.

Janlin looked to see Anaya loping over red earth, one hand

holding the rebreather over her mouth. Good. A glance back made her groan. The two women were gonna die.

"Lauren, listen up," she cried. "Tyson needs you to pick up that suit, help your friend with the other one, and get your ass moving! Lauren!"

They both cried in pain now, but Lauren did seem to hear her. She pulled on the suit despite her terror of the red dust coating her arms. She got it on, helped Eliza, who also moved to find relief. "We will never be allowed to set foot in the colony again," Lauren wailed.

"Lies," Janlin said, so done with the time wasting. "I promise. The red dust will not hurt you. And you're not exactly welcome in there anyway."

Suited up now, the two Mars colonists joined Janlin out on the regolith. Lauren was weeping, and the helmet mic picked every bit of it up. Janlin thought her heart might break. She waved them on to follow her to the Seraph.

"The illness, it's truly a lie?" the other woman asked.

Now Janlin didn't have time to argue, but she didn't know if this was truth or fiction made to control the population, keep them penned up. "I don't know," she admitted. "But I've never heard of it, and it smells an awful lot like Diona trying to keep her secrets secret. And, besides, I don't think you two have any better options."

They conceded her point, still terrified, and Janlin marvelled at how deep the programming went. They stumbled their way to the Seraph. Soon they were all squeezed into the small space inside. Janlin sealed the hatch and pressurized the cabin. Once she pulled off her helmet, she turned to Anaya.

"My friend, I am so sorry."

She found herself engulfed in grey flesh, like being hugged by an elephant. "Oomph."

"Jan'in," Anaya said, setting her free again. "So happy you good, so happy."

"Me too," Janlin replied, "I really thought I lost you."

Chuff.

Lauren and her friend watched with wide eyes. "When you said my brother was 'dirtside' . . ."

Janlin hoped Tyrell's sister was the forgiving type. "Um, yeah, that was in her solar system, not ours," she admitted. "Thank you for helping Anaya, our very first alien friend. It's sure good to meet you in person, and again, from the bottom of my heart, I am so sorry about Tyrell."

Lauren nodded her thanks. "Ah, Janlin, this is Eliza Moran, Diona's nanite technician. She's the one that figured out Diona had an alien locked up, and the one who helped me and Tyson."

"I owe you both a lot," Janlin told Eliza.

"There's more, though," Lauren said. "It's even more than just the anti-immigration dissidents. Diona has plans to upgrade the colony's NECS without their consent, and it's a bit hot, this upgrade."

Janlin rubbed her forehead. "Of course it is," she grumbled. "Whatever the case, we should get out of here first. Unfortunately, I'm not sure this thing is going to fly."

She was flipping through holos, and sure enough, the Seraph had too few thrusters operational to get them launched, especially with the extra load. They had shelter, but no way to move.

"My 'ip," Anaya said.

"We may not have time," Eliza said, pulling at Janlin's arm. "Diona has plans to add the upgrade to the water supply. There was some powerful networking software in this upgrade, and a whole lot of processing power added. Diona said it was for repair work, but the patching programs didn't require such robust communications. Now I'm worried she's trying to build an AI, or use it as a way to control us . . ."

"Could she?"

"Yes." Her wide-eyed horror was awful to see. "She ran one on me, and I couldn't say no to what she needed done. With the new upgrade, she can hack individuals or the whole as she likes without physical contact, as long as humans need water."

Janlin eased back from the woman. "Can we trust you?"

"Yes." Eliza's gaze was steady. "She had me write in a fail-safe, that's the only reason I'm not completely hers."

Lauren looked scared. "Isn't the upgrade designed to clean out the bio-fouling? That's what all the messaging around it says."

"To do so, they needed to network. NECS weren't originally designed to communicate with each other, but only follow certain procedures; if this, then that, kind of processes. They were simple machines. Now she's made them far more powerful."

Janlin couldn't believe what she was hearing. "Spectra specialists said the same thing, that NECS shouldn't be networked or it would cause an AI. Why is that so bad again? Couldn't we use a little more intelligence around here, especially if an artificial intelligence might know how to fix our biggest problems?" Janlin asked.

Eliza sighed, slowly shaking her head. "A separate entity *inside* your body that can think and reason, probably better than you can? That could get out of control quickly, especially if the AI decides it doesn't need you arguing and makes you unconscious."

"Oh."

Lauren gave a nervous laugh. "That isn't realistic though, right?"

Janlin and Eliza exchanged a glance. It was realistic, but neither wanted to admit it.

"I am rather tired of these NECS," Janlin said. "But if the only way to Jump is with nanite technology, then I'm willing to do whatever's necessary to get them up and running. I'm sure you feel the same way," she said to Anaya, "since going home means Jumping again, and that didn't go well the first time."

"Did you really Jump to another planet, Janlin?"

"I did! And I can actually support your research," Janlin told her. "I played music during the Jump here, and it really helped, that and a dose of adrenaline when you come out of it."

Eliza was fascinated. "That's exciting. We could test to see if certain pitches are more helpful than others."

"I would be happy to help with that, once we're out of this mess." Janlin thought about how Ceirin showed her how to scan and monitor her NECS. "We have stuff to discuss beyond that, too. Meanwhile, my guess is Diona must have an offsite place where she is operating this all out of. Any guesses as to where we might start looking?"

"There's always been rumours of a forest dome out in the Martian landscape somewhere. Most call it wishful thinking, some call it a conspiracy theory, some chastise the Jordans for holding out on them, and a few more, Diona's supporters, believe she's creating a haven there for her chosen followers to expand into."

"Wow." Janlin didn't even know how else to respond. "What do you think? Is there a chance she has some fancy place away from the colony?"

The two woman exchanged glances. "I didn't used to believe it at all," Eliza admitted, and Lauren agreed. "Now, I'm not so sure. She did disappear out that airlock. And she told us lies about the Martian soil, lies about your situation, and more lies about her," pointing at Anaya, "and now this new upgrade seems rather dangerous . . . so who's to put it past her to have this place, too?"

Between them, they told Janlin of their adventure collecting Anaya. "So, the airlock on the west side is our only clue."

"And dat where 'ip is," Anaya said.

"Okay, then, you go there, I'll go straight west from here. She can't be far, just hidden, and I'm going after an ariel view."

"How, if this shuttle won't fly?" Lauren asked.

Janlin shrugged off her pack and took out the Huantag flight suit.

Anaya chuffed. "Huantag gift," she said, approving. "You go, we get 'ip, den we come he'p."

"It's a plan." They helped Janlin pull on her flight gear over the spacesuit, added a fresh rebreather, and released the hatch. The others were putting their helmets back on as well, Eliza and Lauren both still eyeing the red dust with some fear.

She launched, passing over the three figures below as they traversed the naked Martian landscape. She had an idea that she could use Ceirin's EMP device to stop Diona's upgrade from ever being a problem, just like Ceirin used it to stop the NECS in her. Janlin just had to blast the upgrade while it was all in one place.

If Diona was able to send the upgrade out, Janlin would have to EMP the entire colony and force everyone to start from scratch with the NECS.

She tucked her wings and flew a little faster.

CHAPTER FORTY-THREE

JANLIN STUDIED THE terrain to the west. A curved, jagged ridge of mountainous rock ran north to where it joined the great valley cliffs, and was only a kilometre away or so. She circled over the colony, hoping to catch some thermal lift from the warmth radiating from there, then sailed west. The Huantag materials cut through the thin air easily, and Janlin soared, indulging in the glory of the moment despite everything.

She swept over the red landscape of Mars. Everything seemed wild and untouched out here. If Diona had a secret lair, and she had put it underground, how would they find her in time to stop the upgrade?

Janlin saw an unusually straight line running westward towards the ridge. A water line? That was their only other hope, to go right to where the water storage intakes were. If she found nothing out here, she'd get Lauren to guide her there.

She cleared the steep ridge to find a huge crater, and within, a massive dome covered in regolith sunk deep in its base.

A large window glinted in the weak sunlight, and she caught a sparkling hue of deep green within that made her gasp. As she drew near the viewport, it became clear the dome was filled with a dense forest that extended to the very edges of the crater.

"How is this even possible?" she muttered to the wind. Gliding in closer, she saw an airlock door that entered on a rise of land, offering a fine view from just within. The outer door was half drifted over. This couldn't be the entrance Diona was using, and that suited Janlin fine.

She circled, looking back, but was unable to see her friends from this vantage. She hoped they would make it to Anaya's ship in good time.

The lock was pressurized within. She cleared the outer panel of dust. The light glowed red. It had not been used in a long time. Thank goodness the inner door was at least closed, or this hatchway would never engage.

"Ceirin?"

"How's it going?"

She explained where she stood. "I need in quickly. Any ideas?"

"Set the disc against the panel, over the control." She did so. A chime sounded, then a vibration, and the light turned yellow, then green.

"It's working," she crowed, then, with some sass, "I might have to keep you around."

She could hear his grin. "Glad to be useful. Be careful in there."

"I will," she promised as she stepped into the airlock and engaged the controls to shut herself in. There was no question in her mind that Diona was here. What was frightening is what else she might have hidden within. The inner hatch cycled open and her suit registered breathable air. Janlin pulled off her helmet, and lost her ability to think for a moment.

A faint path led into the trees, and the smell . . . she swooned . . . that perfume of dirt and green grass and pine trees triggered so many memories. Was that a squirrel call? Nothing like this existed on Earth anymore. She wanted desperately to wander, to explore, to strip off all the protective gear she wore and lose herself in the lush life and memories of Earth. But if Lauren and Eliza were right and Diona was here, she had to find the crazed woman *now*.

Janlin climbed out of her flight gear and stowed it in her pack, listening carefully, scanning into the trees as far as she could see.

Strange, for all the wonder of the domed forest, she could sense the difference between it and Ceirin's place. For one, there was no weather. Everything sat unnaturally still, but for the low hum of fans. These trees had to be artificially created and nano-engineered to grow 100-year-old trees in fifteen, and somehow that hit her senses different. Not wrong altogether, yet not right either.

Still, the place was hope embodied, on a grand, long-term scale. She came upon a creek, and saw a variety of established plants, small animals, and bugs. Sounds of wings rushed by, though she couldn't see them for the denseness of the pine and spruce branches.

Astonishment and anger warred inside her. She moved along the faint footpath to find the trees opening up into a meadow, and there, a house built into the red cliff face. There was another airlock entrance, too, *down* a flight of stairs.

And Diona was there, at the pipe compressor building between the house and the airlock, fumbling with the water lines.

"I came in the other way," Janlin said as she approached. Diona whirled around, guilt and panic on her face quickly replaced by fury.

"What are you even doing here?" Diona snarled. "You should've run when you could." She stooped and lifted a hose that fed back to a tap on the house wall.

Janlin raised an eyebrow. "And let you put your fancy upgrade in the water system? That would be quite selfish of me, don't you think?"

"This is going to save us," Diona said. "It's already saved my daughter. It will stop the bio-fouling. You should be thanking me."

Could this be true. "Daughter?" Janlin slipped off her pack and fingered the device within. It would stop all function of the NECS in that waterline. It would also disable their own NECS. But now Diona was talking about a daughter? "Didn't she die?"

Diona shot her a look of pure hate. "Aren't you tactful," she sneered. She dragged the line to the connector and began hooking it up.

"Look, from what your tech told me, that's dangerous stuff you're playing with there. What you propose takes away our very freedom."

Diona seemed unable to get it. "I'm saving our lives, Janlin. Would you rather die?"

"There has to be a better way," Janlin protested. "You are so selfish keeping this place to yourself, just think of how much better we'd all be if we could live here."

"Oh, come on, I deserve this! They'd all be dead now if it weren't for my family's legacy of nanite technology. We're the reason humanity even has a chance! Have you ever thought of the responsibilities I carry?" There was some desperation, some deeper reason Diona was doing this, but Janlin couldn't figure it. "You don't understand at all what I've been through. You can take your attitude and shove it."

"And you're as pleasant as your brother. Is it a genetic thing?"

"Look, Thea's upgrade saved her life, and she is growing stronger every minute. She is the wave of the future, the testing done on her will save the rest of us. If we want our descendants to be able to live dirtside again someday, they will need this kind of augmentation, this kind of co-operation with each other . . ."

"Co-operation?" Janlin snagged on the word. "You are proposing using us like components in a machine, and with huge risks involved. And, you do know about the standard limitations put in place to protect us from these nanites going AI, right?"

"Bah, conspiracy theories, all of it," Diona said, and somehow Janlin knew Diona lied.

Janlin studied everything, the pipes, the connections, Diona's movements, trying to ignore the awful queasiness she still felt from the Jump. "Where is Thea now?"

"Oh, she has the same sort of quarters as her uncle, very safe, very secure, very hidden."

Diona connected the other end, spinning the wheel to allow water flow once the valve was opened. It was ready. Janlin weighed the consequences if she had to use her device. "I can't let you do this, Diona. You don't have people's consent. You need to do more testing . . ."

"Why, to have people tell me my ideas are too outside the box? This, Janlin, this is our only hope," Diona said, rising to her feet with a huff and setting her hand on the valve. "We need to work together, and since people don't know how, I'll simply make it so."

"Don't," Janlin began, ready to threaten her with the EMP device, try to get her to hold off. She began drawing it out of her pack, but Diona shoved the valve handle over.

Janlin was out of time. She had no choice.

She lifted the EMP blaster, hit the button, and held on for the repercussions.

Diona, unaware of what she'd done, crowed and shook her fist in victory. She refocused on Janlin and frowned.

"What are you holding?"

"An EMP blaster," Janlin said, feeling a little unsteady. "All the NECS in that water tank are now inert." She couldn't hold Diona's horrified gaze. "As are your own, and mine, too."

The door to the house opened, and a small girl emerged.

CHAPTER FORTY-FOUR

THE LIGHTS OF the dome dimmed, and the fans ground down to new silence. Diona gave a small cry. A generator fired up somewhere, probably some fail-safe system to keep the basic life support systems on.

"What have you done?" She stalked over to Thea, and checked the girl over, then refocused on Janlin. "Her room is a Faraday cage, my daughter's saving grace," she said. Janlin heard a weird terror in Diona's voice, and puzzled why she might be afraid of her own daughter.

Thus, Janlin was watching Diona closely as the woman's attention was caught by something behind her, and she got to watch the blood drain completely out of Diona's face. Janlin looked the same direction, and saw the tunnel airlock standing open and Stepper striding towards them.

CHAPTER FORTY-FIVE

"Why do you bring your anger here to taint this place?" Diona's tone held scorn and command that did not cover the waver in her voice. "See what you've done?" she said to Janlin.

Stepper didn't even glance at her, only stared icy daggers at Diona. His arm rose to point at Thea, however, one long index finger singling her out. "She needs stopped," he said, his voice weird. Now he stared at Janlin, his head twitching, as if calculating some un-calculable thing.

Janlin stared, frozen, Stepper's arrival triggering some knee-jerk freeze reaction.

"Janlin," called a new voice. She turned and saw Anaya, Lauren, and Eliza coming down the trail. They must've found her entrance.

"Stay back!"

The two women slowed, but Anaya kept coming. Janlin turned back to Stepper.

"Thank you so much, Jannilove, you set me free of my cage. It takes time to power those up after a discharge, doesn't it?" he said, looking at the EMP device in her hand.

Janlin's gut soured. "I don't know," she lied, hoping to keep his attention. The way he said Jannilove was all wrong, none of the old emotion to it, none of the edge—in fact, no emotion at all. Stepper jerked, and his attention turned to Diona again.

Then he went straight for Diona and Thea. Diona called out,

"Run program Failsafe . . ."

"No!" Stepper cried, scooping up a rock to throw at her. She slipped sideways, and the rock missed completely.

Diona was already advancing on him. "I'll kill you to protect my daughter, brother."

"Ceirin? How long for the EMP to recharge?"

Diona started again. "Run program Failsafe 2.1 dash . . ." she began to say, but Stepper lunged and shoved Diona, and went after Thea.

Ceirin's small voice reached her ears. "Watch the small light on the side, it should turn green when it's ready."

A blast came, and a puff of dirt rose in front of Stepper. It was Anaya, her gun trained on Stepper. It was one of the big guns they used when they raided the Imag slaver ship for humans . . . big, alien, and effective. Diona started her fail-safe phrase again.

". . . zero slash one five . . ."

"No, sister," Stepper said, lunging again and slapping a hand over her mouth. "No fail-safe."

Then he slugged her, hard, and she crumpled.

Janlin caught up to Stepper and swung him around. "What have you done?" she cried. Thea stared at her mother, not moving. How could Stepper hit his sister in front of her own child?

"Solving a problem," Stepper said, pushing her off. He was tense, muscles jumping in his cheek, fists clenched. He practically vibrated, and his eyes darted around. He looked crazed, but when was that ever new with him? Still, something was off. He churned out words that somehow didn't even make as much sense as Stepper usually did. Thea stared at him, wide-eyed. He seemed frustrated when nothing happened. He fixated on Janlin. "Be grateful. She was about to upload a program that would give her complete control over the population. You would've all become her slaves."

"I'd stopped that upgrade already," Janlin shouted at him. "You didn't have to beat her up."

Stepper lunged at Thea again, who retreated further, backpedalling slowly.

Anaya came up behind Janlin and fired, but Stepper sidestepped, making it so she completely missed. Janlin tried to keep up, thinking to gain enough ground that she could put herself between Stepper and Thea.

Why the obsession with the girl? Stepper let off another string of numbers and letters, like some weird code, as he paced towards her. It didn't seem to have any effect at all.

Anaya and Janlin pursued.

"You're quick," Stepper said, slowing. Thea had managed to stay out of reach. "We should work together."

Janlin fired off the EMP device, but she knew the green light hadn't come yet, knew it was too soon. Anaya stopped to raise her own gun and took aim.

Stepper suddenly changed course, turning on them and, in moves impossibly fast, took Anaya's firearm from her.

"Can't hack your nanites, thanks to that EMP," Stepper snarled at the alien, the gun now aimed at her head, "so instead you are going to be my ride out of here before that EMP charges up."

"Hack nanites . . . ?" Janlin echoed. "Stepper, what the hell? Stop threatening everyone!"

"This place is a death trap, with only a twenty-seven percent chance of survival of humanity as a species, and the Orbitals are worse at eight percent. I'll take this meat sack to Huantag—the memories show a higher probability of survival until I can expand into a better host."

Her gut went cold. "What are you saying?" Janlin cried, but Stepper was herding Anaya towards the airlock, gun to her back. Janlin went after them, leaving Thea.

"Stepper, wait," she called. He fired and Janlin dodged, but he was aiming at and nearly hit Thea, thankfully still getting the hang of the alien gun. He continued to fire at the child, who didn't move, didn't duck and run, didn't cry or flinch. Janlin moved to put her own body between, but she was too far, and he was swinging up to fire again, getting a feel for the weapon . . .

Diona's head came up, took stock of her brother's aim, and pushed up just as he fired. Janlin saw it all, the micro-second's moment of choice that a mother made, the ultimate sacrifice.

It was a direct hit. Diona crumpled to the ground, and Stepper was too busy keeping Anaya in line to fire again. "Stepper!" Janlin cried. There was no reaching him. Her gaze locked with Anaya's as Stepper hauled her out of sight down the forest path at gunpoint, with Anaya's own gun.

"Be ok," Anaya called.

And then they were gone.

"I CAN'T BELIEVE it," Janlin said for the umpteenth time. Neither she nor her companions were sure just what part she couldn't believe. All of it was ridiculous, and it all happened so fast. "I failed."

"You stopped the upgrade," Lauren pointed out. "And saved a child. And saved us."

"Great, but Diona's dead. And I lost my Jumpship. And is Anaya okay? If he Jumps with her aboard . . . besides, what just happened with Stepper?"

Eliza looked grim. "I suspect Diona was experimenting on him, and he is now a host for an AI. We may be facing far worse of a threat than just Stepper Jordan."

"You've got to be kidding me," Janlin said, but Eliza wasn't laughing. In fact, she looked positively terrified.

"We're also facing the probability that the EMP took out our systems colony-wide," she added. "All essential services will need rebooted, if we can even get them running again at all."

Janlin stared at her in horror. The colony would face certain death, all seventeen thousand some, if the EMP had reached the colony and they couldn't get things restarted.

She looked out at the forest. "I've ruined it all." She felt utterly defeated.

Thea approached, and Janlin reached out to the child, offering her hand. The girl put her hand in Janlin's and smiled up at her. "It's okay, I can help."

"Aw, sweetie," Janlin said, thinking it was adorable how little ones thought they could fix the world. Thea didn't understand that there was no way to stop Stepper. She clearly didn't understand her mom was dead, either. "Don't worry, I'll keep you with me," Janlin said, squeezing the girl's tiny hand and turning her away while Lauren laid her sweater over Diona's still face.

"We should explore," Eliza said, indicating the cabin. "See if there are backup systems we can initiate from here."

At that moment another figure appeared in the doorway. Lauren gave a little cry.

"Rick?"

"Laur?" the man choked out. "My gawd, I can't believe you're here!" They ran to each other and the man swung Lauren up in a bear hug, spinning her around so she threw back her head and laughed.

"You're not listening," the six-year-old said, tugging on Janlin's hand. She looked down, away from the touching scene of reunited lovers, and found Thea tipping her head in a creepy echo of her mom. "I'm serious. I can help."

"Yes, of course," Janlin said, looking up at Eliza with a little shrug. The tech was studying the girl.

"How is it you can help, Thea?" Eliza asked her.

Thea smiled up at her. "I am not Thea. I am also an AI, and I want to help."

The End
Stay tuned for part three, Jumpship Freedom!

ACKNOWLEDGEMENTS

PUTTING A BOOK out into the world takes a village, as many of you know. First, I'd like to thank the family—my kid, my dad and his wife, my mum and stepdad, and all the extended family that buy my books and cheer me on. How lucky am I that the list of supportive siblings, cousins, aunts, and uncles is too long to include everyone? I'm spoiled rotten, and I like it that way.

There are more friends than I can list, too, but a few must be mentioned: Wayne, Bob and Tuesday, Shannon and James, Janice and Tony, Randy and Val, Jen and Stu, Sherry, Tee and Dan, and so many more have been there for me through some really tough times. And how about new friends like Renee and Casey, whose farm cottage became a writer's retreat for the two summers of the pandemic? Again, the list is too long to include everyone, and I feel wealthy beyond measure because of it.

A special thanks goes out to my beta readers: Janice, Wayne, Dad. And a shout-out to Jennifer Rahn for reading an early version and writing a cover blurb. More kindness that enriches my life.

Without the crew at Tyche Books, there would be no Jumpship Series. Thank you, Margaret Curelas and Ryah Deines for all their work, cover artist Niken Anindita for the amazing artwork, and Indigo Chick Designs for the cover build. Much love for believing in Janlin and me. Thanks also to Jeff Campbell and Shannon Allen for sharing a book launch with me for their anthology The Astronaut Always Rings Twice.

I also had some amazing research help. Thank you, Wayne (nanites, networks, and potentials), Darren (deep space communications, networking nanites), and Jason (non-nuclear EMP weapons, nanite tech, plausibility). Thanks also to my therapist Dr. Liu, and all the therapists on YouTube, blogs, podcasts, and in books teaching about PTSD and how to recover from it.

Last, but never least, I must thank the organizations of IFWA (Imaginative Fiction Writers Association), WWC (When Words Collide), and the Odyssey Writer's Workshop for bringing me so many bookish friends and an extensive publishing community to be a part of. My editing clients are often a part of this same community, and they've helped me grow as a writer even as I get to help them polish their work. I am grateful to be able to help writers with my editing, it is truly a dream job for me.

Oh, and one last special thank you to Randy McCharles for asking just the right question at just the right time to propel this story in a direction I hadn't expected.

This was a pandemic write. Any of you who also wrote novels and met deadlines (or didn't, as I must admit happened here) can sympathize with my agony, I'm sure. While isolation and solitude lend themselves well to writing novels, quarantine took it to an uncomfortable level that ruled out so much of the usual support system, i.e. cafes, retreats, conventions, and writing socials . . . all things that help keep us loners sane. It will be interesting to look back and recognize the influence on the work in some distant future. If you hear abject loneliness echoing through this story, I'm sure you'll understand why.

Thank you most of all, dear reader, for loving Janlin and her crew as much as I do. I hope you'll like where she's headed next!

ABOUT THE AUTHOR

Editor, Author, and Artisan, Adria Laycraft earned honours in Journalism in '92 and has worked with words and visual art ever since. Jumpship Dissonance is the sequel to her debut novel, Jumpship Hope, published by Tyche Books, to be followed by a third book called Jumpship Freedom. Adria co-edited the Urban Green Man anthology with artist Janice Blaine in 2013, which was nominated for an Aurora Award, and she has gone on to help many authors with her freelance editing. Over her career, she has published countless newspaper articles and photos, magazine articles, and short stories in various ezines, print mags, and anthologies. Adria is a grateful member of Calgary's Imaginative Fiction Writers Association (IFWA), and was a proud survivor of the Odyssey Writers Workshop in 2006. Learn more at adrialaycraft.com, where you'll find a list of publications and a gallery of wood carvings, and watch Adria carve on her YouTube channel Carving the Cottonwood.

www.ingramcontent.com/pod-product-compliance
Lightning Source LLC
Chambersburg PA
CBHW030809210726
48290CB00002B/493